Malcolm Hamer is a self-confessed sports addict who has worked extensively in the field of sports management. In 1971 he left Mark McCormack's agency (where his clients included Tony Jacklin and Arnold Palmer) to found his own agency. He has subsequently represented many top sportsmen, among them golfers such as Johnny Miller, Sam Snead and the young Severiano Ballesteros.

As a writer, together with his wife, Jill Foster, he has published a successful series of guide books, *The Family Welcome Guides*, and his previous Chris Ludlow golfing thriller, *Sudden Death*, has been highly praised:

'A bright debut in the sports-thriller genre' *Daily Mail*

'[The author] has used his inside knowledge of the professional game to create a very readable thriller' *Sunday Telegraph*

Also by Malcolm Hamer

Sudden Death

(with Jill Foster)

The Family Welcome Accommodation Guide
The Family Welcome Pub & Restaurant Guide
The Family Welcome Leisure Guide

A Deadly Lie

Malcolm Hamer

HEADLINE

First published in 1992
by HEADLINE BOOK PUBLISHING PLC

First published in paperback in 1992
by HEADLINE BOOK PUBLISHING PLC

10 9 8 7 6 5 4 3 2

All characters in this publication are fictitious and any resemblance to real persons, living or dead, is purely coincidental.

ISBN 0 7472 3817 0

Typeset by Keyboard Services, Luton

Printed and bound in Great Britain by
Cox & Wyman Ltd, Reading, Berkshire

HEADLINE BOOK PUBLISHING
A division of Hodder Headline PLC
338 Euston Road
London NW1 3BH

To Jill

ACKNOWLEDGEMENTS

My sincere thanks to Nigel Bennett, Philip Olsen and Bob Sinfield for their help and advice.

My thanks to Sir Rupert Hart-Davis for permission to quote Siegfried Sassoon's lines on page 42.

Chapter 1

'Do you know how much he got for those lager commercials? Nearly half a million quid.'

The question was asked and answered by Kenny Craig, a pro-am regular.

The pro-am in question was in support of the Give a Child a Chance campaign. It is a well-promoted golf tournament which is held every spring at a course not more than thirty miles from the centre of London. It attracts a few of the top professionals on the European Tour and most of the pro-am regulars – a noisy, eccentric, egotistical and amusing bunch of show-business personalities, sportsmen both active and retired, and well-heeled businessmen. The businessmen not only pay for the privilege of competing and for the dubious honour of rubbing shoulders with the golfers and celebrities, but also pay for most of the drinks.

We were sitting outside one of the many hospitality tents which lined the eighteenth fairway. They are paid for by the companies whose chairmen and managing directors were disporting themselves in the Give a Child a Chance tournament.

Kenny Craig thinks of himself as a comedian and 'all round entertainer', though his show-business success rests on one hit record, made in the sixties. His only other attribute is his Liverpool accent which, he assumes, automatically makes him a funny man. His show-business beat encompasses the clubs, especially in the north, the Christmas pantomimes, and occasional guest appearances on television. Most of the work he does manage to get is due to 'old muckers' from Liverpool. Kenny hasn't yet accepted that he is not a star, and he likes to remind all around of his supposed standing as an entertainer by cracking a joke at every possible opportunity. Very wearing.

Kenny was holding forth on the chief topic of conversation in both sporting and show business circles: money. Who is getting how much from whom. This is normally interlaced with who is doing what to whom, but we hadn't got to that stage yet.

The insiders who know about these things tell me that the high-table chat over dinner at the Oxford and Cambridge colleges is much the same. Elegant and witty discussions of the meaning of life and the nature of the universe come a very poor third behind money and sex.

Kenny had obviously been doing a thorough round of the hospitality tents, and looked and sounded as though he was on his second circuit. He had reached the very voluble stage of drunkenness, his words slightly slurred and his eyes seeming to look somewhere near the left ear of anyone else who spoke.

Kenny was now trying to focus on Jack Mason, a professional golfer, who asked Kenny how his round went. Kenny gave a predictable reply.

'Bloody rubbish, Jack. I think I'm over-golfed. Do you know, this is my twelfth pro-am in fourteen days. When I opened the front door the other day, my missus tried to give me the money for the milk.'

Jack laughed and took another pull at his glass of Rolling Rock beer.

Jack Mason is my boss. I am a caddie; one of those toilers of the fairways who wear bibs or overalls covered in sponsors' names and logos and hump forty pounds or so of golf bag around the courses of the world. Jack's bag had started off a bit heavier than that because he had stowed a couple of litres of Strongarm bitter in his bag. 'Well, it's a hot day, Chris,' he had said when I'd detected the extra weight.

Jack stretched his large frame in the small confines of the wooden picnic seat, which protested under his fourteen stones. He looked over at Kenny Craig and said: 'Kenny, have you met my caddie, Chris Ludlow?'

I half stood and stretched my hand across the table and received just a touch of Craig's outstretched fingers.

'Half a million quid,' he said. 'For Jimmy bloody McCoy.'

Mike Bradbury, the businessman who as a co-sponsor of the event was providing the hospitality and who had been one of Jack's partners in the pro-am, spoke up. He was clearly delighted to have a celebrity in his group, however minor and however drunk.

'What does he do for the money, Kenny?'

'Prances about in that poxy kilt of his and makes a fool of himself.'

'I heard he's got a three-year contract for six commercials,' I said.

'Oh yeah,' sneered Kenny Craig, 'and where would a caddie hear things like that?'

Jack was quick to my defence. 'Chris also works for a stockbroker,' he snapped, 'and specialises in the leisure sector. That's where he hears things like that.'

Even the dulled senses of Kenny Craig recognised that Jack was angered by his rudeness and there was an awkward lull. Mike Bradbury covered the momentary unease by calling for another round. I too resent the attitude that caddies are itinerants, dressed in cast-off clothing, who occasionally stay sober enough to carry a golf bag round a course. Times have changed. I admit though to being a particularly fortunate caddie: my double life is made possible by the connivance of Jack and of the golf-mad head of the City stockbroking firm for whom I work as a salesman.

Andrew Buccleuth runs a relatively small and very profitable firm which has not been swallowed up by one of the conglomerates or foreign banks in the aftermath of the Big Bang. He has a good mix of private clients – rich families whose investments on the stock market he guides, and institutions like the pension funds who are the big players on the financial stage.

It was just after Jack's sharp remarks to Kenny Craig that I first saw Poppy Drake. Fate had some fancy tricks up its sleeve that day: the spring sun, waning a bit as the day wore on, was behind her and framed her as she walked towards us. She was dressed in white and had a glow around her, an aura; and, although she was with two men, she seemed to be totally alone. Shades of that early sequence in *Lawrence of Arabia* as Omar Sharif shimmered out of the distant desert towards the camera.

I wish David Lean had been there to re-direct the scene: cut to travel agency – we see Chris Ludlow buy a one-way ticket to a remote part of the world where the beautiful Poppy Drake will never find him.

Chapter 2

For some time I had been committed to work for Jack Mason through the European golf season, which gets longer every year. In the old days the club professional used to emerge from his shop in May or June, sniff the air and play a few events which would culminate in the Open Championship in July. He would then return to his club to look after his members once more. The new breed of tournament professional can now play virtually the whole year round, if he wants to, for large sums of prize money.

Fortunately, Jack doesn't want to and really only gets going in late March and early April. He doesn't play every week throughout the season either. Not for him the treadmill of airports every Sunday evening, fleeting visits home on Mondays, mainly to get the laundry done, and away again on the Tuesday morning to another anonymous hotel room and the incessant talk of golf, money and girls, girls, money and golf. For one thing he values his wife and family too much.

One of the many advantages to me of caddying for Jack was that I was able to keep track of my stockbroking duties through a somewhat unorthodox working schedule and by the indulgence of clients who don't expect nine-to-five advice.

I have a fax at home and on-screen access to all the current stockmarket prices. I did consider a mobile phone, but when I mentioned it to Jack was left in no doubt about his views. Trenchant as ever, he had suggested two ways of dealing with it: the first would have entailed a great deal of personal discomfort for me; and the second involved his unleashing his one-iron on the offending instrument – or, rather, someone else's one-iron because he didn't want to ruin a favourite club.

It was fortunate on this occasion that Jack had learned fairly early on in the round that Mike Bradbury owned a company which dealt in mobile communications.

Jack is a forthright man. Many people in golf, especially the administrators, would use a stronger epithet. He has been reprimanded and fined by the Professional Golfers' Association too many times for comfort. But it is usually for what he regards as a 'just cause'.

He tries to be on his best behaviour at pro-ams, partly because he can appreciate the terrors that assail many of the amateurs on the first tee, especially the inexperienced ones like our host that day, Mike Bradbury. He had only taken up the game a couple of years before, and was likely to be put off his stroke by the presence of an inquisitive squirrel, let alone the several hundred spectators who had gathered on the first tee that morning to see the stars.

It was difficult to judge the state of nerves of the other businessman playing with us. He was a poker-faced man with an unpronounceable Polish name who owned a chain of jewellery shops.

Jack had spoken some calming words to both of them, ending with: 'Don't worry, they've come to see me and the show-biz boys, not you.'

To me, Jack was really the star of our team, a stalwart of professional golf who has finished in the top ten of the Open on several occasions and has performed with honour for Europe in the Ryder Cup.

He was wrong though about whom the spectators had come to see. The great majority had come solely to see the show-business stars, not the professional golfers; to get close to the celebrities whom they saw in their living rooms on the television screen, and to hang on their every word.

So, most of the fans had eyes only for the fourth member of our team, the celebrated Grant Sadler. In the previous decade he had shot to prominence in a succession of action roles: he was tough and uncompromising and usually in trouble with his boss; he always got his man and always got the girl. He had recently softened his image by starring in a series of light-hearted television commercials for a brand of chocolate.

I tried to be objective and see in him what the fans clearly saw: glamour and success, all the magic created by the 'telly'. I saw a man who might have been good-looking in his youth and early manhood. He was just under six feet tall, with a flat, bronzed and rather fleshy face. His eyes looked small above the pouchy cheeks and his crinkly black hair was probably permed. He was well built, but as he bent to address his first shot I could see a tell-tale roll of surplus flesh around his waist, detectable even under his designer sweater. Perhaps he'd been eating too much of the chocolate he promoted. I suppose that if I'd liked the man, I wouldn't have noticed the perm, the fat or the red veins under the tan.

We all watched Jack hit a one-iron down the centre of the fairway. Then the amateurs hit their shots from a forward tee.

Nervous as he was, Mike Bradbury just connected with his drive and nobbled it about a 100 yards or so down the fairway.

As we walked down the first fairway Jack remarked, 'It's a different crowd, isn't it?'

'How do you mean?' I asked.

'It's a different noise somehow. There's more of a buzz at a proper tournament. This is more ragged, discordant almost.'

'Well, there are more children around.'

'More medallions and lager bellies too.'

'And earrings.'

We waited for Grant Sadler to catch up with us and Jack asked him what he was working on at the moment.

'Oh, a new sit-com for ITV. I set it all up last year. We've nearly finished the first thirteen episodes and they're about to commission another lot. Should be a big hit.'

'That's a new area for you, isn't it – comedy?' asked Jack.

'Yeah. But a good actor can change his style at will. It's not a problem.'

'I wish I could change my golf style at will,' said Jack ruefully.

Clearly Mr Sadler didn't lack confidence in his own abilities and I wondered whether his golf measured up to his reputation. He was said to play a better game than his handicap of ten suggested.

He certainly did. Despite a slightly cumbersome swing, he hit the ball powerfully and well. He played more like a five-handicapper than a ten. His Achilles heel was his putting and a notable tendency to take too short a club for his shots into the green, a mark of the club golfer. The club hacker can often be heard boasting that he 'hit the tenth green with an eight iron', as though expecting everyone to feel his biceps in admiration. Whereas the professional couldn't care less what he hits the green with as long as it's 'on the dance floor', as the old pros used to say, and offering the chance of a birdie.

I noticed that the jeweller had all the latest equipment: graphite shafts, beryllium copper heads on his irons and so on. A golf professional's dream. Sales of wedding rings must be good, I thought, or maybe it was all those earrings that were swelling his profits.

He obviously took the game seriously and played steadily. Jack played solidly too. Mike had a very lucky birdie, which clearly made his day, and Grant Sadler had a couple of birdies too. After nine holes we had a good score.

Jack had been going quietly on his way and seemed a little distracted, though he was ever on hand with a word of encouragement or advice for his playing partners. I knew that he didn't really like pro-ams but felt it was his duty to play in them, and especially for a charity such as Give a Child a Chance.

We took advantage of the refreshment hut between the ninth green and the tenth tee. As we tucked into our sausage sandwiches, Jack said in his genial fashion: 'Well done, boys, we're going well. We could be in amongst the prizes if we keep this up.'

There were smiles all round.

'And don't forget the celebrity prizes. I want to try and win for the Red Cross.'

This sentiment of Grant Sadler's was not as noble as it sounded. His interest was more in boosting his own image than in boosting the coffers of the Red Cross. The celebrity prizes were provided by an opportunistic sponsor, an insurance company, who had put up £50,000 for an Order of Merit amongst a select list of about thirty celebrities. Grant Sadler was one of them.

The Order of Merit would be calculated on each celebrity's four best scores in six pro-ams through the early part of the season. The winner would receive £25,000 for his nominated charity, and there were lesser prizes for those who finished in the next four places.

Most celebrities regarded this seemingly interesting and generous form of sponsorship as a chance to scoop some money for a favourite charity. But one or two behaved as though the Order of Merit was the Open Championship and were determined to win it for its own sake. They were allowed to carry their team score over to the next tournament, even though their amateurs and professional would be different. This had already led to some unseemly lobbying on the part of some celebrities to secure the services of the 'in-form' professionals and, although the teams were supposed to be drawn out of a hat, I had been told that

Grant Sadler had threatened to withdraw unless he played with one of the top pros such as Jack Mason.

It was irritating to listen to his sanctimonious wishes for the Red Cross when I knew that it was only for his own greater glory that Grant Sadler was so eager to win the top celebrity prize.

Perhaps Jack felt as I did; as we walked to the tee Jack spoke to Sadler. 'Just a suggestion, Grant, but why don't you let Chris club you on some of your shots. You're playing well but you're hitting the ball well short of the pin.'

Grant Sadler just nodded, refused a drink from the litre of beer which Jack produced from his bag and strode on to the tee. Jack knew of course that he wouldn't take kindly to any advice from me. From Jack, maybe. From me, no.

Mike had a peck or two at the Strongarm bitter while we waited to play down the tenth, and Jack finished the bottle off in one long glug.

He is an impressive drinker, all right. 'Better,' he said, and crashed his drive miles across the angle of the dog-legged tenth hole to leave himself a simple pitch into the green.

It gave me some pleasure to advise Grant Sadler to play short of the angle of the dog-leg with a three-wood. As he ignored my advice and reached for his driver, Jack winked at me.

Sadler tried to follow Jack across the corner. As he strained for some extra power his swing got faster, his left shoulder turned away from the line of the ball and he hit a horrible shot deep into the trees on the left.

He scowled at me as if I'd played the stroke and told me to keep my advice to myself for the rest of the round – I was ruining his concentration.

Oh well, we caddies know our place. Jack was grinning all over his face, but thereafter he concentrated on his own game and was rather subdued by his standards. But I noticed that he soon finished his other litre of beer. He played rather well and finished five under par, which was good enough to win him a small prize of £100. It was typical of him that he quietly put the money back in the Give a Child a Chance appeal. Grant Sadler, with Jack's formidable help, achieved a very respectable total of points for the celebrity Order of Merit.

Chapter 3

Grant Sadler was one of the two men who were with Poppy Drake on that occasion when I first saw her. The other was an older version of the actor. He was probably in his middle forties and his heavy frame was not disguised by the expensive casual clothes he wore: check trousers, cashmere roll-neck and an elegant jacket. His hair was greying beautifully at the temples and I wondered momentarily if he and Grant Sadler shared the same hairdresser. His face bore the characteristic flush of the heavy drinker. He was introduced to me as Bill Ryan, the producer of *Cap'n Hand*, Grant Sadler's new comedy series.

I wondered what this extraordinarily attractive woman was doing with these two. She had a slender body and long, long legs. Deep auburn hair framed a striking face with dark blue eyes, and those high cheekbones that photographic models always have. But intelligence shone out of her eyes. For some reason I thought I had seen that face before. It was not a face you would forget easily. Had I seen her on television? In a newspaper? I certainly associated it with something unusual, but perhaps my imagination was on overtime. Before I could pursue the thought, however, she was introduced to me by Sadler: 'This is Poppy Drake, one of the writers on my series. This is, er . . .'

I saw her glare at Grant Sadler but he had turned away to help Mike Bradbury organise some more drinks.

'Chris Ludlow,' I said as we shook hands. I offered her my

chair, as she said: 'Actually it's my series. I created it. It's a pity that these actors can't remember that if we didn't write their lines, they wouldn't have a job.'

Jack Mason had moved his chair a little closer; his resistance level to attractive women is low.

'Grant tells me that the series is going to be a great success,' he said.

'Yes. The signs are promising. A second series has been commissioned before the first has been completed. That's almost unheard of these days. But I won't bore you both with show-biz talk, you've probably heard enough if you've played a round with him. I know you're a famous golfer, Jack . . .' Jack attempted a modest smile, without much success, '. . . but what do you do, Chris?'

I explained that I was Jack's caddie and Jack said: 'He's not "just a caddie", Poppy. He's a guide and mentor. He keeps me going in those dark moments when I wonder why on earth I'm doing something so infantile as knocking a little white ball around the countryside, and he calms me down when I think I'm superman and can hit an eight-iron three hundred yards. And he is a friend, too, who never complains when I blame him for my own shortcomings.'

I was rather embarrassed by this uncharacteristic outburst from Jack. Although I knew him as a generous man, he rarely let his feelings surface in public.

Jack finished most of a glass of beer in one swallow and said, 'I must go. Dinner with my accountant tonight. Chris, can we have lunch tomorrow? I'll come over to the City. I need to discuss this year's programme and so on.'

I looked at Jack rather blankly because we had mapped out the year's golfing programme some weeks ago. Oh well, I assumed he had some changes in mind. I nodded my agreement.

'See you in the office at midday then. It's been a delight to meet you, Poppy, and I wish your series enormous success.' He held her hand a shade longer than necessary, gave her a smile and said, 'I'll leave you with my faithful caddie.'

As Jack moved off, shaking hands with all and sundry, thanking Mike Bradbury and giving him an impromptu lesson on how to grip a golf club properly, I took his chair next to Poppy Drake and found those clear blue eyes looking intently at me.

'Chris Ludlow,' she said. 'You're not related to a Max Ludlow, are you?'

My heart gave a nasty thump – oh, no. 'He's my brother.'

Max is my very talented younger brother and if he has a problem, it is with girls. Too many of them and too often. He can charm them into his arms from all corners and particularly out of their husbands' beds and into his own. I have seen him arrange a lunch date with a woman in the hearing of a clearly devoted husband. He usually gets away with it and trouble rarely ensues. He has been married once. It happened in his last year at Cambridge, which is when many young people are most vulnerable to the attractions of marriage. It lasted six months.

'Where is he at the moment?' asked Poppy.

'I think he's in Peru. In the middle of a two-month trek to look for endangered species,' I said with great satisfaction.

It isn't a question of the usual sibling rivalry with Max. There's no contest. While I went to a provincial university, Max got a maths scholarship to Cambridge; whereas I scraped into the university golf team, Max got blues for hockey, rugby and athletics. The only sport at which I can surpass him is golf. Off my handicap of two, I am in theory a much better player than Max off his approximate handicap of seven. The trouble is that I rarely seem to beat him. It's simply not fair.

Foolish optimist that I am, I was harbouring a dream of seeing much more of Poppy, but Max's shadow already lay heavily across those hopes.

A raucous chorus of 'Little White Ball' to the tune of 'Little White Bull' announced the approach of Kenny Craig – it was his joke for the day. Poppy had to lean closer to me so that I could hear her over the hubbub.

'Why don't you give me your number and we'll have a drink together soon.'

I liked her directness. That was the start of it all, and there seemed an inevitability about the course of our friendship.

At this point Kenny Craig, who'd clearly completed his second circuit of the hospitality tents, leaned heavily across the table. 'Here she comes.' He pointed an unsteady finger at the little wicket gate which formed part of Mike Bradbury's terrain for the day.

'She' was Amanda Newhart who had had a rollercoaster career over the past twenty-odd years: originally as a sex symbol in some really awful British films, then as a *femme fatale* in some equally awful British television series; and latterly as one of the stars of an extraordinarily successful American soap opera. She was the star of the tabloids, too, which chronicled her love affairs in mock shock and salacious detail.

'I still wouldn't mind giving her one,' said Kenny Craig.

'No, but I expect she would,' Poppy said.

While Kenny looked puzzled Poppy explained to me that Amanda Newhart was the female star of her series.

'I don't know why she's bothering. But she's got a bee in her Paul Smith hat about being a comedy actress. Her acting has always made me laugh anyway. But the producer, Bill Ryan, couldn't say no to her. He was her third husband, you know.'

'Yes, I do know. She's an old friend of my family. I've known her all my life.'

'Oh dear, I've put my clumsy foot right in it.' Poppy giggled and covered her face in embarrassment.

I knew Amanda Newhart when she was Phyllis Price. Her large family lived a few houses away from us in North London over twenty years ago. I used to go to school with two of her brothers and was mesmerised by this elder sister whose bizarre behaviour was alien to our conventional little suburb. It wasn't just the clothes, the accent or the perfume. Phyllis was simply a world-class show-off.

As I passed through puberty, the awe turned to lust, and I still remember the agonies of realising that she looked upon me as a child. The agonies were softened, though, by the reflected glory of knowing a real live film star and the admiration of friends who were only too keen to share my schoolboy fantasies about her.

To her credit, the great Amanda Newhart did not forget her family and her friends. My mother and father had always liked her, went faithfully to all her films and then watched all her television appearances. She kept in touch with them, even if it was only an occasional postcard from an exotic place, or to send some tickets for a film premiere.

When I arrived in London to work I was always immensely flattered whenever I received a call from her, maybe once a year. 'Darling Chris, come and have tea with me'; sometimes it was a drink and, once, dinner at the Savoy Grill.

The adoration had long ceased, but I still enjoyed her fleeting visits. She had dazzling good looks, which may have owed much to artifice and to her clothes designer. There could, too, have been a little bit of help along the way from the cosmetic surgeon's knife. She was, after all, in her mid-forties and looked fifteen years younger.

Amanda had a huge ego and was still a world-class show-off. But this was outweighed by her sense of humour and the extravagant tales of Hollywood with which she regaled us on her brief and noisy visits.

The delectable Amanda had reached our table in a shimmer of expensive perfume, designer dress and impossibly elegant brocaded jacket. She looked every inch the superstar. There was a flurry of kisses with Grant Sadler and Bill Ryan, who were at a nearby table. Kenny Craig attempted something more enthusiastic and was easily rebuffed by this veteran of thousands of attempted gropes and fumbles.

The superstar turned to our table, saw me and turned on the full power of her dazzling smile. She walked towards me, her arms outstretched.

'Darling Christopher. You look more beautiful every time I see you.'

I enjoyed my moment in the spotlight. With a promise of 'We'll have tea. I'll ring you,' Amanda swept on to give a formal kiss to the air on either side of Poppy's cheeks.

'Darling Poppy, what are you doing here? Shouldn't you be at home writing some good lines for me?'

'That would be a waste, wouldn't it, darling?' Poppy said, deadpan.

I liked this lady.

'And I might ask what you're doing here, Amanda?'

'I'm very involved with Give a Child a Chance. I've come to hand over a cheque from the Hollywood branch.'

'What did you do – a love-in or a coke-in?'

'Very droll, Poppy. We do in fact work hard and play hard over there, and you could perhaps learn a lesson from that.'

I was loath to leave in the middle of this end-to-end showbiz encounter between two well-matched opponents but it was certainly time to go. I made my farewells to Poppy and Amanda and thanked Mike Bradbury. As I left I saw that Grant Sadler and Bill Ryan had moved to a table inside the tent and, with only a bottle of champagne for company, were talking intensely to each other. As they leaned close together, they seemed like a brace of conspirators: Iago in double vision plotting the downfall of their lord.

Chapter 4

London Underground's staff shortages, signal failures and problems on the track at Ealing Broadway made for slow progress to the office the next morning. As we stood in silent misery, crammed together in the aisles, with only the sibilant hiss and thump of personal stereos to be heard above the bump and rush of the tube train, I wondered how many people were seriously considering throwing themselves under a train. 'When a man is tired of London, he is tired of life,' wrote Dr Johnson, complacently.

The good doctor didn't have to deal with the playful Spanish practices of the London transport system each day of his working life. I think I preferred Shelley's judgement: 'Hell is a city much like London.' Looking around at my fellow travellers, which was not easy since I was wedged between a young, blond giant of a man with a huge rucksack, and two city gents who were trying, with difficulty, to read the *Financial Times*, I reckoned that a straw poll would give it to Percy Bysshe and old Sam would lose his deposit.

I was about fifteen minutes late for work in the upended oblong of steel, concrete and glass that thrust itself, brutal and rude, into the City skies.

The firm of stockbrokers for whom I work occupies four floors of this coarse tribute to Mammon, designed by someone with all the aesthetic sensibility of a pit-bull terrier.

It was going to be a busy morning. It seemed likely that

my firm would be handling the issue of shares for Rave Records Associates Ltd, a conglomerate in the entertainment business whose fortunes had been built on the aggressive marketing of pop and rock records and the magazines that go with them. They had branched out from that lucrative source into the ownership of local radio stations, into discotheques, clubs, restaurants and wine bars, into book publishing, video production and marketing, into television and film production, and they had even bought one of the largest and most successful artists' management agencies in Britain.

It was the apotheosis of vertical marketing. In the ideal world of RRA a pop singer, managed by their agency, would cut a record for the Rave Record label. He would be promoted in their various magazines, through interviews, features and 'positive editorial comment', would make a promotional video for the RRA video company, be interviewed on their radio stations, on which the record would be heavily plugged, and would do a nation-wide tour on which most of the venues would be owned by RRA. Eventually a book about the star's life and work would appear from Rave Publishing.

What a way to make money. It certainly seemed easier than stockbroking and was definitely easier than caddying.

I mentioned earlier that my boss, Andrew Buccleuth, is golf-mad; he lives for the moment when he can wave goodbye to the City and spend every day on the golf course. He is a great admirer of Jack Mason and follows his progress on the tour with consuming interest. He was delighted to hear that Jack was lunching with me and even thought about cancelling his own lunch so that he could join us, but the clients concerned were too august. He insisted that I took Jack up to his office for a pre-lunch drink. On the way I gave Jack a rapid tour of the dealing room. The phones were buzzing, the computer screens were flickering with all the latest share prices and the fax machines were humming vigorously. It was busy and noisy and not Jack's scene at all, although he was happy to shake hands and exchange words with several of the dealers.

We were ushered in to Andrew's large and comfortable office which looks south to the towering developments which surround the Thames.

As he took the cork out of a bottle of Krug champagne, Andrew said, 'I'm sorry I haven't got any bottles of interesting beer for you, Jack, but I hope this will do.'

Andrew is well aware that Jack is as much an enthusiast of good champagne as he is of strong beers.

We were waved to some easy chairs by the windows and Andrew lowered his own tall frame into one of them. He took off his gold-framed, half-moon glasses which, perched as they were on his large and fleshy face, gave him the look of a cheerful and intelligent bloodhound.

The two men have several characteristics in common. They are both tall and partly conceal their sharp intelligence behind that bluff style of bonhomie which is often affected by big men. But, as many a City financier and many a golfing opponent would confirm, the inner steel is not too far from the surface. Neither will tolerate fools or charlatans and will deal with them with a sharp-humoured brusqueness that invites no argument.

They are both generous men: Andrew in his relations with his staff and with his peers in the City and as a liberal sponsor of obscure arts projects, especially in the fringe theatre; and Jack as a tireless supporter of golf projects for young people, and a benevolent source of advice for fellow professionals with a problem with some aspect of a horribly difficult game.

These are the outward and visible signs of a generosity that comes from deep within. It also explains why they feel so easy with each other.

Each has a lot of time for the judgement of the other, and values the other's advice. Andrew asked Jack now whether he should invest in a set of metal woods. He felt that his trusty persimmon woods were no longer giving him the length he used to get.

Jack briefly made his recommendations and then asked Andrew about RRA.

'I'm amazed that you're involved with this outfit, Andrew. Rave Records. It doesn't sound your style at all.'

Andrew settled his glasses on his face and smiled: 'You notice that the company is called RRA now. Rave has been discreetly dropped, except as a brand name for records. Rave has been "de-emphasised" as the PR boys would say.'

He refilled our glasses with champagne and continued: 'As for RRA not being our style, I would tend to agree, but the fees are substantial and we will of course get a lot of exposure in the media. It's what's known in the trade as a glamour stock. We should pick up more of the same in the future. Very lucrative. We haven't got the business yet, but I must admit it's ninety per cent certain.'

Andrew went on to explain that RRA were issuing forty million shares which would probably be priced at over £3. The directors wanted the money to finance their expansion and in particular to buy a television production company in the USA.

'We can thank your caddie, to a large extent, if we win the beauty parade.'

'Beauty parade?' Jack queried.

'The pitch for the business. Chris's expertise has probably tipped the scales our way.'

I did my best to smile modestly at Jack, who then asked us if he should buy some RRA shares.

I looked at Andrew, who said: 'Difficult one, Jack. It's my job to move this issue and the last thing I want is for half of them to be left unsold. That would be very embarrassing.

'RRA is not an easy company to assess. Their turnover and profits are respectable and they seem to be good at marketing. But the music and entertainment industry is outside the ken of most people in the City, including me. We're suspicious of it – it's sex and drugs and peculiar people with bizarre hair styles and odd modes of speech. There's a criminal element on the fringes, not even on the fringes in some cases. Of course, it's all to do with fashion. How on earth can I judge whether this or that pop star is going to build a career? My tastes in pop music stop at Sinatra and the Beatles. I can't tell the song title from the name of the group; my daughters are my advisers on this kind of thing.

'Chris will give you as good advice as I can about RRA. But my instinct is to have a quiet gamble, at the last minute, if the omens are right. Watch the comment in the papers because that sways people's opinions. I don't think RRA is one for the long-term investor. I think this is an occasion when you punt a few thousand pounds, take an immediate profit, and thank your lucky stars.'

Jack and I prepared to go off for lunch and as we reached the door Andrew said:

'One more word of advice, Jack, is that your own eyes will help you assess companies like RRA. If your son is playing their records and videos and wearing their T-shirts that may well be a good sign. But if you pop into a retailer and see that their records are in the low-priced range or that their videos are heavily discounted then it's the time to sell the shares.'

It was sound advice and the brand of common sense which Andrew dispensed to his clients.

We strolled a few hundred yards to a wine bar with an agreeable restaurant in the basement. Jack insisted on buying another bottle of Krug and we sat by the corner of the bar to drink it. Jack reckoned that the price he was charged paid the rent for his seat for a year. But the exorbitant prices didn't hold back the City workers around us. A group of young men, with the characteristic looks of money brokers, had taken over the far end of the bar and were piling into bottles of Beck's beer at speed. Nearer to us there were smaller groups of slightly older men, with a scattering of women, spending money even faster on champagne and white Burgundy.

Dark suits and striped shirts were the fashion, as always

in the City, and I checked my theory that there is a relationship between the brightness of the stripes and the optimism of the market. On looking around, I judged the mood to be one of cautious optimism.

We were settled downstairs at our table by the *maitre d'*, or the *maitresse d'*, I should say, a very attractive and cheerful lady. Above her short black skirt, her white silk blouse showed off her cleavage to the best advantage. It was clear that Jack thought her every inch a potential '*maitresse*'.

'Lovely girl,' he said as we studied the menu.

'You noticed, did you?'

'One is allowed to look, but not perhaps to touch.'

I grinned at Jack and reflected that, although he had an educated eye for a pretty woman, he was wholly discreet. As far as I knew, nothing disturbed the calm tenor of his life with his delightful wife of nearly twenty years. It was always a bonus to see Jenny on her regular appearances at golf tournaments, where she assumed her role of loyal supporter with enthusiasm. But she was a detached observer, too, since she has a wide range of interests of her own.

'So what do you really think about RRA, Chris?'

I was surprised that he was again raising a subject which we'd covered and suddenly felt that it was for some other reason that we were lunching. But I summarised Andrew's advice in a slightly different way: that RRA had good profit figures, good income projections and were very good at marketing.

'The figures looked good at several dodgy companies in the last year,' Jack said, 'or, rather, the accountants made them good, and look what happened.'

He was quite right. In particular, a computer company and a food manufacturer had recently gone down with all hands, to the immense surprise of many City experts who seemed to think that the pleasure cruise would last for ever.

'What really worries Andrew,' I continued, 'is the fashion element in the company. What happens if a few of their heavily hyped records don't make it to the charts? If the various TV series they're doing don't get past the first six episodes? If the next European tour by Fiends of the Earth, or whatever loony name the group uses, is a flop?'

'Wasn't Johnny Storm with Fiends of the Earth?'

'Yes, how on earth did you know that?' I asked, because Jack was hardly noted for being immersed in pop culture.

'Oh, it's Nick, my eldest boy. He's heavily into pop now. He wanders around with a personal stereo, clicking his fingers and gently gyrating inside his torn jeans. We'd quite like to have him put down.'

I sympathised and watched as Jack sniffed his glass of Australian cabernet, drank a good quantity of it and looked around the room.

I was more than ever convinced that Jack had something on his mind which had nothing to do with RRA's flotation. And I was right.

'I've got something very difficult to say to you, Chris, and I suppose the best way is to say it straight, without any flannel.'

He studied his glass intently, then looked straight at me: 'I've decided that I need a change of caddie.'

He paused, allowing time for his words to sink in. They wouldn't.

'I hope that this isn't a great shock to you. But I need a change. This is no reflection on you. I meant everything I said to that lovely girl yesterday. You're one of the best caddies around. But I think I need a fresh eye, so to speak. You know every inch of my game and I feel at times that we've got a bit "set in our ways". Like an old married couple, I suppose.'

The speech, which he'd obviously rehearsed, did nothing to soften its effect. Jack had been a shade withdrawn recently on the golf course, and rather noncommittal about his tournament programme. Now I knew why.

I couldn't shake off the sense of shocked disbelief and

there was a sharpness in my voice as I asked, 'And who's your new spouse?'

'My new caddie's Zoe Bernini,' he said with some embarrassment. 'Now, I know what you're thinking and the answer is no, I'm not going to bed with her, and I have no intention of trying.'

He'd be one of the few who wasn't. Zoe Bernini is a bundle of sexy fun, curly haired and cuddly, her dark-complexioned face always smiling. She had played golf on the amateur circuit and had decided to broaden her education by becoming a caddie. Her avowed intention was to carry the bag of an Open Champion before moving into the administration of the professional tour and eventually becoming its executive director. She certainly has the charm and the energy to achieve all those ambitions.

I think my silence unnerved Jack, but for the moment I had nothing to say.

'Look, Chris, I'm thirty-six, which is not old by any standards except sport. Even in golf, which doesn't rely overmuch on fitness, I've only got ten years at the most at the top. I still think I can win an Open, you know.'

I had to agree that he has the talent to do so. His is an admirably solid game in all departments, and especially on and around the putting green which is where championships are won and lost. He has been close on a couple of occasions but I wondered whether he really has the X factor which all true champions must possess. This is the immensely selfish ability to press on to victory whatever the mental cost, to put the fear of winning out of your head. Most people cannot cope with the anguish of coming desperately close and then failing.

I still said nothing. I wanted Jack to talk on until he hanged himself with his own verbal rope. I looked down at my hands which were on the edge of the table. They were tightly clenched, the knuckles white.

Jack continued to justify his decision. 'Zoe is a good caddie. Not as good as you. Yet. But she is devoted full time to golf. And I might have a different approach to the game with her, be a bit more ambitious. Bloody hell, Chris, this is coming out all wrong. It sounds as if I'm unhappy with you. Far from it. I'm sure you know that. But I think a change is advisable. I'm probably a victim of the golfing menopause,' he ended with a strained smile.

'Jack, I think you protest too much. If you think you need a full-time caddie, why don't you say so? If you fancy Zoe, why not say so? Everything's all right at home, I hope?' I asked maliciously. I didn't accept his reasons for sacking me.

'Yes, of course it is,' he said sharply. 'I discussed this with Jenny and she told me that I was an absolute idiot even to consider a change. I won't embarrass you by repeating her words – suffice it to say that she's one of your greatest fans. So am I. But she was also amused at the thought of my having a woman as a caddie.'

Under different circumstances, I might have smiled too at the thought of the imposing figure of Jack Mason, six feet three inches high and tipping the scales at more than fourteen stones, being accompanied down the fairways by the tiny figure of Zoe Bernini. She was only a little over five feet tall, a bubbling and darting figure, always on the go, always chatting. It would be quite a combination.

'Several good golfers have tried to poach me over the three years we've been together, Jack. And I turned them down flat.' So much for loyalty. 'Now, I'd better look for another boss.'

'No need. I've fixed someone for you, if you're interested. In fact I've arranged for you to work with him next month at the Stripes Classic. Rollo Hardinge.'

'You cannot be serious!' Surprise made me quote from the wrong sport. 'Good God, Jack, he's hardly won a cent since he came on tour. And he's as crazy as a coot!'

'I know he seems odd, but he's got an enormous talent. He murdered everybody in the Under Twenty-five tournament last year. Won by nine shots. You'll be good for him. If he gets some good advice he could win a tournament.'

'I'm not sure he's capable of taking any advice. And I'm not likely to make much as his caddie, am I?'

'You'll do OK. He's prepared to put up a solid guarantee. You know his father's loaded, don't you? He's something in Hollywood. TV producer, I think. How much did you make working for me last year?'

'Well, we had a good year. I made around twenty grand, less expenses.'

'That's what I thought and Rollo is willing to put up fifteen as a guarantee.'

This was quite a generous figure, especially from a golfer who was way down at the bottom of the Order of Merit. This league table is based solely on the amount of money won by the professionals in official tournaments. At the end of the season only the top 120 golfers qualify for the next season's tournaments. If you fail to make the grade, the only option is to try and qualify again for the tour at the dreaded qualifying school which takes place in November.

The fees paid to caddies are mostly based on results. The pro pays the caddie a commission out of the prize money earned, and this is normally between five and ten per cent. A guarantee is also agreed and this is designed to cover the caddie's expenses.

It can be a precarious living for a caddie, especially if his boss is someone as unsuccessful as Rollo Hardinge.

I realised what a predicament Jack had found himself in and that he'd tried his best for me under the circumstances. But I wasn't going to let him get away with it so easily.

'Well, thanks for fixing me up, Jack. It would have been nice to be consulted. I wonder if I'll last the week anyway. Didn't he sack a caddie once because he didn't like the colour of his sweater?'

'No, he didn't like his accent. The bloke was from Essex, I believe.'

I looked round nervously in case there were any money brokers or futures traders nearby who might have taken exception to Jack's remark. The likely candidates were several tables away and were too busy punishing the pink champagne to bother about us.

As Jack headed for the Underground and I strolled back towards the office I asked myself whether I wanted to continue as a caddie. I had fallen into the job by chance and was lucky that I was allowed to combine it with a much more lucrative career in the City. A lot of the fun and the excitement might go now that I was no longer to carry Jack Mason's bag. He was, after all, a winner and therein lay the thrill of being his caddie.

There wouldn't be much thrill if I were caddying for a golfer who was battling to qualify for a share of fiftieth place or worse.

I reflected on the little I knew about Rollo Hardinge. The first problem was that he was left-handed. Harry Vardon said that he never saw a left-hander who was worth a damn, and he was a pretty good judge. There have been very few really good left-handed golfers. In fact I could only think of two. There may be a good reason for this. Some say there are so few sets of second-hand clubs for left-handers around that they start by playing right-handed and stick with it. That sounds a bit simplistic to me but it is odd that there are so few, particularly in comparison with cricket where every side seems to have several 'cack-handers'.

Jack was right in saying that Rollo Hardinge could be brilliant on his day. But those days of brilliance had so far been rare compared to his days of mediocrity. He is a man of six feet four and his height makes him look slender. That look is accentuated by his swing which is one to be envied – supple and free flowing. It is beautiful to watch and his long arms and elasticity enable him to get the leverage to propel the ball over vast distances. But he seems incapable of compromise. He's all dash and devil, and when his swing goes wrong it can be disastrous. A round of 66 is often followed by a 78. It happens to every golfer occasionally but Rollo seems to have had more than his fair share of bad days. And this was my new boss.

Chapter 5

I live in a large flat in south-west London. It is on the ground floor of a solid Victorian house, once home no doubt to a large family with a couple of servants, and now split into four.

It suits me well and I like my home, but when I got back to my flat that evening I felt depressed and bitter. It would take time to accept the change forced on me by Jack. I could not settle and knew I was suffering from self-pity. I needed some company, a sympathetic ear.

I made three futile attempts to find a companion. The first woman friend I phoned was already late for a drinks party; and the second told me, frostily, that it had taken me over three weeks to get around to calling her and she was not available at such short notice. I tried a golfing friend who lived nearby, but he was baby-sitting while his wife was at night school. Would I like to join him? I could hear a child screaming in the background and declined his invitation.

My antidote to depression is exercise. I forced myself into a track suit, set up my portable multi-gym in the second bedroom and settled in for half an hour's weight training. It's a fairly monotonous way of getting exercise, but Beethoven soothed my mind while my body suffered a little.

I still felt thoroughly pissed off with life, so thought I might as well do the job properly with a few pints of Young's at the local pub. I was halfway across the hall on my way out when the telephone rang. I only stopped because I thought it might be my neighbour from the flat above, Mrs Bradshaw. A widowed lady of independent mind, Mrs Bradshaw treats me like the son she never had. She keeps a fake-stern eye on me and spoils me to the extent of cleaning my flat every week and occasionally cooking a meal for me. In return I do minor household repairs for her, oversee her substantial investments and sometimes we go to a film or a concert together. She is a great friend and a calming presence.

It was not her voice but the pleasant, if sardonic, tones of Poppy Drake which asked, 'Is that Chris Ludlow, the celebrated caddie? How about that drink? When can you make it?'

'Now?' Poppy Drake was exactly the company I needed. What timing.

She laughed at my eagerness. 'Now? You're playing hard-to-get. OK, we'll make it this evening. Seven o'clock?'

She gave me her address which was not too far away in Kensington and without more ado she said goodbye. She was nothing if not direct and clearly used the telephone only to convey or receive information.

I was surprised at how much her brief call had lifted my spirits. She had the heady effect of a glass of champagne drunk down quickly on an empty stomach. It was a while since a newly met woman had had this effect on me and a warning voice told me to watch out. I should have listened.

Her flat was on the fifth floor of a mansion block in a quiet road just off Kensington High Street. She showed me into a sitting room with wide windows which looked over the zig-zag rooftops towards Kensington Gardens.

'If they hadn't built that damn great hotel I'd be able to see a bit of the gardens – just. But at least I can go running there. It's very relaxing.'

She waved me to one of two broad sofas. The peach-coloured walls had prints and watercolours dotted over them and the shelves in the alcoves were packed with books. I noticed how neat everything was and reflected that it was only Mrs Bradshaw's efforts and my occasional tepid attempts at housework which kept the tide of disorder at bay in my own flat.

I was looking at some of the watercolours when Poppy returned with a bottle of wine.

'Most of those were done by my husband.'

'I didn't realise you were married.'

'Not any longer. He, er, died a couple of years back.'

'I'm sorry.'

'Don't be. The marriage was a disaster. We were about to divorce when he died. He was an actor.'

I suddenly realised why her face, coupled with her name, had rung a distant bell in my mind. I remembered something about his death. Suicide.

With all due respect to Poppy's dear departed, I was glad that there were no complications with husbands or ex-husbands. The presence of my brother, Max, in Poppy's past was bad enough.

'Have you been married, Chris?'

'No, nor even close to it.'

She smiled at me and it was a warm smile, a smile to look at and savour.

'I hope you're not like that brother of yours. He's lovely and he's also bloody impossible.'

I didn't put up much of a defence of my brother's treatment of women and anyway, love him though I may, didn't want to waste time with Poppy talking about Max. Before I could find a tactful way of changing the subject, Poppy had done the job for me in her direct fashion.

'Let's not talk about him. Let's talk about you. Tell me how you manage to combine stockbroking and caddying.'

I explained the happy accidents that had led me to where I am now: university, an attempt to play the amateur golf circuit, marketing jobs in finance and insurance, disillusionment (with work, said my father) and then, by chance, a job caddying for a professional golfer which led, much to my father's disgust, to regular jobs on the tour. He was only mollified when Andrew Buccleuth offered me a job as a part-time salesman with his firm of stockbrokers. In the early days I think Andrew primarily valued me as his golf partner but had since placed his trust in me as a supposed expert in the leisure field.

I thought it was time for me to ask the questions and I wanted to exorcise Max, so to speak. Poppy told me that she had met him in Northern Ireland.

'My father is a soldier, you see, in fact the family has a long tradition in the military. I visited my folks for a couple of weeks, met Max, who was doing something secret over there and, as I told you, we had a little fling which continued in London for a while – a very short while – and that was it.'

That got Max out of the way, which Poppy also clearly welcomed, and I asked her about her writing career.

'I had a conventional education, like you, and joined the BBC after university. Auntie Beeb provides a wonderful grounding, but I really wanted to write, so I moved to Capital TV.

'I was p.a. – production assistant – to several light entertainment producers. I just kept submitting scripts for the various series they were doing, and sketches and one-liners.

'Eventually I sold one sketch, then a few more and then I started to get small commissions. I found myself an agent who represents a lot of well-established comedy writers and through him I started writing episodes of existing series.'

'Didn't the original writers object?'

'Oh no. The originators of these long-running series get bored; they run out of steam and they're often working on something else. They still get a royalty on each script. And that was my ambition – to originate my own series.'

'And you've done it with the Grant Sadler series?'

'Well, yes, he's in it. It's called *Cap'n Hand*.'

She grinned as I did an exaggerated flinch at the awful punning title.

'Yes, I've done it, but I had to make some sacrifices to get it off the ground.'

'Not of your honour, I hope.'

She laughed. 'Worse than that. An independent called RRA is producing the show for Capital TV.'

'The independents are getting more and more of the cake, aren't they? I was looking at the figures the other day.'

'Yes, ITV and the BBC have to take at least a quarter of their production from outside sources. Why were you looking at the figures?'

I explained to Poppy that I was involved in the flotation of RRA on the stock market.

She filled up our glasses and continued. 'My agent introduced me to RRA and I told them about my idea for a comedy drama series which takes place around a little fishing village in the west country. It's a mix of the locals, the shopkeepers and pub owners, the fishermen, the people who hire out boats and, of course, the shifting population of holiday-makers. It's mostly about the impact of the visitors on a small community.'

'A sort of "Archers by the Sea",' I said.

'Well, a little more sophisticated than that,' Poppy said drily, 'and a lot funnier, I hope. But I won't bore you with all the details. Suffice to say that dealing with an independent company is not like dealing with ITV or the Beeb. The people at RRA said it was imperative to present a package to the ITV companies: star, producer, director and writer.

'Before I knew where I was, Grant Sadler was on the scene and his chum, Bill Ryan, was slotted in as producer and director. They are of course clients of RRA, represented by their agency. Then RRA needed more storylines. I'd already written the synopsis of the series, a breakdown of the main characters and the opening episode. But Bill Ryan wanted some more plot outlines. I discussed them with him, as one should with one's producer, and then I heard that he was claiming a writing credit – for listening to my ideas and suggesting a couple of changes.'

'Does it matter?'

'It matters because he didn't write it. And he and Grant Sadler have already grabbed more than their fair shares of the format royalties and ancillary rights.' She could see that she'd lost me and explained. 'The format means the characters, background and so on that I created. Those rights might be sold to an overseas TV company, an American one for instance. And the ancillary rights cover the cinema, publishing, theatre and the like.'

'If they're important, why did you give in?'

'Because there comes a time when you'll agree virtually anything to get the project going. And my agent told me these rights were deal breakers. I had to accept a buy-out – a once-and-for-all fee with no share in future spin-offs.'

There was some resentment in Poppy's voice, but then she smiled. 'It doesn't matter. The fact remains that it's my own series. My first. And I don't think it'll do much overseas anyway.'

I decided to change the conversational tack slightly. 'How do you get on with Amanda Newhart? I didn't discern a meeting of minds at the golf the other day.'

Poppy grinned at the memory. 'Oh, she can be a real bitch at times. And then at other times you know that it's just an act. But I must be careful, she's a friend of yours.'

I shook my head in a deprecating way. 'Just an acquaintance, really. I only see her once in a blue moon.'

'That's what they all say. I know she's a star, Chris, but her acting certainly didn't make her a star. She has an unerring ability to emphasise the wrong word in every sentence. If she can remember the words, that is. Otherwise she makes up her own. As for her timing – huh! And she fancies herself as a comedy actress. And has the nerve to rewrite my lines. Of course she does have Bill Ryan in her pocket and that's a very polite way of putting it. She's trying hard to bring in other writers instead of me.'

'But Poppy, it all sounds purgatory – Sadler, Ryan, Amanda. Wouldn't you prefer to let other people write it?'

'Oh no,' said Poppy with confidence, 'I can handle them. And I'm moaning too much. It's mostly great fun and a lot of the people are charming, including Amanda on her good days.'

I admired her cool determination and laughed as she regaled me with several everyday stories of television folk.

The bottle was empty and Poppy glanced at her watch.

'Chris, I'm sorry, but I must fly. I'm due at a friend's for dinner in ten minutes. Can we do this again?'

I was more than happy to agree and at the door she threw her arms around me and kissed me. I felt briefly her firm and supple body. She pulled away and I turned to the lift. Poppy smiled that splendid smile again and said, 'You will call me, won't you? Over the weekend. We'll make plans.'

There was nothing coy about Poppy Drake. She seemed to be a lady who knew what she wanted and went after it with a will. That was OK with me.

Chapter 6

The sudden termination of my job as Jack Mason's caddie might have left me wan and dissatisfied, especially at weekends, when the closing stages of professional golf tournaments bring their own excitements. It would be a matter of three weeks or so before I took up the bag of Rollo Hardinge, an unknown quantity if ever there was one.

However, the temporary golfing void in my life was filled by Poppy's energetic presence. Any reservations I had about pursuing her – and many men have qualms about pursuing really beautiful women – were overridden by her. She took the initiative and it was a delight.

I have only rarely felt so in harmony with another person; we found that our tastes converged in many things: books, food, theatre and people. It was a perfect start to a new relationship. It had a smooth inevitability to it. Poppy was full of fun and interest, and quirky too, with her sudden telephone calls. It might be to arrange a meal at a new restaurant she'd heard about or a visit to a fringe theatre; once, on an unexpectedly warm and placid evening, we had an impromptu picnic by the lido in Hyde Park.

After nearly three weeks of this whirlwind friendship I felt a real sense of loss when Poppy spent a weekend away with some elderly relations. It was a duty visit and she said she would not dream of disappointing them.

I felt a double sense of loss when I awoke early on the

Saturday morning. No Poppy and no golf tournament with Jack Mason either. On the plus side, I didn't have to tangle with a day in the City. I lay in bed for a while, daydreaming. Eventually I forced myself to get up.

I ran some oranges through the juicer and had a quick look at the morning papers. I looked first at what was happening in the Spanish Open, which Jack had decided to miss, and saw that Mark Buckley, a very consistent golfer from Zimbabwe, was in the lead, with Bjorn Carlssen and a clutch of Spanish, Australian and British players close behind. I didn't know whether my new boss, Rollo Hardinge, was playing there but he certainly did not feature among the top thirty or forty who were listed.

I turned to the pages of the *Daily News* out of loyalty to its golf correspondent and my good friend, Toby Greenslade. He was far too gifted a writer to be purveying words of no more than two syllables for a tabloid newspaper with a predictable and unedifying obsession with the doings of television and pop stars, the royal family and under-talented soccer players.

But Toby accepted the large salary and the even larger expense account and turned an eye blinded mostly by the champagne which was liberally dispensed by the sponsors of golf. One of Toby's minor pleasures was to try to break the two-syllable rule and to slip longer words past the dedicatedly plebeian eye of his sports editor.

Under the headline, 'Tough Buckley Pursued by Spanish Armada', Toby had written:

> In the second round of the Seat Spanish Open, played in the torrid heat of the Costa del Sol, that teak-hard golfer from Zimbabwe, Mark Buckley, recorded his second consecutive score of 68 to lead by one shot.
>
> Right on his tail is the Swedish golfing machine, Bjorn Carlssen, and the fiery Spaniard, Eduardo

Jimenez. The young pretenders from England, Jamie Henderson and Richard Wakehurst, are two shots off the pace.

The report ended:

Can hard man Buckley tough it out in front of these partisan Spanish fans? Will the implacable Swedish ace record his second win of the year? Or will one of the Spanish Armada sail to victory?

I was surprised that 'implacable' had survived in Toby's report and even more surprised that 'Spanish fly' had not been inserted somewhere. Otherwise it was fairly standard *Daily News* fare with the key words which would reassure their readers in place. Scandinavians are always 'implacable golfing machines'; Spaniards and all other Latins are 'fiery' and their supporters are 'partisan'.

The rest of the day passed quickly since I was doing many of the things I most enjoy. I browsed in the local shops and especially in the wine shop, which always has some unusual wines to taste on a Saturday under the tutelage, humorous and well-informed, of the owner; I played golf at Sunningdale and won £25; and ended the day's entertainment by having dinner with some friends who live nearby. Nick works for a large firm of solicitors in the City and his wife, Harriet, is determined to fix me up with a suitable wife. This time she came in the form of a barrister called Jo. We left together and she said with a smile: 'Harriet's always trying to fix me up, too.'

Sunday is a lovely day, especially if you don't have to work. It has a special feel to it which will probably not survive much longer if the men in the grey suits have their way and are allowed to open their stores and supermarkets. It will be degraded to just another day – another victory for wan utilitarianism.

I skimmed the sport and business pages of the quality

newspapers, saw that Bjorn Carlssen was now in the lead in the Spanish Open and that the RRA issue had received a favourable mention from one of the journalists I had lunched recently.

As anticipated, Andrew's firm had won the RRA business and he had asked me to do my best with the financial Press, which is so important to a new issue and especially to one in such a volatile sector of the market as RRA. Like the theatrical critics of New York and London they can make or mar a new venture. They are certainly a sharp-eyed and sharp-tongued bunch. After all, one of their number had ended up as Chancellor of the Exchequer.

The crisp look of the spring day persuaded me to don a track suit and lope off towards the common. The traffic was light as I chugged slowly up the hill and then I stretched my pace along the bridle paths of the common. I passed several other runners and walkers who were strolling through the trees with their dogs and their children. City dwellers need these open spaces, and they are never more rejuvenating than on such a morning.

> Everyone suddenly burst out singing,
> And I was filled with such delight
> As prisoned birds must find in freedom.

Sassoon's words came back to me from some hazy corner of my memory and seemed singularly appropriate.

I showered and followed my usual breakfast of fruit with the indulgence of an egg-and-bacon sandwich with thick slabs of wholemeal bread. Lovely.

I settled down to the newspaper and the various financial magazines and stock market tip-sheets that I had to read. I was amused by an article in one of the magazines that described how the writer had picked some of the more obscure companies out of the stock market listings, and particularly those with bizarre names: Chancer Trust, Spook Industries, Nogo Group, Last Resort Holdings, J & L

Stuff, Stork Enterprises, for example. Over a year he had beaten the average rise in the UK stock market very comfortably, and the best-performing unit trust handsomely. Many people maintain that if you used a monkey to throw darts into the *Financial Times*' listings of shares you would do better with your money than would the average stockbroker. I have a sneaking regard for this idea, which sophisticated analysts call the 'random walk' theory, but have never dared to say so.

A sharp knock on the door, a distinctive note, announced Mrs Bradshaw, elegant as ever in tweed suit and cashmere sweater.

'Are you coming to the pub, Chris? There's some food for you afterwards, if you wish.'

'Yes, I do wish.'

I threw on a sweater and we set off on the five-minute walk to our local pub, a friendly and well-run place which has the enormous merit of serving not only very drinkable beer but also a good range of wines.

I glanced idly at the placards outside the newsagent's shop and stopped abruptly as I saw a photograph of Amanda Newhart and the huge headline: 'Star in Sex Romp Scandal'.

I suddenly realised that she had not called me to invite me to tea as promised. She had clearly been much too busy.

'Would you hang on a moment, Mrs Bradshaw?'

I went in and bought a copy of the *Sunday Chronicle* and the characteristically uninhibited banner headline hit me in the eye:

ONE, TWO, THREE . . . BONK!

The pub was already filling up with eager drinkers, a tribute to the quality of the drinks and the food which the landlord and his family served up.

We managed to find a table and took a pull at our drinks.

I wasn't the only person with a copy of the *Sunday*

Chronicle and there were roars of laughter among one group of men who were studying the report. I laid the paper out on the table and Mrs Bradshaw put on her glasses and said: 'What fun, Chris. Is she a friend of yours?'

'Well, I do know her . . .'

'But not intimately, I trust.'

'Mrs Bradshaw, for a respectable widow lady, you sometimes leave a lot to be desired. She's actually an old family friend,' I said primly.

I read the first paragraph.

> Amanda Newhart, champion transatlantic bonker, is at the heart of a sex-romp ring that has rocked show-business circles.
>
> The sexy star, veteran of five marriages, is usually seen these days in the company of the Italian racing driver, Antonio Peroni. He is well-endowed with money and the other thing that counts with the alluring Amanda!
>
> Our intrepid reporter answered an advertisement to join a couple for 'an unconventional evening'. Imagine her surprise when she was invited to join Amanda and Antonio for an evening's BONKING, and the first course was to be the luscious temptress, Amanda?

There was more in the same vein, much to Mrs Bradshaw's amusement. The intrepid reporter, in the true Fleet Street tradition, 'made her excuses and left' before her honour was besmirched.

'Do they make it all up?' Mrs Bradshaw asked.

'It wouldn't surprise me. I wonder how it will affect the TV series.'

I told Mrs Bradshaw about the *Cap'n Hand* series and she said: 'If anything, the story, true or not, will probably ensure its success. People don't have a strong moral standpoint on sex any more, do they? The so-called stars are expected to do these sort of things, and the general public love the titillation.'

Judging by the amusement among the pub's customers at the 'sex-romp revelations', Mrs Bradshaw was right.

Chapter 7

Poppy telephoned me on Sunday evening to say that she would return to London on the following evening. Perhaps we could meet on Tuesday for a meal.

I asked her if she had read the steamy revelations about Amanda in the *Chronicle* and she told me that her ageing relatives had stuck by the *Sunday Express* for all their adult lives and saw no reason to change. She giggled through my summary of the story and said: 'I'm sorry, Chris, but it does serve the randy bitch right.'

I was in two minds about trying to contact Amanda. I didn't want to seem guilty of prurient curiosity but thought she might feel the need of some support. The story was probably the invention of some jaded Fleet Street hack anyway.

I didn't have a direct number for her and tried her agent first. The fourth lady down the line identified herself as 'Miss Newhart's personal manager'.

'Oh, fancy that, an "old friend",' she spat at me when I explained why I wanted Amanda's personal number. 'My, what a lot of "old friends" Miss Newhart's got. You're the seventeenth to telephone this morning.'

With some difficulty I got her to agree to pass on my name and telephone number to Amanda.

About an hour later her breathy, slightly Americanised tones came over my phone. She didn't want to talk about the Press report on the telephone, 'Never trust telephones, darling – you don't know who might be listening in,' but invited me for a drink at her Barbican flat at five o'clock that evening.

I was delighted. All that awaited me that evening were some overdue domestic chores, and a drink with Amanda was infinitely more interesting than a date with the washing and ironing.

I decided to be a good citizen and use public transport. My virtue was rewarded with the appearance of a bus outside the office right on cue. We had a clear run to the Barbican, with the result that I was a few minutes early in arriving at Amanda's block.

I hadn't visited her since she'd taken this flat and, as I walked through the wide glass doors, I looked for the hall porter. The vast luxurious reception area was quiet and deserted. So much for the security for which the tenants no doubt paid through their teeth. Amanda had taken a penthouse on the seventh floor. I walked across two miles of thick carpet to the lift and pressed the button. The indicator told me that the lift was on her floor. Other visitors for Amanda perhaps.

As I waited, I registered the usual noises of a London street, muffled by the excellent sound-proofing of the building. The sound of the steady dribble of the traffic was occasionally punctuated by the muted thunder of a motor bike and the rhythmic thumping of a delivery van masquerading as a mobile disco, with its windows open and music blasting forth. I thought I also heard the scream of a seagull.

Then my ears picked up an alien sound – a bundle of newspapers being thrown on to the pavement? It seemed to come from the street at the side of the block. It was a noise that didn't fit and I was tempted to investigate but saw that the lift was now on its way down. Seconds later the doors rolled slowly back to reveal the familiar figure of Grant Sadler. Glad to see that Amanda's show business friends were supporting her, I smiled slightly and stood back. He wouldn't remember me.

But he did. He looked uneasy and flustered. 'You're the caddie, aren't you? Amanda's friend?'

I nodded and tried to slip past him into the lift, but he clutched at my arm.

'Hang on a minute. There's something wrong. I popped up to see her but there was a hell of a racket going on in there.'

'What sort of a racket?'

Sadler avoided my eye. He was showing all the signs of severe embarrassment.

'Well, look . . . Chris, isn't it?'

I nodded again.

'I actually thought she was at it. Erm, well, bonking. I listened through the letter box.'

It wasn't difficult for him to see the inevitable look of amusement on my face and he firmly studied the carpet.

'Anyway, I think we should leave it for a minute or two. By the sound of it they can't go on much longer,' he said, aware that this bashful behaviour wasn't in keeping with his tough and sexy image. 'Well, you should hear them,' he said, grinning a bit himself now.

As we hesitated, unsure what to do, I heard the screech of a gull again. Then I knew it wasn't a gull and Sadler too recognised it as a human scream. I raced through the door and down the side street. I remembered the alien sound and my heart seemed to thump in my throat. I saw the twisted bundle on the pavement, the limbs in bizarre attitudes, the long dark hair fanned out on the stone. I knew it was Amanda.

A woman in uniform was kneeling beside her feeling for a pulse. I was glad someone had reached Amanda before me – someone who appeared to know what to do. She looked up.

'Can you get on the phone, love. Ambulance, police. The poor woman's gone, I'm afraid.' Then I recognised her uniform. She was a parking warden.

I ran to do as she had asked. I found Sadler crouching at

the corner of the building, his head in his hands, talking to himself.

'Christ, I didn't understand. I thought she was . . . She must have been weeping, not . . . That noise she was making was . . . I was just the other side of her door and she . . .'

I grabbed him and pulled him to his feet. Inside the entrance to the flats I shoved him roughly towards the porter's desk.

'Make yourself useful. Get on that phone. Nine nine nine. Ambulance and police. I'm going up to her flat.'

I left him to it and ran for the lift, which was still waiting at ground level. I didn't know what I would find in Amanda's flat but I was happy to be doing something. Anything rather than wait by that broken body.

I felt sick. Had the humiliation of the *Sunday Chronicle* story been too much for Amanda to take? That was difficult to believe. She was a fighter; her unnerving egotism would carry her through any problem. But Sadler's words implied that she was in such distress that she had killed herself. Or had he really heard two people in there? The sounds he heard could have been the sounds of a struggle to the death. But I couldn't face up to the idea of murder or suicide and tried to tell myself that it must have been an accident.

As I stepped out of the lift on the seventh floor, I realised that her door would be locked.

I decided to follow Sadler's example, so I knelt down and peered through the letter box. It did not tell me much, apart from the fact that the hallway looked at least twice as long as a cricket pitch. Straight ahead were two double doors. They were open on to what was apparently the living room. I could see right through that to Amanda's terrace.

I was still gazing through the letter box when I heard the lift doors open behind me and I stood up, guiltily.

A very broad man, with thick grey hair, was watching me with an amused look on his face. Tinted spectacles sat uneasily on top of a large beaky nose. He was flanked by two uniformed policemen.

'Surveying the scene of the crime are we, sir?' he asked cheerfully.

The policemen smiled dutifully. The large man announced himself as Chief Inspector Brand.

'And who might you be, sir?'

I began my explanations and continued them at Tower Bridge police station. I was interviewed for over two hours by a detective sergeant, who chewed gum hypnotically throughout. With his jacket off and tie undone, he looked every inch a character actor in a television cop series. The big gun, in the shape of Brand, had obviously been brought to bear on Sadler.

The main thrust of the questioning was about timing. Was I sure that Sadler was on his way down before I heard Amanda hit the pavement? No, I wasn't, but he was probably just entering the lift at that time. Was I sure that my attention hadn't wandered? Could there have been a longer gap? Yes, I was sure; no, he did not have time to heave Amanda over the balcony and still get downstairs in the time available.

What was my relationship with Amanda? A family friend. Oh yes, really. And my relationship with Sadler? And his relationship with Miss Newhart?

So it went on and Detective Sergeant Prynne made it abundantly clear that it was only my testimony that stood between Grant Sadler and a charge of murder.

I had to repeat the words that Sadler had said to me several times and had to listen patiently to the policeman's various interpretations of them.

'Mr Sadler says he thought he heard her making love. If he did, there must have been another person in there. It takes two to tango,' he said with a smirk.

'Not necessarily. The sounds of passion are very close to the sounds of human distress.'

He wasn't convinced and I'm not sure that I was, either.

But I was sure that there had been no artifice in Sadler's despair at realising that he could possibly have saved Amanda. He wasn't that good an actor.

Initially, Prynne wasn't convinced either about my memory of the time between the sound of Amanda's fall and the movement of the lift. The persistent questioning was designed to shake my story but I clung fast to the knowledge that Sadler had simply not had the time to do the awful deed. The police hinted at various motives – jilted lover, professional rivalry. None of them rang true.

Tiring under police pressure, I was tempted for a moment to tell them what they wanted to hear and profess to uncertainty about the exact sequence of events. Sadler was such a creep, I would have enjoyed dropping him in it up to his flabby neck. But the one thing I could be certain of was that Grant Sadler hadn't the guts to commit murder.

Chapter 8

I felt slightly ashamed that my main emotion on reaching the comfort of my flat was not horror or sadness at Amanda's death, but one of overwhelming tiredness. I had great need of a drink before I listened to the two messages which my answering machine flashed that it had for me. First the familiar and trenchant tones of Toby Greenslade told me that he would see me at the Stripes tournament and perhaps we could get together for a drink and a meal sometime. And then Poppy asked that I please please ring her as soon as I got home. She answered immediately. She'd heard about Amanda's death on the radio. Could she come over?

Less than half an hour later she was at my front door. She marched straight past me into the hall. She was in a distraught state; her face was pale, the collar of her shirt was half in and half out of her sleeveless sweater and one of the laces of her trainers was undone.

'Oh Chris, thank God you're here.'

'Only just. I've been with the cops for half the evening.'

As I told her what had happened, she went even whiter in the face.

'My God. Poor Chris. Poor Amanda. Those bastards on the *Chronicle* killed her.'

She began to tremble as the tears welled up in her eyes.

'Jesus Christ. I feel so awful. I've been so nasty about her.'

She put her hands to her face and the tears started to fall. I was at a loss to know what to do or say, so I just put my arms out to her and she fell against me. I held and stroked her and the comfort of it seemed to help as her sobs gradually subsided. She started talking again, her face pressed into my chest and her voice muffled.

'The radio said it was being treated as a suicide, "following recent revelations about her private life".'

'It seems out of character. I've always thought of her as a real toughie. But what other explanation could there be?'

She sat up, grimaced and withdrew slightly to her end of the sofa.

'Yes. I thought of her as tough too. The original show-biz harpie. But she's turned out to be a tart with a heart. You must think I'm a dreadful hypocrite after all I've said about her. She was an awful pain in many ways but she was a vital part of the series, and you had to like her as well as loathe her. God knows what we'll do with the show now.'

Concentrating her mind on her television series rather than on what had happened to Amanda seemed a good idea.

'What will happen, do you think? Will they abandon ship?'

Poppy winced at the unintentional pun and said: 'No fear. Do you know what they've invested in it?'

'I've no idea.'

'Well over two million quid. Each episode costs over two hundred thousand pounds and we've already done ten of them, plus all the location filming.'

I nodded silently at her.

'Chris, can you run to a very large gin and tonic? Then I might have the courage to ring Bill Ryan. We're recording another episode next week and he'll want a major rewrite.'

I moved towards the kitchen to get her drink and Poppy followed.

'At least we've got the location scenes in the can.'

'What do you mean?'

'Locations. The scenes we film outside the studio. Fortunately it was all finished weeks ago. We were going to shoot the rest of the next episode in the studio on Monday. Then it's Bill's job to knit it all together.'

'Don't all sit-coms use location scenes?'

'They'd like to, for the sake of realism and variety. But it's expensive. There's transport. The actors, technicians and other production people. You can imagine how much it costs to feed all that lot just for a start.'

We took our drinks over to a sofa where she sat close to me and continued my lesson on situation comedy production. She seemed much calmer now and I was happy to listen to her talk.

'Then just as you've set everything up and the scene is set to go, it starts to rain or some moron goes by playing his tranny, or a plane or a motor bike roars by and the sound is ruined.

'But the biggest single problem is the lighting. You have to be meticulous. It's a real pain. On a really good day you might only get four or five minutes on to film.'

'A whole day for four minutes?'

Poppy explained other problems to me, especially those of continuity; of having to wait for the sun to be in the right position, for instance, or having to scrap a whole scene because the tide has refused to stay in the same place during delays.

'Because somebody out there amongst the great British telly-viewing audience, comatose and almost brain-dead though they are supposed to be, is bound to spot it.'

'So it's much easier and cheaper to shoot everything in a studio?'

'Yes, but if you're trying to produce an interesting series with some good production values, then you must include some location shots.'

Poppy had now entirely regained control of herself and I suggested that she phoned Bill Ryan. I felt it was tactful to leave her to it, so I spent a few minutes in the kitchen to see if my supplies were up to providing a meal.

When I returned Poppy was staring out of the window at the dwindling light.

'Bill's only just past the gibbering stage,' she said. 'He was of course married to her once. He said that copies of the *Chronicle* were scattered around her flat and that the adverse publicity had made her flip her lid.'

'Hadn't he seen her or talked to her about it?'

'Yes, but she had laughed it off. Said it was a put-up job and that she was going to sue the *Chronicle*.'

'She might have won, too, and walked off with half a million quid.'

'What a bloody mess. Anyway he needs some rewrites. I'll have to plant a few clues in the current episode and then we'll have to get rid of her in the next. Perhaps I'll make her run off with a toy boy. I'll have to rewrite the other episodes too. Poor Amanda. But at least we might get a decent actress in now.'

Poppy smiled grimly and I asked her if she would like some food.

'No thanks, Chris. But would you do me a favour. I don't want to go back to my flat. Can I use your spare bedroom?'

I was happy to agree. After all she might lose her way to the bathroom and end up in my bedroom.

She did.

When I entered the kitchen the next morning she had already juiced some oranges, made some tea, and was standing by the toaster. Two slices popped out of it as I walked in.

'Superb timing,' I said.

'I don't know what you have for breakfast but this is a start anyway. What are you up to today? Is it the City or the golf course?'

'The City, unfortunately.'

'Do you mind if I work here, Chris? I don't want to go to my flat. The phone will be ringing non-stop about Amanda and I've got to do those rewrites. Can I use your fax, by the way?'

I nodded in agreement, my mouth full of toast.

As it was Tuesday I knew that Mrs Bradshaw usually came in to do some tidying and I popped up to her flat to warn her of Poppy's presence.

On the way out Poppy said:

'I noticed your multi-gym, Chris. May I use it? I like to stop at midday and have some exercise, a run or a swim or sometimes a work-out. The break, or the change of tempo, seems to do me good.'

'Watch out Jane Fonda.'

'I'm younger, Chris, and fitter – as you know,' she said with a smile and kissed me.

I was still smiling to myself as I walked towards the Underground and congratulated myself, smugly, on knowing such a resilient and enchanting woman.

The headlines in the newspapers brought me back to earth. The story of Amanda's death was splashed over every tabloid. The police were treating it as suicide. Grant Sadler was mentioned as 'having found the body'. Although the presence of 'a family friend' was also noted, to my great relief my name did not appear. I was sheltered by Sadler's fame.

Chapter 9

A note from Poppy awaited me on my return home. She was at a meeting with Bill Ryan and had more meetings on the following day – could she hide out at my flat again on the Thursday? Was that OK? As Thursday was the day of the first round of the Stripes Classic, I agreed. Poppy had arranged to borrow Mrs Bradshaw's key. Was that OK? It was.

The following day would bring my first encounter with Rollo Hardinge at the pro-am which preceded the Stripes Classic. This event was one that counted towards the celebrity Order of Merit and most of the regulars would be on parade. I wondered if Grant Sadler would make it and whether the gentlemen of the Press, obsessed by scandal and show biz, would give him space to swing a club. Thank God they were not aware of my walk-on part in the tragedy.

Jack Mason had used his influence to get Rollo invited even though he was certainly not one of the leading golfers. Usually the sponsors only invite the top forty or so professionals, the real drawing cards. The rest of the field is made up of celebrities and of businessmen who pay substantial amounts of money to play. The whole exercise is devised to raise money for charity, but it is also a chance for the sponsor to place favoured customers in the pro-am field. In general, both the customers and the businessmen want to play with well-known professionals and not with the likes of Rollo Hardinge.

I sought him out on the practice ground, as agreed, and had no trouble in finding him.

For a start he was the only left-handed player there. But he would have stood out anyway mainly because of his hair, sun-bleached and drawn back into a ponytail. Professional golfers are relatively conventional people in dress, despite the bright clothing, and I hadn't seen a ponytail on the circuit before. His other unusual item of attire was a personal stereo. At least he removed the headphones when he saw me. I wondered what music he was playing. Something slow and rhythmic, perhaps, to help his swing?

We shook hands and I gestured at the headphones.

'Strauss?'

Rollo Hardinge shook his head.

'No fear. It's my sports psychologist. Dad introduced us in California. He's recorded some key thoughts for me. Psychological triggers. To keep me positive and make me into a winner.'

I nodded and decided to say nothing. But I wondered gloomily just what Jack Mason had got me into. However, I was there to carry Rollo's bag and to offer him whatever help and advice he required. I know that psychologists are gaining a foothold in sport. They had long ago infiltrated some of the major American sports such as football and baseball and some of the European soccer teams have a resident psychologist. It seems that every top tennis player has one – along with a trainer, a coach, a dietician, a beautician and a 'movement specialist'. Most of them ought to invest in a dialogue writer while they're about it. Well, they have to spend all that money somehow.

I watched Rollo hit a few shots and he certainly had an impressive swing. Because he is a tall man, with proportionately long arms, he is able to generate tremendous power. He is young and fit and swings the club 'high, wide and handsome' in an uninhibited fashion. The ball was fizzing off the club head, and I noticed that he had attracted a little gaggle of spectators. It was great fun to watch.

I wondered what he was like in moments of high pressure: the drive that must be hit into a precise area of the fairway; the pitch shot that must be floated close over a bunker; the downhill putt with a fifteen-inch break that must be holed.

Those are the moments to which a golfer's hours of practice are dedicated; the moments when he lets the muscle memory take over, when he must relax and hit the all-important shot on which thousands of pounds may rest. I was not optimistic.

While Rollo hit a few shots with his woods I checked his bag: a good supply of golf balls, all of the same manufacture, waterproof trousers, extra sweaters, both short-sleeved and long, bananas, an apple, some chocolate, tee pegs, markers, pencils, a book of the rules, umbrella, two types of hat, sun cream; all the necessities plus no more than fourteen golf clubs. It all added up to around forty pounds for me to carry for five or six miles.

My new boss pronounced himself satisfied with his practice, stowed his personal stereo away in the bag and moved off to hit a few putts on the practice green in front of the club house, a charming series of buildings which had grown around the original wooden pavilion over the past century.

The banners of the sponsors, Stripes, a brand of lager, were everywhere and they featured the unmistakable image of Jimmy McCoy, the spearhead of their current advertising.

Naturally the 'real McCoy' was playing in the pro-am and I could hear his rapid and harsh Glaswegian tones on the side of the putting green. He had risen to fame as an alternative comedian whose act was based on a gallery of misanthropic Scottish characters. I was glad that he was not one of Rollo's partners since his brand of humour was relentless and he so clearly *knew* that he was funny.

He had gathered quite a crowd around him and was rattling off his famous and inexhaustible collection of one-liners. Some cameras were flashing and I saw McCoy in a characteristic pose with his arm around a young lady whose charms were all too evident.

'Her name is Mikki Boone,' a voice said from my left, 'and I'm Felton Butter. Toby told me to introduce myself. I'm one of his colleagues and I have the dubious privilege of covering show business for the *News*.'

'Well, Mr McCoy will give you plenty to write about, won't he?'

'Not as much as Amanda Newhart and Grant Sadler.'

'Oh, is he here?' I enquired innocently.

'Yes, with two bloody great minders hovering about. I heard that you saved his bacon the other night. Otherwise, he might have been the prime suspect in a murder case.'

'I thought it was being treated as suicide?'

'At the moment, yes.'

Butter waited for me to say more. I didn't.

'Your friend Toby told me to treat you well, Chris, so I'll change the subject – for the moment.'

He gestured towards McCoy. 'What a ghastly bore he is when he's parading in front of his public. It makes me ashamed to admit that I'm a Scot. And my editor has told me to be nice to him.'

Felton Butter had the mere trace of a Scottish accent, only just discernible to me. He was lean and fit-looking and was suitably attired for the golf course in elegantly cut plus-two trousers in a very dark check, bright yellow socks and two-tone brown golf shoes. The outfit was topped off by a maroon cashmere sweater. A checked cap sat at a casual angle on his blond hair. It was very studied and as I shook his hand, he said: 'I hope I look the part. But I'm really here as a *Cap'n Hand* watcher. The series Amanda Newhart was making. You probably know all about it.'

'A little,' I said carefully. 'Is McCoy in the series?'

Poppy had mentioned that McCoy had a part in the series, but I felt I should be very careful with this particular show-biz journalist, whether a friend of Toby's or not.

I could sense that he was assessing me, weighing me up in his quiet way.

'Oh yes, he has an important character role in the series. In other words he's not expected to act, which is just as well. I assume that McCoy got the part because he's big buddies with Neil Anderson, the boss of RRA. And of course the RRA management agency represents him.'

'It all sounds very neat.'

'Or incestuous.'

'Maybe, but McCoy is a big star in his own right whether you like him or not and I suppose that he must have been acceptable to the network who have bought *Cap'n Hand*.'

'True. But it's that bloody Glasgow mafia that I can't stand. Anderson and McCoy go way back into the murky depths of Glaswegian clubland. And of course my MD, Dick Finlay, has some connection too. He's from Glasgow and never lets anyone forget it. No doubt Anderson and McCoy supply him with introductions to willing starlets.'

'There is a financial connection, Felton. The *News* has a small holding in RRA and Anderson owns some shares in the *News*. So it's no wonder that your editor has told you to be nice to McCoy. Be nice to McCoy means be nice to RRA and thus ensure that the *News*'s shareholding shows a big gain.'

'Yes, I should have guessed that the reason for all this wasn't friendship. It had to be something to do with money or power.'

'Well, at least Anderson has made it under his own steam. He's certainly a self-made man.'

'Is he hell! His old man left him a thriving business. He was a real hooligan. He came through the ice-cream wars in Glasgow in the sixties and seventies.'

'The ice-cream wars?'

'Battles for the best territories between the ice-cream vendors. They used everything short of guns. Broken bottles, knives, heavies with coshes. Molotov cocktails as well. And old man Anderson was the toughest and nastiest of the lot. He ended up ruling the roost.'

'The ice-cream king, eh?'

'He went on from there into betting shops and pubs. He caused ruin to many a small and honest businessman, and misery to many a happy family.'

'You seem to know a lot about it.'

'Just some research I did at university. I was daft enough to study sociology amongst other things.'

'You're a long way from sociology now. Are you happy in your work?'

He smiled thinly. 'It's a means to an end. And this *Cap'n Hand* business adds a modicum of excitement.'

'Talking of work, I must do mine. See you later.'

I watched Rollo hit some putts with a smooth, repetitive action and then we joined our partners on the first tee. The celebrity in our group was a young snooker player who had already made millions from his sport. The two middle-aged businessmen made it plain from their lukewarm response to Rollo's words of welcome that they were irritated; they had clearly expected to be playing with an Open champion. Obviously they had never heard of Rollo and looked even more disenchanted when they noticed his ponytail.

Rollo shrugged off their coolness and prepared to hit his drive down the first. It's an undemanding hole, as long as you can carry your ball over a rather unfriendly strip of rough which had been allowed to grow across the fairway about 200 yards from the championship tee.

Rollo not only carried that bit of trouble but also the bunker which lay about 250 yards from the tee. His resounding shot of over 300 yards left him a simple pitch to the green. The snooker player grounded his club and applauded and the businessmen began to look interested.

When I got to Rollo's ball I would be able to tell him the precise distance to the hole by using my chart of the course.

In the good old days caddies used to measure distances by eye. It was one of the skills of golf. Then caddies began to pace out the distances because the players, who know precisely how far they can hit with any given club, insisted on being told the exact distance to the flag from any point on the course. Not the distance to the front of the green or the centre of the green, but to the flag. Woe betide any caddie who cannot supply the right yardage.

Science has now taken a hand, with the use of a measuring wheel. Even more precise is the use of a wire which is anchored into the front edge of the green and then played out back to various points on the hole. This technique was pioneered by an American caddie and he includes measurements from the rough and the heavy rough. These are marked JICYFU and JICYRFU. Loosely translated this means Just In Case You Foul Up and Just In Case You Really Foul Up.

I use several of his charts and they are very accurate. He was famous a few years ago for his exploits on the women's golf tour in America, where he was known as the 'kissing caddie'. Every time his employer registered a birdie she gave him a smacking kiss.

A television interviewer once asked him what he got for an eagle but he wouldn't tell.

Today was an opportunity to recheck the distances I had on my chart and also to assess Rollo's game. I had to discover how far he expected to hit the ball with various clubs and try to get some idea of his temperament.

Did he really have the potential, as Jack Mason had told me, to be a winner? How would he react to advice and criticism?

The first nine holes were relatively uneventful because Rollo was crashing his tee shots huge distances, finding the green with his second shots and holding the putts. He was already four under par and I was beginning to believe in Jack's assessment.

The tenth hole looks innocuous. It is a mere 340 yards to the edge of the green and I was thinking in terms of yet another birdie. So was Rollo. His enthusiasm got way ahead of his technique and he hit a monumental hook which sailed on and on into the woods on the left of the fairway.

He told himself what a bloody idiot he was and turned to me. 'I thought I could hit the green. Stupid.'

He played a provisional ball down the centre of the fairway and we headed for the woods.

One of the advantages that the professional has over the humble club golfer is that there are usually plenty of spectators who are more than willing to look for his ball. With success, in this case, because a little knot of fans had gathered around Rollo's.

It had settled into a horrible spot and was sitting about six inches off the ground, on top of a patch of tough-looking brambles. Dozens of trees lay between Rollo and the green.

We both looked at the various options but only one was realistic. I wondered how his sports psychologist would have advised him in this situation. I was far from hopeful about the outcome and had visions of several despairing hacks and a very high score for the hole.

Rollo eventually settled over the ball and said: '"There is a pleasure in the pathless woods."'

My heart warmed to him.

His wedge then smashed through the brambles and the ball soared through a tiny gap towards the green.

'"There is a rapture on the lonely shore,"' I said. 'You're in a bunker.'

Rollo grinned. 'So, you know your Byron as well, Chris. Jack Mason said you were a man of many parts.'

Rollo ended up with a one over par five for the hole. But his concentration wavered several times over the closing holes. The result was mediocrity when brilliance had promised to show itself.

I anticipated that the mediocrity would mean a long session on the practice ground, but Rollo merely confirmed our starting time for the next day and insisted that we all joined him for a beer in the sponsor's tent.

The snooker player slipped away because he needed to practise and I hoped that his example was not lost on Rollo.

Chapter 10

We entered the familiar hubbub of the sponsor's tent and were seized upon by one of the legion of Stripes' public relations people. The man was out of the PR manual of stereotypes. He was stockily built and clothed in a dark, double-breasted suit and a shirt with wide pink stripes. A silk floral handkerchief flowed out of his breast pocket and his pale and rotund face was shiny with effort and bonhomie.

He was very good at his job and had soon established that Rollo's two partners for the day were, in one case, the owner of a chain of off-licences and, in the other, the director of a cider manufacturer whose products were distributed by the Stripes' parent company.

In no time at all he had us sitting at a table with one of his assistants, Penny. She was an attractive woman with the wary blue eyes of someone who had been on the receiving end of too many suggestive conversations in sponsors' tents. She disguised well the signs of too regular an attendance at such junkets as today's with a ready smile and a keen interest in everything that her company's two guests said. I noticed that she kept darting looks at Rollo and her eyes opened a little wider as she did so. He was toying with a beer and merely playing a walk-on part in the conversation. But it was clear to me that Penny would rather be in a quiet corner with him than at a table with two businessmen and an unknown quantity – me.

I looked over at the bar and noticed Felton amongst a noisy group of people, including Grant and Bill Ryan, the inevitable Kenny Craig and one other pro-am regulars, whose faces were as familiar drinking styles. Two very large men, the minders standing just behind Sadler. The sponsor's product being fully tested, especially by Kenny Craig, whose ing handicap would, in golfing parlance, probably be scratch.

Felton saw me and waved me over. As I excused so did Rollo and I thought I saw a tiny shadow cross face.

'I'll see you tomorrow perhaps?' she said.

'I'm sure,' said Rollo.

'Nice girl,' I put in my bit of PR on Penny's behal walked away.

'Yeah. But she's probably past her "sell by" date, said lightly.

As I moved towards the bar Sadler looked up, smil gave me half a wave. I still didn't like him any better a feeling he saw me as his friend and saviour. I joined at the bar. With his slim figure and plus-twos he sho elegance which belonged more to the twenties than nineties, particularly among the garish clothing whi on view. I noticed that he was drinking mineral wat

'Don't let Toby catch you drinking that stuff. He for a stewards' enquiry.'

Toby Greenslade takes a very serious view of his as a golf correspondent. He feels that not to drink a alcohol, preferably of the fizzy variety from Cham that a sponsor can reasonably provide amounts to a Since he has great charm and usually seems imper the effects of booze he is welcomed and indulged b of them.

'I'm afraid that I don't subscribe to everyone's the typical journalist – drink-sodden, grubby, lec unreliable, unscrupulous . . .'

'Even working for the *News*?'

'Some of us try, Chris. Toby tries. I try.' He smiled at me and continued. 'Forgive me. I'm getting pompous. Tell me about some of these people – as golfers, I mean.'

He waved at the rest of the group.

'Well, Grant Sadler is a competent golfer, but he thinks he's better than he really is. Self-confidence is necessary in golf, but a touch of humility never comes amiss. Sadler doesn't have any of that. I don't know about Bill Ryan but drinkers are always a bit suspect, as Toby will tell you.'

'And Kenny Craig?'

'He's a one-off. He can play as well after a bottle of champagne and six brandies as he can stone-cold sober. Which is impossible of course.'

'You've seen the results so far for this inane celebrity Order of Merit, have you?' asked Butter. I shook my head.

'Mr Sadler will not be pleased. He's so far amassed, courtesy of his two teams, over one hundred and sixty points, but "the Real McCoy" is only one point behind.'

'Why should McCoy bother Sadler, particularly?' I asked.

'Because they loathe each other. The atmosphere on the set of *Cap'n Hand* is poisonous apparently. McCoy is upstaging Sadler like mad and he knows every trick in the book. Sadler can't take it because he's supposed to be the big star. And now McCoy is at it again. On the golf course.'

Butter chuckled happily. 'It's lovely stuff. Anyway, what about your new boss, young Rollo?'

'You keep up with the gossip, don't you?'

'Gossip is my business. He's a very handsome young man, isn't he?'

'Rollo could be a fine player, if he wants to be. The question is whether he can put enough devotion into his game and ignore the distractions of the easy life. As you say, Felton, he's a handsome young man and I'm told that his father is well-off. Those are his two immediate problems.'

'"Enemies of promise"?'

'Exactly.'

'You're not suggesting a monastic life-style, are you? Early to bed in a hair shirt and so on?'

'No. But to get to the top he'll need to be single-minded to the point of being boring. He has lots of friends and lots of interests which will easily divert him from the real aim, which is to beat the hell out of everybody else on the golf tour.

'There are dozens of kids out there who hit the ball as well as Rollo. In theory, they've all got the game to win tournaments. They can drive the ball two hundred and eighty yards, they can hit their irons consistently to within a few yards of where they're aiming, they've got smooth putting actions. But do they have the real desire to win, that real sickening ache which runs right through their whole being? Have they got the guts to be champions?'

'My goodness, that came from the heart.'

'Well, I had aspirations to be a pro golfer a few years back. And I realised that I didn't have the talent needed. But Rollo has. In fact, he's more equal than the others in many ways.'

We then moved from golf back to show biz and the topic of the moment – Amanda.

'The late-lamented Amanda had ambitions as a scribe,' Felton told me. 'Intended to write some of *Cap'n Hand* as well as star in it.'

'I don't suppose Poppy Drake would have been too happy about that,' I said before I could stop myself.

'Ah, so you know the beautiful Poppy, do you?'

'I've met her,' I said stiffly. Felton Butter looked at me knowingly.

'A little bird tells me that it's more than that. You're obviously smitten.' So, he already knew, the sod.

'Of course, Poppy has no control over the series. The control lies with the big guns, including those two over there.' He gestured towards Grant Sadler and Bill Ryan. 'They'll make all thc big money out of *Cap'n Hand*.'

With those words in my head I moved off towards the car park. I was worried about Poppy, who had created what promised to be a highly successful television series and might not get her due reward. But on reflection I reckoned she was tough enough to take care of herself.

Chapter 11

On the following morning I threw my bag into the boot of my elderly Porsche and headed for the M4. The sun was trying hard to shine through the clouds and that wasn't a bad metaphor for how I felt: I had the uncertainties of a new employer in the shape of Rollo Hardinge to face but a new and interesting woman had come unexpectedly into my life.

For once the traffic along the motorway was light, although I noticed that the average speed of the company-owned Cavaliers seemed to have moved up a notch. I kept to my usual eighty mph or so, on the grounds that I could lift off the accelerator if I saw a police car and soon be down to a legal speed. It was my feeling that, compared to a year ago, many more cars were passing me, and at higher speeds. With a mobile phone in one hand and a cigarette in the other, I wondered what they were steering with. I fear for my life on motorways.

However, I arrived at the golf course early and in one piece. I wandered off in search of a cup of tea and as I was passing the front door of the club house, it opened and Rollo Hardinge greeted me. He came excitedly towards me, waving a book. Not just a book, *the* book; it was a copy of the Bible.

'I didn't know the Gideon Society were placing the good book in golf clubs as well.'

'No, no, but it's there. I've found the secret.'

I looked about me cautiously and hoped that none of my fellow caddies were within earshot. There are of course many Christians among professional golfers and especially so on the American circuit, where a sizeable group of born-again Christians holds regular prayer meetings. Some of their number have won important championships and I remember that Jack Mason, during one of his infrequent visits to the USA, went to a couple of their gatherings 'just in case the God-botherers know something I don't' as he put it. Whatever divine guidance was on offer escaped him because he missed the cut that week. I'd never met one until now who ran around waving his Bible like a new convert; I feared shouts of 'Hallelujah!' might come next and steered Rollo towards a refreshment tent. I ordered two teas and asked him what was the secret and to what.

'It's in Isaiah, Chris. I knew I'd seen it somewhere in the Old Testament and here it is.'

He thrust the book into my hands and pointed at a sentence which was heavily marked in pencil.

'Strengthen ye the weak hands and confirm the feeble knees,' I read.

'And this, look,' Rollo said excitedly as he turned the pages back. I read another of the prophet's sentences: 'By the strength of my hand I have done it and by my wisdom.'

'Your hands are strong enough, Rollo, it's your wisdom I'm worried about.'

He ignored me. 'I spotted this a few weekends ago at a wedding. The bride was late, of course, and I was thumbing through the Bible and I saw it. I didn't realise the significance until a few days ago and then I'd forgotten which prophet I'd been reading. So I spent last night researching the Old Testament.'

'So, you think Isaiah was a golfer. Maybe you should write some articles with him for *Golf World*. That would put the real meaning back into ghost-writing.'

'You're not taking me seriously. You probably think I should have been on the practice ground, not studying the

Old Testament. But he was right. You can't play good golf unless your hands are strong and your balance is good.'

'I agree. It's what any good teacher would tell you. It was what Henry Cotton always said.' I wondered what his psychologist would make of this other source of inspiration.

I decided to change the subject. 'Good wedding?'

Rollo, his mind on higher things, looked blankly at me for a moment. 'Oh fine, good fun. Actually the vicar married the wrong people. Their names are Nigel and Sue, but the vicar, who'd presumably been at the communion wine, called them John and Joanna for most of the ceremony. We reckoned that they weren't legally married.'

I smiled and suggested that we really should now get down to the practice ground. When we got there he tucked the Bible in his golf bag and said; 'There's a lot of good stuff in there, you know.'

They're not all locked up.

Rollo had been drawn to play with Jose Miguel, who always ends up amongst the top ten players in Europe, and a young Swede who was in his first year on the tour. Miguel has won only a handful of tournaments but is a model of stern consistency. There is no flamboyance in the man; he merely hits the ball down the middle, knocks his next shot on to the green and either gets a birdie or two-putts. It's an easy game, really.

I hoped that his remorselessly steady approach would rub off on Rollo. It didn't. He scored a 74 which should have been a 68, while Miguel scored a 68 which never looked as though it would be anything else.

Rollo missed a couple of putts, fluffed a chip shot into instead of over a bunker, and hooked one drive out of bounds late in the round. Those were the differences between an encouraging opening round and one that would mean a severe struggle on the following day to qualify for the final two rounds. Despite that, I'd prefer to watch Rollo any day.

As we headed for the practice ground, Rollo removed the Bible from his bag, thumbed through it and said: 'Second Kings, nine, twenty.'

'Would you like to translate?'

'"The driving is like the driving of Jehu, for he driveth furiously."'

'Yes. We've got to sort that out.'

'Well, as Isaiah says . . .'

No self-respecting caddie is going to accept competition from a centuries-dead prophet.

'Your hands are strong, Rollo. It's your concentration that's at fault. Look at Miguel; you could explode a bomb behind him when he's playing a shot and he wouldn't notice.'

'You're going to tell me the "what train?" story now, aren't you?'

'Not if you already know it, no.'

He was right. I had been about to tell him the story of the legendary Joyce Wethered. Bobby Jones thought her to be the best golfer, man or woman, that he had ever seen. She was renowned for her concentration and is said to have holed a putt to win a championship as a train rattled by on the track alongside. When asked why she had not delayed her stroke until the train had passed, she said, 'What train?'

Rollo hit some long irons and was trying to keep the clubhead driving on down the line to the target. He was striking the ball superbly and I suggested that he should make more use of his one-iron off the tee.

'Occasionally, for safety. Or you could carry a metal wood like Jack's. It has the loft of a two-wood.'

Jack was just a couple of places away from us on the practice ground and turned round when he heard his name. He came over to us and asked how Rollo had scored that day.

'Not well enough,' Rollo admitted, 'and Chris thinks I should be a bit more cautious, especially off the tee.'

'And he's undoubtedly right. We all play the occasional

bad shot in a round of golf, but you must try to limit the damage. No one wants to inhibit you, Rollo. God knows we need exciting players on the tour, not just a bunch of journeymen who turn up every week, try to finish in the top thirty so that they can still pay their mortgages and then go home to their nice suburban semis in Penge or Surbiton, where they kiss their wives and settle down to watch *Emmerdale Farm* with their slimline dinner on a tray from Tesco.

'We'll be in the same state as the Yanks before we know where we are. The television ratings for golf are dropping like a stone over there because every pro is a college graduate with a degree in general arts and communication. They're interchangeable, from their white visors to their two-tone shoes, and no wonder the general public can't identify with them.'

'I was at an American university,' Rollo said.

'Yes, but you don't wear a visor. Just do me a favour and listen to Chris occasionally. Golf isn't all blood and thunder.'

Rollo was a strange mix and I couldn't quite work out what made him tick – tall, tanned and good-looking; talented; Bible reader; psychologist user; poetry quoter. Jack couldn't be accused of landing me with one of the golf clones he'd described.

Jack went back to his own practice, mainly because his caddie, Zoe Bernini, was energetically waving him back to work.

'Which university were you at?' I asked.

'Southern California. My dad set up his business in LA about ten years ago. He's British and so am I. When I play in the Ryder Cup it will be for Europe. Dad produces original television programmes for the networks and he's been involved in some UK changed-format deals.'

'Ah, I've been hearing a bit about formats – changed formats?'

'Yeah. You remember *Twice Around the Bend*? Dad

took the changed-format rights for the States – changed the setting, cast American actors, commissioned new scripts and so on. It became *Here We Go, Larry*. It was a great success. And then he sold the American version back to British television.'

'He sounds a smart operator, your dad. What did you study at USC?'

Rollo laughed and said, 'Don't tell Jack, but it was general arts and creative writing.'

'Ah. That explains your familiarity with some of the English poets.'

The conversation took place as Rollo was thrashing one-irons down the practice ground. I was determined to try and harness his great power to produce better scores. As the hardened pros love to tell you, golf is played mostly between the ears.

After some chipping and putting practice we arranged to meet at 7.30 the next morning as Rollo was due on the first tee at just after nine o'clock.

I decided to go in search of Toby Greenslade and I thought that the sponsor's tent would be the most likely spot. Plenty of journalists were there, trying manfully to dent the company's considerable profit. But there was no sign of Toby and without much hope of success I tried the Press tent.

I saw his familiar figure at one of the desks and I was astonished to see that he was writing. The nearest TV screen was blank, so the race meetings had obviously finished, and Toby was bent in deep concentration over the desk. His tie was undone, his sleeves were rolled up and his hair was awry. He looked every inch the committed, hard-working journalist.

'What's up, Toby? Are you trying for the Pulitzer Prize?'

'Hello, dear boy. It'll take more than a Pulitzer Prize winner to pull this one out of the bag.'

'Are you late with your copy?'

'No, no. That's already in, every syllable polished to

perfection for my faithful band of readers. No, it's this accursed autobiography of Carlssen. If there's a more boring person in the world, I wouldn't care to meet him. But I've been given an ultimatum by the publisher. I've got to deliver the first twenty thousand words by tomorrow night or he'll cancel my contract.'

'And how far have you got?'

'I've limped and stuttered to fifteen thousand and I reckon honour will be satisfied with another two or three. Christ, I need a drink. No, I need lots of drinks, but I daren't. What about dinner? Can you make it on Monday? I'll pour out my troubles then.'

We agreed where to meet and I headed for my car. The scoreboard told me that Rollo was way down the field, but Jack Mason was three off the lead with a 68.

It was after eight o'clock when I got back to my flat and, as I put my key in the lock, the door was flung open by a smiling Poppy. I was slightly taken aback since I imagined that she would have returned to her own home. She pressed a glass of champagne into my hand.

'What a lovely welcome.'

'It's a thank you for giving me sanctuary, especially from the damned phone. I've worked flat out and managed to do most of the rewrites. I only stopped for a work-out at lunchtime and a cup of tea with Mrs Bradshaw. What a smashing lady! I've invited her out for lunch tomorrow.'

'Why don't we go out for dinner now?'

'Because I've cooked us a meal. I consulted Mrs B and she told me that you like pasta and so I've cooked my own very special tomato sauce.'

Poppy filled my glass, kissed me on the cheek and headed for the kitchen. This is the life, I thought, as I sipped the champagne.

It certainly was: the very special tomato sauce was very special, as was the bottle of Barolo which Poppy had bought to go with it.

During the meal Poppy brought me up to date with the progress of *Cap'n Hand*.

'Things aren't going too badly considering the very large spanner Amanda's death has thrown in the works. I'm trying to rework the storylines for the last three episodes. It's not easy because she had a pivotal part in the series – she wouldn't have agreed to do it otherwise. But if we can finish the first series without losing our credibility, we'll have time to insert a new character or two. Not that I'll be quite so involved next time around,' she finished with a frown.

'Why won't you?'

'Because RRA wouldn't agree to my writing more than fifty per cent of the second series. And my fool of an agent didn't even get that for me. He let himself be bullied into agreeing that I write only five out of the next thirteen episodes.'

'That doesn't seem fair.'

'Fair doesn't come into it. Companies like RRA want all the slices in the cake and the wrapping and the knife you cut it with. You've got to be pretty tough to stand up to them and dear old Victor isn't up to it.'

'Your agent?'

'Yes. He prefers a quiet life. He just likes to get back to Chelsea to his boyfriend every evening. He doesn't want to spoil his day with an unpleasant confrontation with those RRA people. They're just nasty yobs to him.'

'Why don't you change agent?'

'Oh, Victor's very sweet. I couldn't hurt his feelings, even though I know the money I'm getting is too low. I should probably be getting another couple of thousand an episode. And, of course, I'm sharing the writing credit with bloody Bill Ryan too.'

'So, all in all, you're not ecstatic about your first big break.'

'It's not so bad, just not what I expected. I was so excited when it all began. My series, my name on it. And it looked like good money for several years. But it has turned a bit sour. It'll make my year if they sell the US rights and everyone earns a bundle except me, not that I think that'll happen.'

I declined coffee and explained that I had to be on the road before six o'clock the next morning in order to meet Rollo at 7.30. We debated where Poppy should take Mrs Bradshaw for lunch and finally agreed that she would enjoy a lively Italian restaurant in Chelsea which we both knew.

'Well, time for bed, Chris. Are you going to chuck me out or can I stay another night?'

'Please stay.'

I reached out for her. She moved into my arms and started behaving in a very provocative manner.

'Usual payment, love?' she said in tarty tones as she pulled me to the bedroom.

It's not all bad being dominated by a masterful woman.

Chapter 12

I had set my alarm for 5.30 but it wasn't needed since Poppy's cool fingers on my forehead woke me from a dream. I was glad because I was stranded in some impenetrable woods with a driver in my hand, trying to reach an unseen fairway. I hoped it wasn't a portent for Rollo's forthcoming round. The dream I prefer is the one in which I win the Open. Poppy put a cup of tea by my bedside and turned off the alarm clock just as it gave out its first buzz.

I thanked her and reached out towards her from under the covers. She pressed my hand and asked me if I wanted anything for breakfast. When I told her what I'd like for breakfast, she reminded me that I had to get a move on and that she did not like her pleasures to be hurried. I gulped down some of the tea and left the comfort of my bed.

Poppy wished me luck with Rollo and I wished her a good lunch with Mrs Bradshaw. I headed out of the door with my bag in one hand and a banana and an apple in the other. Poppy waved from the window. I felt like a kid going off to school.

On the practice ground Rollo's swing looked to be in its usual good order and we agreed that a score of 70, two shots under par, would be enough to ensure his appearance for the final two days. After two rounds the field of 144 players is always reduced, roughly by half. We also agreed that it would do Rollo no harm to exercise some caution occasionally. This was not to be a death or glory day; far from it.

We had one major alarm late in the round when Rollo hit another of his spectacular hooks, but the ball hit the trunk of a tree and bounced back into the semi-rough. In the circles in which I play we call that a 'woodpecker' and it would have resulted in the claiming of a forfeit of a couple of pounds by the opposition, but Rollo looked extremely pleased with himself and said, '"The woods shall to me answer and my echo ring."'

'You're a lucky sod,' I said. 'Let's take advantage of it.'

Rollo did, by scoring a birdie, and he ended up with a hard-fought 68. Very satisfactory – it shot him up the field and he qualified with ease. On the crest of this minor golfing wave, Rollo decided that he didn't need any practice beyond some putting and I was in my office by mid-afternoon.

Andrew Buccleuth was anxious about the RRA issue in the light of the adverse publicity which had followed Amanda Newhart's suicide. So I decided to do some basic market research of my own. I spoke to several clients, a mixture of institutions and private punters, about the issue. When all the qualifications and prevarications were stripped away I calculated that they were good for over five million shares. I had to bear in mind that Friday is often a good day for selling shares; the approaching weekend makes everyone a little more sanguine and relaxed.

Andrew said that he would enjoy his weekend that little bit more.

It cheered me up, too. I was also encouraged by Rollo's performance that day and felt more optimistic about his immediate prospects in the Stripes Classic.

When I got home I noticed that all signs of Poppy's stay seemed to have been eliminated and I glanced into the guest bedroom. On the bed was a package with a note of thanks taped to it. Inside was a bottle of Veuve Clicquot. Poppy clearly knew the way to a man's heart and I decided the gift should be put to immediate use. I rang Mrs Bradshaw and asked her to share it with me.

Half an hour later she was sitting in an armchair opposite. She reiterated her sorrow, already expressed in a note to me, about what had happened to Amanda. She didn't overdo it and was soon telling me what a splendid lunch she had had with Poppy.

'What a lovely girl, Chris, and so generous. She wouldn't let me pay for a thing, not even my taxi home.'

'Yes, she's a determined lady, isn't she?'

'She'll go far, I'm sure. She was telling me about *Cap'n Hand*. So interesting. She's going to arrange for me to see the last recording in a couple of weeks' time. You're going to the one on Monday, aren't you, Chris?'

'Not to my knowledge. I'm actually having dinner with Toby Greenslade that night.'

'Oh well, forget I mentioned it. But I think Poppy was making plans.' Mrs Bradshaw gave me a searching look. 'In fact, Poppy seems to have lots of plans for you.'

I rather liked that idea.

After his round of 68, Rollo was just below halfway in the Stripes Classic field, which had been cut down to seventy-six players. We were out with a morose Spaniard called Luis Dando who was clearly determined to play his game without thought for his partner. He gave a stony response to Rollo's cheerful greeting in Spanish and was one of those golfers who, however successful the shot, would always find something wrong with it.

Here was a man who was angry with himself, his game, the golf course and probably the whole world. He was particularly angry with his caddie, a young man who had only been working on the circuit for a short time. Time after time Dando, with an air of disgust, threw his club in the general direction of his golf bag or the caddie.

It was a graceless performance and I know caddies who would have hurled the offending club back and left the player to carry his own clubs. There are several professional golfers who simply cannot help themselves; their pressure valve is the hapless caddie. There is a golfer on the American tour who gets through several caddies per tournament. At one stage there was a vogue for the American caddies to wear a little badge which read: 'I caddied for O'Sullivan for one day.' Or two days. I never saw a badge which claimed a longer period.

Dando clearly felt that he had the right to go round the course in thirty-two shots. After a few holes I asked his caddie how he put up with it. He explained, in his pleasant Geordie accent, that he had no choice; he needed the money and unemployment where he came from was at an appallingly high level.

Perhaps the muttered curses and the slamming of the clubs into the turf after every shot affected Rollo because he was certainly not the confident player of the day before. At least one of the cylinders was not firing and he spluttered his way to a level-par 72.

Whatever the reason, Rollo had had one of those days which all golfers experience, when the flame is not fully alight and however hard he tries he cannot make things happen.

Things happened in the final round but not as either of us had planned. At a short hole early on Rollo found an appalling lie in a bunker at the back of the green, was forced to play out backwards and, just to compound the misery, three-putted. Neither his psychologist nor Isaiah could help him and the more he tried to recover those three dropped shots the worse he fared. He was more in the rough than he was on the fairway and he went out of bounds twice. The result was an ignominious finish down at the bottom of the pile and Rollo earned just over three hundred pounds. My share of his purse money wouldn't have paid much of the mortgage and I was thankful for the generous guarantee which he had agreed.

It was some consolation that we had finished by lunchtime. We drank a subdued beer together and made our arrangements to meet for the next-but-one tournament. I would not be at next week's Belgian Open at Royal

Waterloo with Rollo. He would employ a local caddie and we would join forces again for the next two tournaments in Britain.

I was home by the middle of the afternoon and watched the final few holes of the tournament on television. Jack Mason won after a play-off and I felt a real and unexpected jolt as I watched Zoe Bernini jump for joy. Everybody loves to be a winner and that goes for caddies too. Unfortunately I had been kicked into touch by a proven winner and was now working for a steady loser.

There were several messages on my answering machine and one of them recorded the incisive tones of Poppy Drake. Would I phone her? It was urgent.

She answered on the second ring and asked me whether I could join her for the *Cap'n Hand* recording on the following day. I told her of my plans to have dinner with Toby but she soon won me over.

'I do need your moral support. It'll be the first time that I've seen the cast since poor Amanda's death. And you can see Toby any old time. Thank you, it's sweet of you.'

We arranged our meeting place and I reflected on how death alters one's perceptions of people. To Poppy, 'that bitch Amanda' had become 'poor Amanda'.

I decided to cycle down to the local swimming bath and take advantage of that quiet period in the evening after 7.30. It isn't my favourite form of exercise but it is a relaxing way to keep fit. Even Toby, whose antipathy to all aerobic activity is complete, goes for the occasional dip. I got him on the telephone when I returned, refused the offer of 'just a quick one' at his local and we agreed lunch on the following day.

Before bed I skimmed the Sunday newspapers and saw that they all had delved into Amanda Newhart's past. The quality papers gave earnest assessments of her place in film and television history – a footnote if she were lucky – but did not omit some passing references to her 'vivid' marital and social life. In more reticent days she would have been called 'fun-loving'. The inside pages of the *News* and other tabloids dwelt in salacious detail on her various husbands and lovers.

As I idly flicked over the pages towards the sports section, I saw Felton Butter's column. Amongst the mixture of hard show-business news and gossip there was a piece on Amanda:

> The cast of the new sit-com *Cap'n Hand*, which is due to hit the small screen in a month's time, don't know whether to laugh or cry. The sorrow of some of them at Amanda Newhart's untimely suicide is no doubt tempered by delight at hearing that a new series of thirteen has got the green light. Even better for RRA, who are producing, is confirmation of a pilot version for the US of A.
>
> If it goes with a bang in America (whoops, sorry Amanda) RRA will make big bikkies. Good news for RRA whose shares will be offered to the public shortly. Not so good news for the creator of the series, the elegant and beautiful Poppy Drake, who won't have a share of the expected American bonanza.
>
> It's a funny old world – 1: Poppy's new boyfriend is Chris Ludlow, who is masterminding the sale of RRA to the stock market. I'll bet his loyalties are at full stretch, so to speak.
>
> It's a funny old world – 2: I wonder what the old dad of RRA boss-man, Neil Anderson, would make of it all. Old Tommy started with ice-cream carts and a few betting shops and now his son is high-flying in the world of multi-million pound deals in America and spending his time in the company of pop stars and pneumatic TV actresses.
>
> It's a funny old world – 3: Neil, who never forgets a friend and certainly not an enemy, is going to take his

old mate, Jimmy McCoy, all the way with him. The Real McCoy not only has a starring role in *Cap'n Hand* but he has a stake in Neil's company – or so a little bird told me.

I groaned mentally at what my colleagues would make of that and was not disappointed on the next morning by the breadth of their imaginations. Well, depth of their imaginations. It was assumed that I'd laid the entire female cast of *Cap'n Hand*. I was asked by one broker how I rated Amanda Newhart out of ten, and by another if I had a good source for cocaine.

I was curious about Felton Butter's reference to McCoy's stake in RRA and rang him to ask what he knew. Having established that I wasn't ringing to give him a bad time about the article, he was prepared to impart a clue.

'Why don't you find out who are the directors of Sporran Holdings,' he suggested. 'They own half a million shares in RRA.'

Before I could ask any more questions, he said, 'Australia is on the line' and put the phone down.

I asked one of the research assistants to contact Companies House and get hold of the latest accounts filed by Sporran Holdings.

I was relieved to escape the office at lunchtime to meet Toby, but had to undergo some of his gentle teasing.

We had hardly settled into his favourite watering hole, a restaurant-cum-wine-bar just off Ludgate Hill, when he remarked how nice it was to see Jack winning again and how well he seemed to be getting on with his new caddie.

'And such a good-looking girl, too. I hope Jack isn't going to do anything silly.'

'Everyone is waiting for the first rumours,' I said. 'He might be daft enough. I used to think I knew Jack, but now I'm not so sure.'

'Well, he's at a dangerous age. For a sportsman, I mean. Mid-thirties, when he might think his powers are on the wane, you know the scene. And Zoe is such a pleasant girl for one so young.'

'Do I detect a slight yearning in your cynical breast, Toby?'

'Well, I'm not sure I've totally got over Fiona.'

Fiona, also a journalist, had caused the break-up of his second marriage, but the affair had recently petered out.

'Most of the young things I meet might as well comc from another planet. I'm only just in my forties, but they either treat me as if I'm in my dotage or as if I'm beneath their contempt. The generation gap, I suppose.' He looked mournful.

'It might not just be that, Toby. Have you thought that they might be frightened of you. Despite the column you write, you have a sharp tongue . . .'

'Thanks for the compliment.'

'. . . and you look formidable. Like a taller version of Dylan Thomas, especially when you wear one of your bow ties.'

Toby was studying the wine list with close concentration. The nod went to a bottle of Cotes du Rhone and we discussed the merits or otherwise of the RRA flotation. Toby decided to buy a couple of thousand shares if the omens were good.

'But it all depends on the biography of boring Bjorn. The publishers are paying me twenty grand for my peerless prose, so God knows what the Swede is getting. Christ, he bores for Scandinavia. I could summarise his life on the back of a postcard and I'm supposed to deliver eighty thousand words.'

I sympathised as Toby emptied half his glass in one emphatic and well-practised motion. He explained that he'd already had half his fee, which had gone to placate an aggressive tax-man who, said Toby, had no understanding of creative souls like his. But if he delivered more of the manuscript in about a month's time, he would have some money to invest in RRA.

'I've delivered nearly twenty thousand words and that was a miracle. How can you make an interesting book out of a bloke like Carlssen? He's Swedish for a start. His parents are both teachers and live near Gothenburg, his sister is also a teacher. He had an idyllic boyhood. He's gone from success to success. He's a Christian. He's just got engaged to . . .'

'A Swedish schoolteacher from Gothenburg?'

'She isn't a schoolteacher. She works for Scandinavian Airlines. I need to be a novelist, not a sports writer. I'm reduced to asking him to do an instructional chapter just to spin it out.'

'That should be interesting. He's a marvellous player, and stylish too.'

'Unfortunately for his autobiography, it's all so simple for him. I got enough material to cover about two pages. Everything in his lite is nice, nice, nice – never any difficulties and certainly not a trace of scandal.'

I changed the subject by asking Toby, who was demolishing the last of the Cotes du Rhone, his opinion of Felton Butter. Toby stared somewhat moodily at his glass and said: 'He's an odd cove, a loner, although his business is gossip. He's very good at trawling the murky waters of show business. And that's what my paper is interested in – anything to do with the telly, or the supposed stars of football, or royalty. A footballing prince who does a weekly chat show and is bi-sexual would be sheer heaven to my editor.

'Felton is very skilled at his job and you should be very wary. He's convinced that you're holding something back about Amanda's death. He reckons the business is a lot murkier than it seems. A routine suicide just doesn't add up.'

'He could be right. But Grant Sadler couldn't have killed her, he didn't have the time.'

'Well, just watch young Felton. He's nice, but he's dangerous. He's already on to you and Poppy, I fear.'

I told Toby, rather ruefully, that I had offered a haven to Poppy Drake for a couple of days and that I would be at the *Cap'n Hand* recording that evening.

'Yes. I can just imagine the headline: "Writer and upper-crust caddie in love-nest riddle. Link with death of sex-bomb Amanda." How would your mother or, worse, Mrs Bradshaw react to that?'

'There's no possible link between Poppy's and my private life and Amanda's death.'

'Totally irrelevant, Chris,' he said in a magisterial tone that stunned several nearby tables into silence. 'Butter would write whatever he thought he could get away with and that abominable editor would print it. Would you fancy taking on the *News* in a libel action? Of course not. You couldn't afford it. And that's why they usually get away with it.'

Toby waved for the bill. It came with two large ports 'on the house'. I can't drink port at lunchtime if I want to remain compos for the rest of the day and Toby kindly took on both glasses.

He glanced at the bill without any real attempt at a proper scrutiny and continued on the subject of Felton: 'It's difficult to see what makes him tick, except that it's obvious that he's very ambitious.'

'You can't see behind the veil?'

'No, and why should one be able to?' he asked sharply. 'You're a bit the same, Chris. I've known you for years but there are many occasions when I wonder what goes on behind those watchful blue eyes of yours. They change to a rather flinty grey when something displeases you and that's when I'm glad that you count me as a friend.'

If someone talks about your eyes, you want to hide them. I looked down at my coffee cup and Toby continued: 'Very little is known about his background. He never mentions any family and he tells everyone that he was born near Edinburgh. His voice seems to suggest that, but I heard that his birthplace was nearer Glasgow than Edinburgh.'

'So it suits him to suggest a more genteel background than is true?'

'Maybe. He was at Durham University, by the way, and he's a lot tougher than he looks. He boxed for the British Universities on several occasions and was a good soccer player.'

'He doesn't look the type.'

'That's another mistake that people make. He's so elegantly turned out, and he looks so studious, even artistic, that he's sometimes assumed to be homosexual, but he's not. All in all, he's very difficult to fathom; like Russia, a riddle wrapped in an enigma or whatever it was the man said.'

'Sounds like a description of putting to me.'

Toby strode away towards the Underground, 'back to my lonely garret to invent some more of Carlssen's life'. In fact he had a very comfortable small house not too far from Clapham Common and in his soberer moments he thanked his lucky stars that both his ex-wives had agreed to the very equitable divorces which enabled him to buy it.

My two or three hours in the office were mostly spent in fielding enquiries about the RRA issue and trying to convert them into firm intentions to buy. Andrew Buccleuth's pre-weekend palpitations about the flotation seemed to have eased and he was more interested in confirming the arrangements for our day's golf on Wednesday.

Chapter 13

Eventually I set out for the studio in the docklands where RRA were recording *Cap'n Hand*. The taxi driver entertained me with his trenchant views on the latest Middle East crisis ('we should knock seven shades of you-know-what out of 'em, sir – the price of petrol, it's diabolical, I can't make enough money to take the missus out for a steak and chips anymore'), on England's prospects in the Test series against the West Indies ('course, we shouldn't be playing these nig-nogs, sir. I mean, I got nothing against 'em, but we should stick with our own kind, like, you know, the Aussies'), on drugs ('well, I'd stick 'em up against a wall and shoot 'em, sir').

There's no point in arguing, is there? An occasional grunt and a nod, which he could see in his mirror, was all that was needed to assist the flow. He suddenly got my attention though when he said, 'You're a City gent, aren't you, sir? Well, I've had a good tip I don't mind passing on.'

He mentioned a small company in the stores sector, about which there had been some comment in one or two of the tip sheets recently. The tip sheets are newsletters, sold on subscription only, which supposedly unearth companies whose share price is said to be too low or about to rise significantly. These tips can be self-fulfilling prophecies because the brokers also read the newsletters, which are delivered to the subscribers at the weekend, and mark their prices up on Monday morning. This, added to the purchases made by the subscribers, invariably moves the price up, and lo and behold the newsletter has been proved right yet again.

I thanked the driver automatically and reflected that Joe Kennedy, the millionaire father of President John Kennedy, was moved to liquidate all his holdings in the US stock market when a shoeshine boy began to give him tips. He reckoned that if the shoeshine boy had become an expert it was time for a real expert to throw in the towel. It was just before the Great Crash of 1929.

Perhaps I should do the same tomorrow morning – it was something to ponder, if not too seriously.

We were now in docklands, that much-trumpeted area which was to regenerate East London with its mixture of spacious dwellings built in reclaimed warehouses and new industrial and commercial buildings. The latter, high-tech structures in strong primary colours, look unnatural and alien to me in this waterfront wasteland.

As he took my fare, which was not much more than my monthly mortgage payment, the cabbie said, 'These yuppies've caught a cold with the flats down 'ere, 'aven't they, guv?' and with a cheery grin he was off. With the fares he was getting, the price of oil or not, I thought he could probably afford half a dozen of the flats that were now being offered at knock-down prices.

Poppy had told me to meet her in the studio bar, whose wide windows looked across the water to the old brick warehouses. She was in a far corner with two men and waved when she saw me. I was introduced to her agent, Victor, a large crumpled man in a shiny grey suit. He had quite a full beard, which looked suspiciously as though it held bits of his lunch, and below it sat a slightly stained Old Wykehamist tie. I wondered whether he knew Andrew Buccleuth and while I was wondering I was introduced to Victor's friend, Tony, who was as neat as Victor was untidy. He had the drawn, tanned face of the habitual dieter and sun-bed user. He gave me a quiet but welcoming smile and asked me what I would like to drink.

I wondered why Poppy had introduced me as Christopher. Only my mother calls me Christopher and then only in rare moments of excessive irritation.

As Tony returned with a glass of tired-looking beer, Bill Ryan appeared at the table. The producer/director of *Cap'n Hand* was clutching what looked like a very large Scotch in one hand while he ushered another man into the group with the other.

'Let me introduce Johnny Storm's manager,' he said, 'Kevin Lagrange.'

The manager was stocky, with a drooping moustache, and had one of those fashionably casual looks that must take several hours a day to achieve. He had thick black hair combed straight back and kept there with a liberal dose of hair gel. He had the latest in designer jeans (with holes randomly punched in them) and they were tucked half in and half out of a pair of cowboy boots. A black leather jacket draped over his shoulders completed the ensemble. He stood poised on the balls of his feet, with his head pushed slightly forward, as if he was ready for action. He reminded me of the bear in those awful lager commercials.

He ordered a Southern Comfort and Coke from the attentive Tony and concentrated his attention on Poppy.

'Look, darlin', you're not getting the best out of my boy. Johnny's gonna be a great actor . . .' he waved his foot-long cigar to silence Poppy as she tried to speak '. . . OK, he's a bit raw at the moment, but you gotta give him more to do.' Kevin's voice was an unnerving mixture of South London and mid-Atlantic.

Poppy had given Kevin Lagrange a freezing look when he had called her 'darlin'' but her glare now was Antarctic.

'Given his talent, Mr Lagrange, I've given him more than enough to say already. I've had to cut out the big words, but I refuse to write dialogue that consists only of grunts.'

That's my girl.

Bill Ryan spoke manfully into the frigid silence and, as he assured Lagrange that he would 'talk to Poppy about the problem', he steered him away to another table.

'Don't get upset, Poppy,' Victor said placatingly.

'I'm not upset, just bloody amazed that an ignorant little oik like Lagrange has the cheek to tell me what to put into my scripts. I've had it up to here with these people. First Amanda Newhart had the bloody nerve to rewrite my lines and then eases one of her friends in to write some of my series; then Bill Ryan, who's already wormed a co-creator credit, tells me to expand the even-more-talentless Johnny Storm's part; now his manager has shown up to shout the odds.'

Poppy's anger was splendid and quite frightening and who could blame her? Just as she uttered the last furious words, Felton Butter glided silently up to the table. A light grey suit sat elegantly on his wiry frame.

'Hello, Poppy, do I hear harsh words? Is it something I should know or, even better, something I shouldn't know? Victor and Tony, nice to see you. And Chris, you're here at Poppy's invitation, I'm told. You've forsaken the smooth fairways of golf for the rough and tumble of show business. Temporarily, I trust,' he said with a short smile.

Poppy rose and, with a barely perceptible nod and a 'See you later' to the others, said, 'Let's go, Chris. We can sit in the director's box. It's more interesting than being stuck with the audience.'

I followed her out of the bar thinking that these show-biz people made money brokers look tame.

To ease the tension, I took Poppy's hand and murmured, 'Darling, you're beautiful in your wrath.' She spluttered with laughter, her good humour quickly restored. She pulled me past the back of the steeply raked seats which faced the stage sets, and up two flights of stairs to the director's box, the control room for the whole operation.

Bill Ryan was sitting in front of a bank of television monitors, row upon row of them, some of which were tuned in to receive the *Cap'n Hand* pictures. He had four assistants, two on each side, and was very much in charge. We were separated from his control room by a glass panel. A loudspeaker played over the conversation between Ryan and someone called Charles who, Poppy told me, was the floor manager, the man who controlled matters on the set. We could hear, too, the sound of the audience. Though we couldn't see them it was clear from the excited hubbub that most of the seats were occupied.

I asked Poppy whether we could look at the audience and she led me a short way along a corridor, opened a door and we peered out over a small balcony to the people below, most of whom had probably, like me, never been in a TV studio before. They were looking eagerly at the two stage sets in front of them and at the various television monitors which were strung at intervals above them. These would show the scenes which had already been shot on location and which eventually would be interleaved with the studio sequences.

Charles now spoke to the audience and introduced Freddie Bentley whose function was to 'warm up' the audience – to put them in a good humour so that they would laugh at anything – and also to introduce the members of the cast.

Freddie Bentley was a fatherly looking man in his middle fifties, with a dark suit matched by a sober tie. He was clearly no Max Miller or Arthur English, but Poppy told me that he was much in demand.

He had an instantly acceptable manner, with a comforting smile and a slightly conspiratorial air. He seemed to be saying to the audience, 'Don't be afraid, join in with me, it's only a bit of a giggle.' He was very easy to like. He began with the old gag of asking everyone to stand up and shake hands with the person behind them. That got a good laugh and he followed it with a few rapid-fire jokes. Then came the little homily about how the audience were there to enjoy themselves, but would they please let the audience at home *know* that they were enjoying themselves. Let the laughter go, 'because you can't hear *smiles*'.

It was so beautifully timed that you were unlikely to object to the patronising tone, although I could hear Poppy groaning quietly in mock anguish. He went on to welcome groups from Westminster Council ('Marina's in charge, stand up, boys and girls') and Sainsbury's, and a party of Irishmen on a mystery coach tour ('they haven't arrived yet').

After a few more jokes, Freddie Bentley began to introduce the cast.

'Not a word about the poor bloody writer,' Poppy said in my ear.

The actors playing the very small parts had already gathered on the set and some of the other players were introduced. Freddie Bentley's comments were so flattering that I wondered why they weren't all superstars. He then went on to the main actors.

'And now that grand old man of the theatre, Eliot Stonehouse, who plays the harbour master. You've all seen Eliot in countless roles in the cinema and on TV and he is also, of course, a very distinguished stage actor.'

Eliot Stonehouse, clad in a vaguely nautical uniform and carrying his cap, looked like everyone's conception of a British actor with his upright carriage, fine head of snow-white hair and matching pencil-line moustache. He resembled an amalgam of David Niven, Douglas Fairbanks Jr and Wilfred Hyde-White.

'Not so much of the old, Freddie,' he said into the microphone, much to the delight of the audience.

'It's a great pleasure,' the comic continued, 'to introduce to you that superb singer and budding young actor, Johnny Storm.'

Not so much of the young, I thought to myself, because Johnny Storm had been around since the early seventies at least, when he had burst upon the public with a string of hits in the 'Glam-Rock' manner. His career in the charts had been brief, although I dimly remembered a so-called concept album, a rock version of the Planets Suite. Thereafter it had been a familiar tale of alcoholism and drug abuse, broken marriages, and now bit parts in films and television.

I asked Poppy why he had been resurrected for the series.

'Neil Anderson. Johnny was a part of a nostalgia tour he set up a couple of years ago. It did well and Anderson recommended him to Bill Ryan. Anderson has great plans for him, apparently.'

I had to admit that he was looking well on it, from a distance anyway. He seemed fit and lean and his face bore none of the ravages that were seen so clearly on the faces of many pop stars. Johnny Storm said a few words of welcome and sang a few bars of one of his hits – to thunderous applause.

This was the cue for the entrance of Grant Sadler, the star of the show, and our cue to re-enter the director's box. On the monitors we watched Sadler's entry. Congratulations were due to the make-up people: he looked very good. Gone were the bags, the puffiness and the red veins. He gave a modest smile as Bentley provided a remarkably unctuous summary of his career and he then stepped up to the microphone.

'Ladies and gentlemen, thank you for your generous welcome,' he oozed, 'and I do hope that you are going to enjoy the show.'

He paused and held the pause just long enough for one or two people to fidget and to wonder whether he'd forgotten what he intended to say.

'I want to say a few words about one of our colleagues, a great star, who has just been taken from us.'

He paused again and the whole studio was silent except for the murmured instructions of Bill Ryan.

Grant Sadler continued. 'You will all have read about the tragic death of Amanda Newhart. I called her a great star, but she was much more than that, she was a staunch friend to all of us on this series and was of course an ornament to her profession.'

Another pause. Poppy muttered in my ear, 'Pass the sick bag.'

'I would like to ask you all to observe, with me, a minute's silence in tribute to her. Thank you.'

At that point an image of Amanda Newhart appeared on all the monitors. I knew I'd laugh if I looked at Poppy, and there was a notice alongside us which asked for quiet as we could be heard in the director's box. I stared resolutely ahead until, after about fifty seconds, we were put out of our misery. The monitors went blank and Bill Ryan said, 'OK, let's get this show on the road.' Poppy winked at me and said, 'That's show business.'

The first two scenes went reasonably smoothly. The first took place in the local police station where Johnny Storm played a harassed constable and the second in an up-market harbourside pub where Grant Sadler was the land-lord.

There were two or three retakes, mainly because Johnny Storm fluffed his lines and then had grave trouble with the word 'opportunity'. Poppy was concentrating on every syllable with great intensity and was particularly peevish about the timing of some of the lines. At the end of Johnny Storm's scene she told me that he'd 'completely messed up the emphasis and ruined the exit line'. It didn't seem to worry the audience; they were laughing at everything. I realised that it was unwise to sit next to a writer during a performance of her work.

The next few scenes involved several retakes, mainly because an actress playing a dizzy blonde barmaid was type-cast and couldn't string more than three words together without a prompt. It was noticeable that, in contrast, Eliot Stonehouse was word perfect.

'She's only got five sodding lines and she can't even learn those,' Poppy said resignedly. Nevertheless, the audience continued to love every minute of it.

I glanced at my watch and realised that the recording had been going on for nearly an hour and a half.

At one point there was quite a long delay when one of the four cameras which were in use broke down. Bill Ryan asked Charles to send Freddie Bentley out to keep the audience happy and he did it admirably.

The real problem was the last scene which had to be shot by one specific camera. It lasted about four minutes and comprised a conversation in the pub between Grant Sadler, Eliot Stonehouse and the dizzy barmaid, interspersed with various comings and goings to their left and right.

Grant Sadler fluffed his lines twice early on, the barmaid again forgot her two lines and was then afflicted with a fit of the giggles, and the other actors could not get the timing of their exits and entrances right. Throughout it all, Eliot Stonehouse remained impressively calm and charming.

In the end, after nine takes, the scene was 'in the can' – to everyone's relief.

Once it was completed the indefatigable Freddie Bentley stood up to tell the audience what was going on. 'We're waiting for a "clear",' he said. 'You see, God up there, otherwise known as Bill Ryan the director, is waiting for the film to come back from Boots, and if it's all OK you can go home. I expect you're dying to go. I'll bet you need a wee, dear, don't you?' he said, gesturing at a row of elderly ladies near the front. And still they all laughed.

'Right, we've got a clear. Thanks for being a wonderful audience. You can come back anytime.'

I turned to Poppy. 'Was that OK?'

'If you ignore the last scene, and these problems do occasionally crop up, and Johnny Storm's inability to say more than two words without a moronic pause, and that silly bitch of a barmaid, and Grant Sadler's total indifference to his stage directions, not bad. Grant is such an idiot, he likes to keep what he thinks is his "best side" to the audience. The trouble is, he doesn't have a best side any more. It almost makes me long for Amanda's return. Well, perhaps not,' she said with a grin.

We saw through the window that Bill Ryan and his assistants were well down their glasses of champagne and by mutual consent we set off towards the bar.

'I thought Jimmy McCoy was in the series,' I said.

'He is, but he's not in every week. He plays the owner of the local caravan park and is slotted in to about eight out of the thirteen episodes. Come on, let's join the thespians and the other poseurs for a drink, shall we?'

On the way to the bar I asked Poppy why they didn't dispense with an audience altogether and use canned laughter as they do in America.

'They think it sounds more spontaneous, which it does. As you heard, the audience will laugh at anything.'

The bar was very crowded but Poppy saw her agent, Victor, flanked by his friend Tony, in the act of ordering and called out to him for a couple of glasses of wine. Victor thought that the episode had gone well and congratulated Poppy on her rewrites.

'I couldn't see the join, darling,' he said, with a smile, which turned to a worried frown when Poppy asked him how many episodes she had been guaranteed to write for the next series.

'Well, it's still five, Poppy, as you know. They had promised four to Amanda . . .'

His voice trailed off as Poppy cut in, 'Exactly, and I want at least three of the four that Amanda won't be writing. So, will you go back and negotiate with RRA, please.'

Victor sighed and finished off his glass of red wine. I noticed that he was sweating slightly. With a woman like Poppy around I wasn't surprised. Clearly, she was not the sort of client who gave her agent an easy time.

'Look, Poppy. Bill Ryan wants to bring in more writers, experienced writers, to share the burden. Another series of thirteen is already agreed and I know that RRA are talking about a third series. There's even a chance of a sale to the States.'

I watched Poppy flush suddenly and a little scar showed up white alongside her left eye.

'A lot of bloody use a sale to the States is to me, Victor. I agreed a buy-out for those rights, on your advice and against my better judgement. You shouldn't have let me. If the US deal goes ahead and I don't get something out of it, I'm going to cause a lot of trouble to a lot of people.'

After this short exchange, vehement as it was, Victor seemed to go grey and was sweating heavily. He looked desperately at his empty glass and then smiled with relief as Eliot Stonehouse joined us. Urbane and upright of posture he put his arm around Poppy and said, 'Marvellous script, my dear. Well done. I hope you're looking after her, Victor.'

'Trying, Eliot, trying,' Victor said. I wondered which meaning was foremost in his mind. 'I hope you won't think me rude, but Tony and I must go. Heavy day tomorrow. Lovely to see you, and I'll call you tomorrow, Poppy.'

With a wave, he ambled off with Tony in his wake. A big gentle bear of a man who only wanted a quiet life but wasn't going to get one from Poppy Drake.

I was aware of a hand on my shoulder and the clear tones of Eliot Stonehouse asking Poppy, 'Who is this handsome young man?' He seized my hand and said, 'I'm Eliot Stonehouse. One L and one T, like the poet. You know what I do for a living, but how do you earn a crust?'

He was holding my hand overlong and I was uncertain whether to tug it away or pretend I hadn't noticed.

Fortunately, as I appealed mutely to Poppy, Eliot Stonehouse let my hand go and I began to explain that I was a caddie for a part of my working life.

'Oh, a beautiful game, golf,' he said. 'I had an Italian friend a few years back. I was doing a film for de Sica. He was such a beautiful boy. He had a house by a golf course in Tuscany.'

He smiled nostalgically and Poppy told him that my 'real job' was with a firm of stockbrokers. Eliot asked me with whom and continued: 'I had a charming financial adviser. He went to Harrow, but I didn't hold that against him. He seemed to put me into some frightful stocks though. He left his firm last year. There was some sort of scandal. He also pinched a couple of first editions from my library.'

Poppy grabbed my arm and said, 'I want Chris to meet Bill Ryan.' As she steered me away, Eliot cried out, 'Come and have lunch. Perhaps you can help me sort out my investments, my dear.'

'It's probably more than lunch that he's got in mind,' she said, 'but I'm sure that you can handle it.'

Poppy pointed out Bill Ryan in a distant corner of the bar where he was deep in conversation with Grant Sadler. They seemed to spend a lot of time together in conversation and I wondered what they found to talk about at such length and with such concentration. It had to be money, sex or religion and my bet was firmly on the first.

As she headed toward the two men Poppy asked me to get a couple of glasses of wine and I veered towards the bar, only to find the gap I was aiming for filled by Felton Butter.

'Did you enjoy the show?' he asked.

'Yes, very interesting. It's all new to me but I was very impressed.'

'Your friend Poppy isn't a bad writer. She's laid the trail for Amanda Newhart's exit from the series with great skill. One might almost have thought it was a labour of love,' he said with a mischievous smile and continued, 'it's a good job they had all the location work in the can.'

'Yes, I hadn't realised they did all the outside filming in advance.'

'Oh yes. Much simpler and more cost-effective. And talking of cost-effective, I've just been talking to Kevin Lagrange and he told me that CBS in America have already bought an option on the series and that a pilot will be made within a few months. I wonder if the fair Poppy knows?'

'Does it stand a chance of getting on the network in the States, do you think?'

Felton Butter drank reflectively from his glass of mineral water and said, 'Every chance. Series that have originated in Britain and been adapted for American television have been doing very well. In fact they're rather the flavour of the year.'

I looked up and saw Poppy waving at me with her empty glass. I managed to attract the attention of the languid barmaid and bought a couple of glasses of tepid white wine. As I walked towards Poppy I wondered what her reaction would be when she found out about the American deal, in its formative stages though it was.

I saw Poppy gesticulating and caught the end of her sentence '. . . and I've got every right to do more episodes. Five is ludicrous; I should be doing at least seven.'

Bill Ryan put his hands up placatingly and said, 'Look, your agent has agreed that you will write five episodes. And, I'll be honest with you, we've got to have plenty of writers on tap if this series is to run smoothly. OK, Amanda was going to do four with me and I could possibly offer you one of those, but to be co-written with me.'

Grant Sadler cut in. 'I agree with Bill. We've got to give other writers a chance. If we're looking at another three or even four series you couldn't possibly keep up the pace, Poppy.'

'Five episodes is hardly overdoing it, is it?' said Poppy. She pointed at Bill Ryan. 'Bloody hell, you're the producer and the director and you're doing four for the second series. It's not fair.'

'Fair doesn't come into it,' Grant Sadler said. 'It's what the contract says that counts.'

Bill Ryan glanced at me. 'All this business talk must be very boring for Chris. Let's change the subject.'

'Not at all,' I protested. 'It's of great interest. After all, my firm is handling the issue of RRA shares. I'm encouraged to hear of the possibilities of overseas sales of

Cap'n Hand. Do you think it will do well in America for instance?'

I was waiting for some sort of reaction from the two men and caught the involuntary look that passed between them.

Bill Ryan smiled. 'There's very little chance of that,' he said. 'Why should the Americans buy our stuff when they've got material from their own studios coming out of their ears? No, I'll be honest with you, no chance.'

'That's not what Felton Butter told me.'

'What would he know about it? He's just a bloody journalist. More like a gossip columnist. He makes up most of his stuff,' said Grant Sadler dismissively.

He put his hand on my shoulder in a friendly way. I wanted to squirm away but stood unmoving. 'Chris, I'm in your debt. I haven't thanked you properly for backing up my story the other night at Amanda's. God knows what they'd have pinned on me if you hadn't been there.'

'I told the truth about what I saw. That's all,' I muttered stiffly.

'And so did I,' he said sharply and then added, 'anyway, if there's anything I can do . . .'

Not bloody likely, I thought to myself.

Sadler continued, 'Chris, I'd value your advice on golf clubs. I need some new irons and can't make up my mind between buying Pings or a traditional blade. What do you think?'

I automatically went through the pros and cons while I watched Poppy, who seemed to be having a regulation show-business chat with Bill Ryan and one of the actresses with a minor part in the series.

The crowd in the bar was beginning to thin out as Felton Butter came over and congratulated Poppy on her script.

'It must have been frightful having to do those rewrites at such short notice,' he said. 'I'm finding it hard enough to complete a first draft. To go back and rejig a finished script must be purgatory.'

'I didn't know you wrote for TV,' said Poppy.

'I've just started. My clever agent put up an idea of mine to North Western and they've commissioned a pilot. So I'm just a beginner.'

'Well, make sure that you've got a good agent to protect you,' Poppy said, glancing quickly at Bill Ryan. 'Otherwise you'll get screwed.'

'I hear that *Cap'n Hand* is about to be sold to the States,' Felton said, with an inquiring look at Bill Ryan.

I saw Grant Sadler stiffen and before Bill Ryan could reply he moved toward Felton and said, 'I don't know what you're trying to stir up from your gutter in Fleet Street, but there is no US sale of *Cap'n Hand*. Now, is that understood?'

'Perfectly,' said Felton. 'Can I quote you on that?'

But Sadler had already turned away and was heading for the exit with Ryan in his wake.

'Have I said the wrong thing?' asked Butter.

Poppy said, 'Judging by their reaction, yes. Where did you hear this rumour?'

'From Kevin Lagrange, amongst others.'

'It's probably not worth the foul air it was expelled on,' said Poppy. 'Let's go,' she said to me.

As we said our goodbyes, Felton Butter told me that he would be seeing 'Poppy's colleagues' on Wednesday since he would be playing in the United Charities Pro-am. This is one of the major pro-ams of the season, which is followed in the evening by a gala dinner at which the entertainment is provided by the show biz/pro-am regulars. I was due to play in it with Andrew Buccleuth.

'I'll see you there,' I said. 'I didn't know you played, Felton.'

'All Scots can play golf, Chris.'

'I hope so because Neil Anderson is in our four-ball.'

'Keep your hand on your wallet.'

As Poppy drove us quickly and efficiently home through the darkened streets, I asked, 'Phew, is it always like that?'

'Not usually. I'm sorry you got caught up in it all. It must have been boring for you.'

'Not at all,' I protested. She said very little more as she drove the small and lively car with great verve. I assumed that she was concentrating on her driving and sat back contentedly. It was good to be driven by someone else for a change.

We were soon outside my flat and I asked Poppy in for a snack and a coffee.

'Not tonight, Chris. I've got so much on my mind. It's this *Cap'n Hand* business, as you can guess. I must do some thinking. They're not going to get away with it. The first thing I'm going to do is talk to Victor. He can start working for his ten per cent.'

She turned to me and gave me a long kiss. 'I'm sorry that this is such a fraught time. I'll call you tomorrow.'

Chapter 14

On Tuesday morning I entered my office bright and early, and found a note on my desk from Andrew Buccleuth: would I see him at ten o'clock?

I scanned several of the morning papers and saw only one or two desultory comments about the RRA flotation. One was distinctly unfavourable and questioned whether RRA should be flirting with the US market, where so many British companies had met with disaster. The writer had a good point as the American market represents the Holy Grail to so many British businessman: it's so huge and the Americans have such large disposable incomes. But the American market is much more diffuse and volatile than the British, and we still make the mistake of assuming that because their language is the same as ours, so are their business methods. They're not.

The writer had learned that one of Neil Anderson's objectives was to acquire an American TV production company and pointed out how rarely such a take-over had brought success 'over there'. There had been several disasters and he cited one in particular: the take-over by a British television company of an American company with a string of hits to its credit. They had paid over half a billion pounds but, after the take-over, the successes dried up and the British company realised that it had acquired a very expensive turkey.

The tone of the article was not good news for the RRA

flotation, but it could easily be countered by some positive comment in the days leading up to the actual offer for sale of the shares. As long as the sentiment in the market was not unfavourable the issue would go well enough.

At ten o'clock I went upstairs to Andrew Buccleuth's office and received a guarded smile from his secretary-cum-personal assistant, Veronica. She is a tall lady in her late forties whose style of dress harks back to another decade. I'm not quite sure which decade, but her careful make-up is reminiscent, according to Toby, of the stately mannequins of the early fifties.

She always greets me in a rather forced way. I feel that she doesn't approve of my double life and thinks that I enjoy myself too much. I know she disapproves of the way Andrew appears to indulge me.

'He's ready for you,' Veronica said, as if Andrew were waiting to drill my teeth without an anaesthetic.

Andrew's desk was more than usually cluttered and I noticed that the clutter contained nearly as many golf magazines as financial journals. He was now thinking of buying a new putter and was doing some serious homework.

Andrew flicked a piece of paper across the desk to me. 'Here's the draw for the pro-am tomorrow. We're off at eleven o'clock. You've met Neil Anderson, haven't you?'

I had once shaken hands with the founder of RRA and wondered what sort of a golfer he was off a handicap of fifteen. 'Only briefly. What's he like?'

'He's quite lively, quite amusing, but he does affect a hard-headed businessman pose. Makes you feel he's expecting us to fall over with fright or admiration at his toughness and shrewdness. Still, he is good at what he does. I can never understand, though, these people who boast about how many hours a day they work, eight days a week.'

'They've read too many of the colour mags with all those boring profiles of tycoons who say that they're workaholics and expect us all to beam our approval.'

'Yes. We come across the type often enough, don't we? Got no other real interests, that's their trouble. I believe in working civilised hours. Can't play to my handicap if I spend too long in the office. I'm looking forward to tomorrow. I'm trying out my new metal woods.'

I consulted the draw. The professional in our four-ball was Russell Cope who had played on the British circuit in the sixties and early seventies and was still a very solid performer on whom you could happily put your money to score level par or better.

I saw that the team next to us in the draw and starting eight minutes later comprised Grant Sadler, a banker whom we both knew slightly, my old boss Jack Mason and Felton Butter. I wondered how Felton had wangled it. I noticed that McCoy was in the team behind them.

Andrew said, 'What a pity that we haven't got Jack as our pro. Or would it have been embarrassing for you, Chris?'

'Not embarrassing, no. But both of us might have felt uncomfortable.'

Only when he'd confirmed that he would send a car to pick me up in the morning and that I could use his house, which is near the golf course, as a base, did he turn to the RRA flotation. He dealt with it briefly, stressing the need to feed positive stories to the Press and the institutions.

He then returned to the more interesting matter of the golf. 'We've all got to change into our glad rags for the dinner, so why don't you stay with us, Chris? Or my driver will take you home. It's up to you. Now, I'm leaving after lunch because I'm going to have an hour or two's practice at the club and you can do the same. I imagine that there'll be some fairly stiff bets flying around tomorrow, especially between Sadler and McCoy, and I know that Anderson likes a punt.'

'Show me a Scotsman who doesn't.'

Chapter 15

The bets were struck over coffee – and, in the case of Jimmy McCoy, Grant Sadler and Andrew Buccleuth, brandy – in the clubhouse on the next morning.

The format for the competition was that each team comprised four players. The two best scores on each hole would count towards the total score. The bet between our two teams was £100 per man and, in addition, Neil Anderson had individual bets with McCoy and Sadler for £200. This was the third event in the celebrity Order of Merit and McCoy was one celebrity who was obviously looking forward to it. He waved his second large brandy of the morning at Sadler and said: 'Here's to you, Grant. I'm in the mood today. I'm gonna leave you for dead.'

Sadler didn't even smile, but said: 'Put your money where your mouth is, Jock. How about five hundred. Straight bet. Just you and me.'

'That's fine by me,' was the reply and they nodded grimly at each other to confirm the bet.

This was a little heavy, even by show-biz standards, and it underscored the vehement dislike the two men had for each other.

Felton Butter, as smart as ever in dark blue trousers and a pale yellow cashmere sweater, was saying very little and I wondered if he was nervous about the golf to come or the money he might lose. He had the great advantage of having a very accomplished tournament golfer on his team in the shape of Jack Mason, who led us all to the tee. Zoe Bernini was waiting there. At only a shade over five feet she hardly looked as if she could lift Jack's golf bag, let alone carry it for four or five miles around the course.

Jack was one of several pros playing the pro-am who had decided not to travel to the Belgian Open, where I hoped Rollo was doing his stuff even now.

Waiting to play from the first tee when we arrived was the unmistakable figure of Kenny Craig, who was giving the Minister for Sport the benefit of his views on soccer hooliganism. The MP was probably already regretting leaving matters ministerial for a game of golf with our Kenny. A battering in the House would be preferable to five hours of his non-stop chat.

There were more greetings, followed by the tedious and slightly embarrassing ritual of McCoy and Craig trading one-liners. Craig's behaviour with Zoe was just as tedious. He put his arm around her and held her too close until she wriggled free and said: 'Chris is getting jealous. He's a caddie too and you haven't given him a hug.'

Craig looked at me and eventually the tumblers fell into place.

'Oh yeah, I remember you. Are you a better golfer than you are a caddie?'

Jack Mason spoke up: 'Why don't you try him, Kenny: I'm sure Chris will have a small bet with you.'

We struck a bet for £50 on our individual cards, and I reflected that with all these side-bets being contested, and the consequent need for everyone to hole out on every green, it was no wonder these rounds took so long.

We eventually got off the tee several minutes late and after our group had all played their second shots towards the green of the opening par-five hole, I looked back towards the tee to see how Felton Butter would fare.

He was playing off a handicap of eighteen and I watched him make a slow and smooth swing at the ball, which landed in the middle of the fairway. Toby had told me that he was a good games player and first impressions seemed to confirm his words.

Both Russell Cope, the professional, and I had put our second shots on the front edge of the green and I noticed that he still had that rhythmic and unfussy swing that really good golfers always retain. He has never hit the ball long distances but is deadly accurate. I wandered over to him and asked him how the world was treating him. He is the professional at quite a big club about forty miles west of London.

He leaned on his bag. 'Well, sir . . . .'

'It's Chris.' Most of the professionals of his generation address amateur golfers as 'sir'.

'Times are not easy. I do my teaching and thank goodness for that. But the members are not easy to please. If they can save themselves a couple of pounds by buying from one of those golf supermarkets, they will. There's not so much loyalty now, sir. Not that I'm complaining. They've been very good to me over the years.'

We walked towards the green and I thought how those words would be echoed by hundreds of club professionals around the country. I know Russell's club and reckon that his income – a retainer from the club, sales through his shop and lessons to his members – would bring him not a lot less than £50,000 each year, and a proportion would no doubt be in cash and undeclared.

We both putted up the green and got our birdie fours and so our team had made an encouraging start. A watery sun had broken through the clouds as we stepped on to the second tee and it highlighted the many different shades of green of the course, the majestic trees which lined the fairway and the light brown of the bunkers etched at intervals down the second hole.

For once my swing felt fluid and uninhibited. It was one of those mornings when any doubts about technique had vanished; my mind was uncluttered and I just stood up and gave the ball a crack. I was also able to watch Russell Cope's simple action and that helped enormously.

Neil Anderson and Andrew were hardly needed, but I noticed that Anderson, with an abbreviated swing, was sticking pretty close to his handicap. He was a stocky man, with a dark complexion and crinkly, thinning hair, and had a swing which is typical of short strong men. All the emphasis was on the arms, punching the ball through from a wide stance. It looked very effective, very competitive, just like the man himself.

As we waited on the tee at the ninth hole, where there was a considerable delay, Anderson asked us how the RRA issue was shaping up. Not that he had to worry; the forty million shares were sold as far as he was concerned. If the institutions and the public did not buy them all, Andrew's firm would have to come up with the money for the remaining shares. Nevertheless, such an outcome would suggest a lack of public confidence in RRA and the share price would certainly fall. What everyone wanted was a mad rush for a piece of the action and a healthy premium on the first day of trading. There is nothing so heartening to a company new to the market, or its stockbroker, as the sight of investors crowding into the bank at the last moment with their share applications.

Over the next few holes Andrew and I did our duty, asking Anderson his plans and making all the right noises.

'As you know, I want to buy a production company in the States. It'll complement RRA over here; I've got my eye on an outfit in LA. I want a share of the vast American market and I want to create a better market for British product and British performers out there. If Dudley Moore can do it, so can Jimmy McCoy.'

'I see that he's got a stake in your company,' I said, as I idly swung a club up and down.

'Yeah, I gave him a few shares way back. He and his wife will make a nice little pile out of that. Good luck to them.'

'You and he go back a long way, I'm told.'

Anderson looked sharply at me and then smiled. 'Jimmy started in the pubs in Glasgow and got his first real breaks in some of our clubs. There isn't a tougher baptism. The old-timers talk about the Glasgow Empire, but that was a Tupperware party compared to our clubs. That's why Jimmy's so good, and why he's a stayer, a real pro.'

Anderson talked on as the round progressed. He talked about expanding his magazine interests into other areas, such as fashion, and said that he was quietly building up a stake in one of the main television franchise holders.

'But all that's relatively long term. *Cap'n Hand* is of immediate importance. We're already committed to make twenty-six. Between you and me we'll probably make fifty-two, and then we'll make one more series to get to the magic sixty-five.'

'What's so magical about sixty-five?' asked Andrew.

'Well, it's four less than sixty-nine.' Anderson smiled and continued. 'It's all to do with the States. CBS have got an option on the series, and believe me, they'll exercise that option. They'll change everything for the US market, as you know, and twenty-six episodes is neither here nor there in terms of money. It's nice, but it's not big money even for us as the producers.'

As we walked down the next fairway Anderson expanded on the 'magic sixty-five' episodes.

'It's in the lap of the gods whether an outfit like CBS will take sixty-five episodes of anything. They're absolutely ruthless and if the audience declines they'll drop a series without hesitation. But if *Cap'n Hand* goes to twenty-six and holds its audience they could well commission another thirty-nine over a period. That's when you hit the big time.'

Anderson paused and hit a very respectable mid-iron shot on to the edge of the next green.

'When you've got sixty-five episodes in the can, CBS will not only repeat the series at regular intervals on their network, but they will put them out to syndication for all the other American stations. You're then talking very big numbers for everybody; for the producers and the originators over here.'

'And the writers?' I asked.

'Well, that depends on the deal. As far as I know the writer sold all rights to Grant Sadler, Bill Ryan and RRA. If it all falls into place, those two guys will become millionaires several times over.'

I thought ruefully of Poppy Drake and wondered what her reaction would be if she could hear our conversation. I hit a horrible iron shot towards the green as a result, a half-topped effort that did, however, have the virtue of flying straight towards the flag, even if it was at neck height for most of its journey. When we got to the green my ball was sitting about six feet from the hole, much to the delight of my partners. As I holed out for an undeserved birdie, Russell Cope uttered the old golfing saw, 'If you're going to miss 'em, miss 'em straight.'

We had another long delay on the seventeenth tee. The team ahead of us was waiting to tee off and from our elevated position, which gave us a clear view down the fairway, we could see three other matches on the same hole.

Kenny Craig came over and asked me how I was doing. I did a rapid count of the last few holes and told him that I needed two fours for a 68 which, with my two handicap strokes deducted, would give a score of four under par.

'Not bad for a caddie,' he said. 'I need two fours for a net sixty-five.'

He was called to the tee by his partners and I reckoned that the odds for the fifty quid were just in his favour. Craig played off a handicap of nine and had a shot to come down the next hole, a par five, but the final hole was a very demanding par four. He hit a good drive down the right of the fairway and I thought that the odds were now certainly in his favour.

Russell Cope came over and asked me how I stood against Craig.

'Right, sir, no problem. I'll tell you where to hit it and I'll show you the right line on the greens. No point in giving away fifty pounds is there, sir?'

At this point the opposition – Grant Sadler, Felton Butter, Jack Mason and the banker – arrived on the tee. It was decided to count up the respective team scores to add a little spice to the final two holes.

Our combined total was seventeen under par and our opponents were one better. All to play for and two rousing holes on which to finish.

Russell Cope hit his drive dead centre and, as I prepared to play, he said to me quietly: 'Don't follow me, hit it right of centre where Craig went. By the way, he's in the bunker on the right of the green but we won't be going there, sir.'

I did as I was told and our two partners were also safely on the fairway.

As we walked towards our drives, Neil Anderson told us more about the significance of *Cap'n Hand*.

'We've managed to persuade CBS to take two of our actors on board for the American series. Jimmy McCoy and Johnny Storm. This is unusual to say the least, but Johnny is known in the States anyway as a pop singer and Jimmy has done a few spots on various shows.

'They've agreed to use them and this is important in two ways. Storm's career over here is going to be geed up by *Cap'n Hand* and this will make double sure that his new album sells really big. Well, it'll be the same routine in America. He'll become a nationally known celebrity and his records will sell like crazy. And of course the videos to go with them. That's real money.'

Anderson stopped and counselled by Cope – 'Make your shot count, sir, we want to make sure of our net four' – punched a mid-iron to within about a hundred yards of the green.

Cope walked on and hit a wood straight as an arrow on to the middle of the green and then turned his attention to me.

'Now then, you're forty yards nearer the green than me.

I want you to fade a five wood on to the pin. It's at the back of the green on the right. Line up on the centre of the green and slide it through.'

Again, I did as I was told and when we got to the green I saw that I had a virtual tap-in for an eagle three.

Russell nodded his encouragement and told me that Craig had taken five shots and all I needed was a steady par down the last. He told me where to hit the ball again and I registered, with great relief, a par. Andrew, to his great pleasure, had a net birdie. As a team, we had finished twenty-one shots under par.

While we waited for Jack Mason and his team to finish, Andrew asked Neil Anderson whether he had any grandiose plans to further McCoy's career.

'Oh, yeah. He's capable of becoming a big star over there and when we've bought that company in LA, we'll place him in various series out there. With Jimmy in them we'll be able to sell them to the UK network.'

The best Jack's team could do on the final hole was two pars and they had scored two birdies on the previous hole. So we had won the team match and were better off to the tune of £100 each.

Jack said: 'I thought you were swinging well, Chris you beggar, and I suppose Russell went round in his usual two under, did he?'

'Three under, Jack,' Russell said with a smile.

As the others headed for the clubhouse, a welcome shower and a late lunch, Jack lingered a little and then stopped. 'I'm glad you won the money, Chris, because I'm afraid we had a cheat in our team. As it happened, it didn't affect the overall team score or I suppose I'd have had to speak up, but Mr Grant Sadler is pretty adept at improving his lie. A nudge here and a roll there, and he's none too clever at counting either. Isn't that right, Zoe?' He turned towards his caddie.

'Yes, I spotted him several times. And, boy, doesn't he fancy himself.'

We both grinned at her and Jack said: 'Did he promise to make you a star?'

'Not quite that old cliché. But he's one of those blokes who stands too close to women and thinks his magic will make them fall on their backs.'

'Well, you can't blame him for trying,' Jack said.

As Jack went off to get changed I asked Zoe how she was faring with my former boss.

'Fine. He's a lovely man inside that rather spiky façade, isn't he? And of course winning a tournament helps.'

I nodded, a shade ruefully and Zoe continued: 'And how are you doing with Rollo? I reckon he could be a fantastic player if he put his mind to it.'

'That's the problem – his mind. No one doubts his talent, but does he take the game seriously enough? I'll find out over the next few weeks.'

Zoe looked at me thoughtfully from under her long dark lashes. 'I'm surprised, Chris, that we've never had a drink together or a round of golf. We'll arrange something, shall we?'

She patted my arm in an admonishing way and said: 'And soon, too.'

She gave me a brilliant smile, perfect white teeth flashing in her tanned face, and strode off.

'I'll see you at the dinner tonight,' she called over her shoulder.

That woman had more than a passing interest in me, I could tell. Perhaps it was going to be a bumper year for lovely women. It suited me just fine.

Kenny Craig was waiting for me in the changing room.

'Finished with two-thirds of a State Express,' he said. 'Five, five. I saw your eagle at the seventeenth and knew I was in trouble. Well played.'

It gave me a lot of pleasure to take his £50 note. 'I'll see you in the bar. A large brandy should soften the blow. Stuffed by a caddie, my God,' he muttered as he went out.

I joined the rest of the team and my erstwhile opponents

in the bar and the outstanding bets were settled. Russell Cope particularly enjoyed taking £100 from a current tournament player, Jack Mason, who handed it over with a show of mock reluctance.

I noticed that Neil Anderson had beaten Jimmy McCoy but had lost to Grant Sadler. And Sadler had beaten McCoy and relieved him of £500. As the money changed hands I looked very hard at Jack Mason. He shrugged his shoulders as if to say that it was none of his business.

At the end of the queue for the buffet lunch I was joined by Felton Butter who congratulated me on my round and asked me how we had all got on with Neil Anderson. I assured him that we'd had a friendly and interesting round.

'He's a very ambitious man, isn't he?' I said rather superfluously.

'Not half. Did you know that he's in the process of taking over Johnny Storm's management company? Kevin Lagrange is not happy, but there's very little he can do.'

'Why should he sell out if he doesn't want to?'

Felton stepped a little closer to me and spoke quietly. There was so much hubbub in the dining room that he was in very little danger of being overheard but he looked over his shoulder to make sure that no one was within eaves-dropping range.

'Our friend Kevin Lagrange hasn't got much talent on his books these days, except for Johnny Storm. He's been lying semi-dormant for several years. He developed some very expensive habits when his pop groups were dominating the charts, and expensive habits don't go away.'

Felton tapped his nose in an ironic gesture: 'Exotic substances and plenty of them. And guess who bailed him out of his financial difficulties? No need to guess, eh Chris? Our other friend Neil Anderson. He was apparently very casual about the loans. He led Lagrange to believe that he could pay him back any time. "When the good times roll again. After all, what are mates for." I can just hear him saying it.' There was bitterness in Felton Butter's voice.

As we walked towards a table with our plates, filled with an eclectic selection of smoked salmon, rare roast beef, seafood and salad, Felton said quietly to me: 'The good times are of course about to roll again. And Anderson wants his money back. Now. So Lagrange has no option but to sell out. He'll clear his debts, but little else. So he'll end up working for Anderson and see Johnny back in the big time, but with the big-time money going straight to RRA.'

His mouth tightened in cynical amusement and he suggested that we join Zoe, Jack Mason and Andrew Buccleuth for lunch. After a conversation with Felton, I sometimes thought business in the City was fairly decent compared to show business. A silly thought.

Chapter 16

Three hours later most of us were together again, with the addition of wives and lovers, boyfriends and business associates, in one of the function suites of a large mock-Tudor, four-star hotel not far from the golf course. We were there to celebrate the United Charities pro-am at a gala dinner. This is designed partly to entertain the participants in the pro-am, but primarily to continue the fund-raising exercise which had begun early that morning.

As befitting one of the biggest pro-am events of the year, a true cavalcade of celebrities from sport, show business and commerce was lined up. As Andrew and I entered the reception room for pre-dinner drinks, it seemed that they were all talking at once. We joined in with a will and it was noticeable that, despite the crush, the waiters and waitresses were super-efficient. No glass seemed to get more than half empty.

After an hour or so we were seated at round tables, each laid for ten guests, and the dinner began. It was acceptable but uninspiring hotel food. The wines were remarkably expensive but Andrew insisted on buying champagne, some buttery Australian chardonnay, and an excellent second-growth claret.

Felton Butter and Jack Mason were more or less opposite and Bill Ryan and his wife were also with us. I was lucky enough to have Zoe Bernini sitting next to me, although I discovered that it wasn't luck when Zoe announced that she'd changed the place cards. She looked gorgeous. She was wearing a simple sheath dress, which she had the figure to carry off. I saw several male heads turn to get an eyeful of her beauty and vitality. Bill Ryan's wife, Sheila, was sitting on my other side and did not compare well. She was almost as small as Zoe, but without any of her animation. Her flowery frilly dress was buttoned tightly up to the neck and she wore a pair of half-moon gold-rimmed specs which were called granny glasses when John Lennon made them famous in the sixties. She looked as if she were nursing some secret sorrow and only smiled after careful consideration – and she chain-smoked. Not an ideal dinner companion. Apart from Andrew's wife, the party was completed by Jack Mason's bank manager and his wife. Some time ago Jack had promised them a night out and this was a painless way of fulfilling his promise.

The conversation swayed to and fro between show business and golf and I noticed that Andrew talked at length to Jack's bank manager about the forthcoming RRA flotation.

Reluctantly, I turned from Zoe and tried to make conversation with Mrs Ryan. It was hard work at first – I asked her questions about herself which she answered slowly and in tedious detail. I discovered she taught design at adult evening classes and clearly considered that this made her an expert on all matters educational. And so, regrettably, we were on to education, a subject along with feminism and the environment which should be banned from the dinner table. Sweet reason can be changed to unbridled aggression and anger when it crops up. At this dinner table everyone joined in the row. She and I got into a heated argument; Felton Butter tried to lighten things by musing on his dislike of homework in his youth and told of how his father, eager for his youngest son to go to a good university, had encouraged and cajoled him.

The bank manager's wife, Pat, said that she wanted her two boys to go to university, too. 'To Surrey University, we hope, so that we can keep an eye on them. They'll get better jobs then, won't they?'

'Education has nothing whatsoever to do with getting a better job,' said Felton emphatically.

The bank manager, Eric, joined in: 'Well I can't see any other reason for spending three years at a university at their parents' expense.'

Then all hell was let loose, but Felton managed to shout us all down: 'Education isn't about making money. It's about opening people's minds, about showing them how to lead a decent life, a good life, a moral life if you like. It's about learning to appreciate literature, music, painting, science, other people. If you want to train your kids for some grubby little job in a suburban bank then send them to the local tech where they belong.' What lung power.

Pat turned to Felton and yelled, 'You're just an intellectual slob.'

Andrew choked into his glass of claret and was able to cloak his amusement with a coughing fit. Jack Mason was grinning openly and winked at me as Bill Ryan's wife got stuck in again: 'Children should be left to follow their natural inclinations. We didn't push our daughter, Posy. She spent most of her time at the Kensington Café and in my view got a better education there than she'd have got from regimented homework.'

'Went to a good school, did she?' asked Felton.

'Oh yes, St Vincent's, and then a final year at Benenden. She had no need to go to university. She's in television now.'

'That figures,' hissed Felton. 'What a waste. My father'd spit in your eye, if he were alive.'

I was surprised at how passionate Felton was about education. He had clearly been much influenced by his father. Education is certainly a subject worth being passionate about.

I saw that Jack's bank manager was about to launch himself into the fray again, but we were saved by the master of ceremonies. He announced that the entertainment was about to begin. It was a tradition at the United Charities dinner that half a dozen of the stars did a turn, and first on to the little stage was Kenny Craig.

Accompanied by a three piece combo he sang his old song 'Down on the Street' and then told a few jokes. I have to admit that he made all of us laugh.

The MC then announced Johnny Storm 'by courtesy of RRA, whose Chairman and Managing Director, Neil Anderson, is a great friend to United Charities. Stand up, Mr Anderson, please.'

With a great show of modesty, Neil Anderson, at an adjoining table, rose to acknowledge the applause. His dinner companions included Jimmy McCoy, Grant Sadler, Kevin Lagrange and several ladies who seemed to have strayed off the set of *Dallas*. Without exception they were tanned, had masses of long blond curls and a startling collection of jewellery worn over tight-fitting, low-cut dresses. All beautifully packaged. I thought I recognised one of them.

Felton Butter noticed me eyeing them and leaned towards me across the table. 'You know one of them, Chris. It's Mikki Boone and she's with McCoy. The rest are starlets, bimbos, page-three girls, call them what you will.'

'I wouldn't mind, whatever they're called,' Jack said.

'Yes you would, you'd catch something,' Zoe said with a nasty grin.

Johnny Storm sang a couple of his old hits, returned to Anderson's table and Jimmy McCoy took his place. I noticed that he had moderated his Glaswegian accent for the occasion. He was good, very good; even Felton, not McCoy's greatest fan, smiled at some of his jokes. I could see that Jack, who had given the claret a thorough and searching test over the last hour or so and was now drinking port, was looking for any opportunity to heckle – a dangerous thing to do to a man who had learned his craft in the pubs and clubs of Glasgow. But an opportunity did not present itself because McCoy's barrage of one-liners kept everyone laughing. His final gag was about the best kind of after-dinner speech: 'It should last as long as the average Englishman takes to make love. And in conclusion . . .'

Not a bad way to finish: to thunderous applause, too.

There were two or three more performers and then it was time for table-hopping. Andrew and his wife decided to go home and said they'd send their car back for me; Bill Ryan and his wife joined Neil Anderson's table, and the bank manager and his wife said their farewells, rather stiffly, to Felton. Jack Mason wandered off to talk to some other professional golfers.

The noise from Anderson's table had now reached a formidable level and it was noticeable how some of the women's low-pitched, sexy tones had turned into the shrill squawk of the London suburbs. McCoy's harsh voice overrode them all, until a bellow from Grant Sadler stopped everyone in mid-sentence.

'Don't you call me a cheat!' His chair fell backwards as he flew out of it and went round the table towards McCoy. His face was dark with anger.

'I can beat a poxy Jock like you with one arm.'

'The way you count your score you'd beat Jack Nicklaus,' was McCoy's reply. He too was out of his seat. But Neil Anderson, who clearly kept himself and his drinking under close control, was faster than either of them. He stepped between them and said: 'Whoa, you two, calm down. We don't want any nonsense. Now sit down and enjoy yourselves.'

After a bit of nominal pushing and shoving, order was restored. Felton was taking in the whole scene avidly. He grinned sardonically at me: 'That'll make a nice piece for the column.'

It was noticeable how many people paused at our table to talk to Felton. The Press is even more potent in show business than in sport. A middle-aged man in an immaculately cut dinner suit greeted Felton. He was about Felton's height and his heavily tanned face was crowned with silver hair, which was complemented by his thin silver moustache.

He was introduced as Bill Morris, the agent, and Felton asked him how his business was going.

'Never better. Since I suddenly realised that I've got FU money, I've really enjoyed myself. If I don't like a deal, I walk.'

Zoe asked him what FU money meant.

'It means, Miss Bernini, Fuck You money; I've got enough now not to have to worry ever again.'

He strolled off, beaming, to another table. A happy man.

Felton told us that he was one of the toughest negotiators in the business. 'He's done everything. He was on the boards himself. A singing-dog act, I think. Then he put shows on, did some script-writing and ended up as an agent. He looks after Eliot Stonehouse, by the way. And used to represent Sadler.'

'Used to?'

'Yes. As he said, he's got FU money.'

We were all standing by this time and Zoe and I were talking to a young insurance broker who clearly fancied Zoe like mad. I knew that he played golf off a very low handicap and lived in Holland Park with a wife and a young child. He was insisting that Zoe play golf with him soon. 'It's never too early to sort out some basic insurance plans.' I didn't feel that golf or insurance were uppermost in his mind.

As he weighed in I noticed that Johnny Storm's manager, Kevin Lagrange, was talking to Felton. He was holding on to the table with one hand and had clasped Felton around the upper arm with the other. He was clearly very drunk but was talking earnestly to a bored-looking Felton, whom I saw shake his head several times.

I couldn't hear what was being said but saw Felton try to move away from Lagrange; with difficulty, because Lagrange still clung to his arm. I could see that Felton was getting irritable. Perhaps Lagrange was airing his views on education.

What happened next was confused. I saw Lagrange relinquish his hold on the table and grab at Felton. There was a rapid movement from Felton and I saw Lagrange double up. Then came a mixture of thud and crack as Felton's fist met Lagrange's face, dead centre.

No one else had noticed. The guests at the table next to ours had all gone, either home or to other parts of the dining room, and everyone else nearby had their backs to Felton and Lagrange. I dashed round the table, took a quick look at Lagrange, who was sprawled on the floor, and said loudly: 'I think he's broken his nose. Must have hit it on the table. Let's get him off to hospital.'

A volunteer emerged in the unlikely shape of Johnny Storm. Between us we levered Lagrange into a chair and Storm dabbed at his bloodied nose as Lagrange mumbled 'What happened? What happened?'

As Storm and Bill Ryan took over, I steered Felton out of earshot and said: 'I think I saw some very fancy footwork just then, but I'm not sure. How's your hand?'

Felton smiled a little sadly and said: 'It's OK. I didn't hit him very hard. Just the old one-two.'

'Why?'

'He was coming on strong. Made a very heavy pass. I told him that I'm not of that persuasion but he kept on. Even if I were, I wouldn't touch a bit of rough trade like that.'

He laughed. 'It's been an exciting night. I must go, Chris. Thanks for your help.'

He waved a good-bye to Zoe, at whom the insurance man was still talking forty to the dozen and walked quickly away. Lagrange was on the move in the same direction, supported between Johnny Storm and Bill Ryan.

As I watched their uncertain progress, Fred Onslow, Andrew Buccleuth's chauffeur, gardener and handyman, appeared at the door. I waved at him and indicated that I would be with him in five minutes.

It was less than that as Zoe, clearly anxious to get away from the eager attentions of the insurance man, asked me if she could cadge a lift back to London. A few minutes later we were settled in the comfortable rear seats of Andrew's Bentley.

Zoe and I talked a little about golf but after a few minutes her head fell against my shoulder and she was dozing comfortably. So much for my scintillating company. But it was relaxing to have her so close; I gently moved my arm and in her sleep she snuggled warmly against me.

Fred, a taciturn man, was concentrating on the road ahead, and I had some time to think about that evening's events. There's nothing like a nice friendly dinner.

One thing was obvious: Grant Sadler hated McCoy and could not bear his rivalry either on stage or on the golf course. His fierce will to win the Order of Merit had been multiplied by his urge to defeat McCoy. He was even prepared to cheat blatantly to fulfil this obsession.

It seemed to me that Sadler was on the edge of a nervous breakdown and these clear signs of instability made me wonder again about his role in Amanda's death. Could he have had an accomplice who had actually done the deed while Sadler made his escape? What could be his motive?

I re-ran the scene in my mind's eye: the thud outside the flat, Sadler's arrival on the ground floor shortly afterwards, the scream, my dash to the side road. Had I seen anyone else? Only cars and vans passing the front entrance, and then the warden who was tending Amanda. On the way back with Sadler I had seen several vehicles waiting at the traffic lights at the far end of the main street and a man on a motor-bike. Just the normal City traffic on an average working evening.

Then there was Felton Butter's unusual behaviour. His convictions about education were clearly very deeply held and I guessed that these were based on some strong emotions from his past. His father had obviously been very important to him and I wondered what his childhood had been like. I also wondered at his strong reaction to Kevin Lagrange's pass. Lagrange was an odious man, particularly to someone as fastidious as Felton, but surely fisticuffs, even concluded swiftly and clinically, were going too far. Perhaps Felton was guilty of protesting too much?

My ingenuous, cut-price Freudian musings were interrupted by Fred's inquiry, as we approached the western fringes of London, about where to go. Zoe stirred, gave the name of her road just west of Marble Arch and whispered in my ear: 'Why don't you stay with me?'

Although I don't have my brother Max's facility for drawing girls into his charmed circle from all points of the compass, I like them, and I particularly liked Zoe Bernini. She was bright and intelligent, with a carefree spirit. She was very desirable and, above all else, she was as crazy about golf as I am.

But the image of Poppy Drake inserted itself forcefully into my mind. I began to feel uneasy, even though I had made no discernible commitment to her. Did I have some vague feeling that she needed me? Whatever the reason, the thought of Poppy prevented me from accepting Zoe's offer.

I kissed her. 'Not this time. I've got to be up very early. A presentation to prepare.' It came out rather prissy, so, as I walked her to her door I said, 'Anyway, I've got a headache.'

She smiled and I hoped like mad that she was a girl who would take my excuse at face value and not as a slight.

I should have jumped into her bed and stayed there for a month or so.

Chapter 17

There was a considerable pile of messages waiting for me in the office the next morning. Many of them were from clients who wanted to confirm their view of the RRA issue. After returning several of the calls it seemed that the tide of sentiment was strongly in favour and I began to feel confident of its ultimate success.

An early call came from Felton Butter who was concerned that he might have caused me some embarrassment. 'It's the little scuffle with Lagrange that worries me, not my firm advocacy of education for education's sake,' he said in his precise way.

I assured him that, as far as I could tell, no one had noticed the incident, only the result. Felton thanked me for my 'forbearance' and hung up.

Poppy was next on the line and we arranged to meet for dinner that evening.

Business was desultory that morning as the stock market was in one of its periodic moods of introspection. The pound was under pressure, the retail price index had risen more than expected, a gloomy forecast for the economy had emanated from the widely respected Cambridge Institute and the latest trade figures, to be announced in the next few days, were expected to be what the Government would term 'disappointing'. On all counts it was a day to disappear for an early lunch. I was about to do that when Felton Butter's voice greeted me once again on the telephone.

It had the metallic, disembodied sound that car phones make.

'Chris, one favour deserves another. I'm *en route* to Jimmy McCoy's house. He's dead. My information is that he was found in his swimming pool with most of his head blown away. I thought you should know. I'll tell you more when I know more. Call you later.'

My plans for an early lunch and a browse in one or two bookshops had to be revised. I rang through to Andrew Buccleuth's secretary and asked to see him.

'I can get you fifteen minutes tomorrow at three o'clock,' she said with steely disdain.

'No, it must be now, Veronica. It's important.'

'Nothing is that important, Mr Ludlow.'

I wasn't going to waste time arguing with her. I told her I was on my way up.

As I entered Veronica's office, the vengeful dragon's lair, I met Andrew. He was clearly on his was out.

As Veronica began to say that she'd told me he was busy, Andrew said: 'Come and have a glass of wine and a sandwich, Chris. I haven't properly congratulated you on your golf yesterday.'

He ushered me out of the door and I could almost feel Veronica's resentful glare like a laser in my back.

As we whizzed down in the lift Andrew said, 'She's over-protective, I'm afraid. It gets me down at times. But she's devoted most of her adult life to her mother who's a semi-invalid, apparently. Veronica was jolly attractive in her day. Should have had more fun. Should have married. A shame.'

I wondered whether Andrew had once had a fling with her and then rejected the thought. Marriage certainly wasn't the antidote to all ills. On the contrary, according to Toby. But I wasn't going to start a sociological/philosophical debate about marriage with Andrew. I know nothing about it. In any case there were more important matters to discuss.

As we settled into a corner of a nearby wine bar, I told him of Jimmy McCoy's sudden and violent death.

Andrew chewed thoughtfully on his sandwich, swallowed and said calmly: 'Yes, I know. Neil Anderson phoned me about an hour ago. He wanted me to assess how it would affect the flotation.'

'Badly presumably. *Cap'n Hand* is a vital part of their strategy, as Anderson explained to us yesterday. The series has now lost one of its main character actors as well as its star.'

'Yes. It seems doomed, doesn't it? The press are bound to seize on it. "Jinx on top TV series" and all that nonsense. On the other hand the people who are going to buy RRA shares won't necessarily know about the significance of *Cap'n Hand*, will they?'

I thought about this and agreed that the average punter would not have either the knowledge or the sophistication to assess Jimmy McCoy's death as detrimental to RRA's future prospects. But it was worrying that so much bad news was attaching itself to *Cap'n Hand*. At this rate it would attain *Macbeth's* unlucky tag. Superstitious thespians always refer to it as 'the Scottish play' on the grounds that even the mere mention of its name is a bad omen.

I wondered how the death of McCoy would affect Poppy. Thank goodness he played a minor character; on the other hand he was an important part of the narrative. From what Felton Butter had said, it did not appear to be another suicide. My thoughts turned to his possible killer. After last night's shenanigans, Sadler had to be a prime suspect. *Cap'n Hand* would surely be finished if he'd killed McCoy.

My suspicion that Amanda Newhart's death could not be suicide erupted again. I wondered if there was something in Sadler's past or hers that might provide a motive for murder. But how could Sadler have done it? Only with an accomplice.

Andrew must have been tuned in to my thoughts because he said, 'I wish I'd never touched this RRA offer. Of course, the fees are good and it's very high profile, as those ghastly PR people call it, but it's not really my scene. As you know, I love the theatre but this world of TV and pop music and promotion is foreign to me.

'And now we've had two sudden deaths. If there's any more nonsense I think we'll be in serious trouble with this issue. The market is volatile enough and many investors are as nervous as someone with a six-foot downhill putt to win the Open.'

I told Andrew that when I saw Poppy that evening I would ask her what effect McCoy's death would have on the rest of the series.

'Oh yes, I'd forgotten that you have friends at court. That would be very useful, Chris.'

We strolled the few hundred yards back to the office and the placards at the newspaper seller's pitch on a nearby corner already had the news: 'SCOTS COMEDIAN SHOT DEAD' they proclaimed.

Andrew bought a paper which he read in the lift. There was not a great deal of information: merely that McCoy had been found by his cleaner that morning floating in his 'luxury indoor pool', one of the features of his 'multi-million pound home in the stockbroker belt of Surrey' and that, as no weapon was found, the death was being treated as murder.

'He only lives a few miles away from me,' Andrew said thoughtfully.

There were messages from both Felton and Poppy. Business first, I thought, and I got through to Felton on his car phone.

'You've probably read the midday papers by now,' he said. 'Most of his head was blown off with a shot gun. It seems that the murderer caught him in the pool. He or she must have known McCoy's routine. Apparently he swam every morning at eight o'clock, whatever time he went to bed.'

'Are there any theories about the murderer?'

'Plenty. But I'd put my money on Sadler, wouldn't you?'

'I'm not sure. It's too obvious, isn't it? And despite all his bombast and macho nonsense, I don't think he's a violent man. Some strutting and posturing, fists clenched, is as far as he'd go. Fisticuffs might mess up his curls.'

'Well, OK. There are plenty of other candidates, because McCoy wasn't the best-liked man in show biz. On the other hand it's a rather extreme form of dislike that results in murder. He did snort a lot of cocaine, so maybe he got in with evil men. But, even if he was heavily in debt to them, why should they kill him off? After all, he's very successful and he was all set to continue laying those golden eggs. Why kill the goose?'

'An intruder?'

'Possible, but a bit unlikely.'

'What about his personal life. All those girlfriends.'

'That's also possible but unlikely. He's been going about with Mikki Boone for nearly a year now, but his wife won't agree to a divorce. She knows she's on to a very good thing financially. So I can't really see either woman having a motive, can you?'

My other line was buzzing, so I broke off the conversation with Felton and spoke to Poppy. She had rung to tell me the news but seemed surprisingly relaxed about it.

'Oh well, more rewrites. There'll be more rewrite than original material if this goes on,' she said with a dry laugh.

My lines were busy all afternoon and included a call from the veteran actor, Eliot Stonehouse. I was surprised that he had remembered me but, in his finely modulated voice, he modestly reminded me who he was and where we had met. He asked me if I would advise him about his investments and, with some small misgivings, I agreed to have lunch at his home on the following Monday. When he had put the phone down I thought how beautiful his voice was; it had a richness of tone which put me in mind of Richard Burton. Lovely voice or not, I hoped he wouldn't try to hold my hand again.

Chapter 18

The vagaries of the London Underground had already made me late for my date with Poppy and the ringing of the telephone as I entered my flat made me look nervously at my watch.

The answering system was on and I decided to listen to the identity of the caller before committing myself. It was Felton Butter and I picked up the phone.

'So you're doing some positive vetting of your callers, are you, Chris,' he said in his precise voice.

'Not really,' I lied, 'I've just walked through the door.'

'I have more news of McCoy's demise for you. The police story is that he was full of alcohol and cocaine and was done to death some time between six and ten in the morning. Apparently the temperature of the water in the pool, which was quite warm, made the time of death difficult to establish.'

'Have they any clues yet about the murderer?'

'Plenty. But nothing conclusive. They know that he was killed by someone who was familiar with his morning swim routine. Mikki Boone has been eliminated – from the inquiries, I mean,' Felton said with a faint snigger. 'She was picked up by a taxi at her house at just after five o'clock that morning. On her way to do some location filming for a P. D. James thriller. Very appropriate.' He gave another quiet chuckle.

There was one other message, from Chief Inspector

Brand. He would welcome a chance to talk to me about Amanda Newhart's death. Tomorrow, please, at Tower Bridge police station. I didn't relish the thought.

When I finally arrived at Poppy's flat she cut my explanations short with a kiss and told me that she'd cooked a meal for us.

'It's more relaxing than going out to eat.'

It was probably much better than most restaurants, as a beautifully flavoured soup was followed by salmon *en croute*. Poppy was a marvellous cook.

We talked a little about *Cap'n Hand* and, as on the telephone earlier in the day, I was surprised at how unruffled Poppy seemed by McCoy's death. The rewrites were minimal for the last two episodes and McCoy would simply be written out of the next series and replaced by another character.

'It'll be the end if Sadler is pinned for McCoy's murder, won't it?' I said.

'Is it likely?'

'He's the strong favourite at the moment.'

Poppy sighed. 'Christ, it's getting more and more like a Greek tragedy or a Tennessee Williams' play. Suicide, murder – only the incest is missing.'

'Are you sure you'll get any actors for the next series? It's unhealthy to be around *Cap'n Hand* and they're a superstitious lot, aren't they?'

'Oh, they'll overcome that for a guaranteed part in a thirteen-part series, with a good chance of another thirteen to follow. Remember how insecure actors are – worse than writers. At least we can plough on with our work whether or not we've got a commission. Most actors spend ninety per cent of their time out of work. They're just hanging around waiting for the phone to ring and have to make do with casual work. What a life.'

Musing as I had been about Sadler and his capacity for violence, I asked Poppy: 'Do you believe that Amanda's death was really suicide? Did she jump or was she pushed?'

'You know more about it than I do, Chris. You were there. Surely there's no real suggestion of dirty work, is there? It's the usual "suicide while the balance of the mind was disturbed", isn't it?'

'I no longer know what to believe. But I do know that I've been summoned to another interview with Inspector Brand and I'm not looking forward to it.'

Poppy's face clouded. She got up from the table and walked a little stiffly to the windows. She half-turned to me and said: 'I'm sorry, Chris. I'm still very upset by the Amanda business. Whatever anyone says, those bastards on the *Chronicle* caused her death and they're going to get away with it scot free. It's the injustice of it I can't take.'

I saw that she was trembling. I couldn't tell whether in sorrow or in anger. But the whitening of that tiny scar on her otherwise flawless skin told its own tale of her distress.

The embrace I offered her soon turned to something more urgent.

Quite a while later I cycled home in the brisk coolness of the early morning.

I woke up early and my lack of sleep made me feel as if I had grit behind my eyeballs. I showered, felt no better, and set out on my bike for the swimming pool. A half hour in the pool, even with my laborious style, did the trick, and I arrived at the office only half an hour late but feeling an ease of mind that verged on the smug. Even the forthcoming visit to Tower Bridge police station no longer bothered me.

The death of Jimmy McCoy had made the front pages of all the newspapers. In the case of the *News* a banner headline shouted: TV STAR MCCOY MURDERED. The slightly smaller sub-heading read: COMEDIAN DIES IN SHOTGUN BLAST MYSTERY.

The reporter told no more than Felton Butter had already relayed to me. His own tribute on one of the inside pages was a carefully phrased, if not particularly warm, tribute to McCoy's talents.

I turned to the sports pages and, amid the welter of trivia about football and horse racing, found a brief account of the Belgian Open. Rollo Hardinge had made a reasonable start with a score of 70 – two under par.

My first call of the day came from Poppy who, brisk as ever, suggested that we went to see a film that evening.

'I'll meet you in the foyer at eight,' she said.

'Why don't we meet inside,' I said, 'back row, last two seats on the right.'

'Smutty,' she said and rang off. These comedy writers have no sense of humour.

I had the very dubious privilege of an interview with Chief Inspector Brand himself, who, after taking me through my original statement, didn't waste his time on any niceties.

'Do you know of any reason, Mr Ludlow, why Sadler might have wished to kill Amanda Newhart?'

'No. On the contrary, she had an important part in *Cap'n Hand . . .*'

'. . . and Sadler stands to make a lot of money out of it.'

'Yes.'

'It couldn't have been a love affair turned very sour?'

'I doubt it. Amanda's current beau is that racing driver, Peroni.'

'Yes, we've interviewed him. Could Miss Newhart have had anything on Sadler? Perhaps she was blackmailing him?'

'She's not the type.'

'Of course, you knew her well didn't you, Mr Ludlow.' He put a heavy emphasis on the words that made me feel that merely knowing Amanda made me a suspect.

'I used to see her about once a year. She was a friend of my family.'

'And you were in love with her?'

'No, absolutely not.'

'Do you think Sadler contrived, with an accomplice, to kill her?'

'No.'

'No, neither did I, until McCoy was killed. And then I heard that Sadler had had a stand up row with him at dinner. Not much charity between those two, was there? Certainly no love affair going on there?'

Inspector Brand gave me a rare smile and carried on. 'I just wonder whether Mr Sadler is actually a very violent man, but also a very clever one. We can't shake his alibis on either occasion. Of course, you could give us the leverage to unsettle Sadler. Perhaps you mistook how long he took to arrive downstairs in the lift . . . ?'

He left the question hanging invitingly.

'I told you everything that happened, as it happened.'

Chapter 19

The next morning I woke at my habitual seven o'clock. The sun was streaming through the windows and falling on to Poppy's serene and beautiful face. I eased my way towards the edge of the bed. It was enough to wake her and she rolled over and smiled at me.

'Tea?'

She nodded. As I waited for the kettle to boil I thought fleetingly about Poppy's intensity. It applied to her love-making, as in other things. Oh well, I might as well lie back and enjoy it.

As I re-entered the bedroom Poppy was pulling on a tracksuit.

'Come on,' she said, 'tea, and then a run round Kensington Gardens. It'll do us the world of good. You can use one of my tracksuits and you've got some trainers with you.'

It was true that Poppy was only a couple of inches shorter than I and the tracksuit trousers fitted me, if a shade tightly. An old sweat shirt completed the ensemble and off we went into the park.

At that time on a Saturday morning there were very few people about: one or two exercising their dogs, including one eccentric lady with about a dozen of them, and some dedicated joggers.

I noticed how gracefully Poppy moved. She flowed along and I thought how awkward I must look beside her. She was also very fit, as I realised when she turned into Hyde Park and then St James's Park. It was quiet and the sight of the lush grass and the immaculately kept banks of flowers was enough to lift anyone's spirits. Everything smelt so fresh, too, renewed at the start of another day.

Poppy was bounding along enthusiastically and I asked her if she was a recent convert to running.

'Not at all. I ran a lot of cross country at school but then I got very keen on swimming. It was only a couple of years ago that I began running again. I did the London marathon last year.'

I had a moment of panic at the thought that I'd found another running bore, who would pepper me with details of her training programme and her diet. They're all over London these days, chatting away about 'running highs', 'carbohydrate loading' and where they finished in this or that half-marathon.

Poppy read my thoughts: 'It's OK, I'm not going to do another marathon. I did it because it was there and I only run these days for fun and a bit of fitness.'

When we got back to the flat we had some more tea and some fruit and Poppy told me that we had covered over five miles. We decided to have a shower together. It was a bit cramped and one thing led to another and then we had another shower together.

While Poppy grilled some kippers I went in search of newspapers. There was more about the McCoy death, including tributes from many of his show-business associates. I read a particularly nauseating one from Grant Sadler and then checked on Rollo's third round at the Belgian Open. He wasn't listed. I assumed that he had missed the cut, that he had been eliminated after the first two rounds. It looked as though we would have some hard work to do in next week's tournament, one of the most important of the year, the British Masters Championship which is played on a very tough course near Bristol. If Rollo were not at his best I foresaw another early exit. If I continued as his caddie and his game did not improve, I thought unhappily, I'd better find a hobby to occupy my weekends.

We sat companionably in Poppy's living room and drank our way through several cups of tea. Towards ten o'clock I rang one of my regular golf partners and confirmed our game for two o'clock that afternoon.

As I replaced the telephone I was aware that Poppy was looking at me sharply. She spoke quite sharply too: 'You're playing golf this afternoon?'

'Yes. I always try to play if I'm not working. Got to keep my hand in.'

'But I'd planned lunch and then a look at the French Impressionists exhibition. Surely you can forego your golf for once.'

'No, I can't.' Her face hardened a little. 'I'm sorry to spoil your plans, Poppy, but I didn't know about them.'

'It was a surprise.'

'Well . . . I'm sorry.'

'You played last Wednesday.'

'Well, yes, but that was business. Not that that's got anything to do with it. How many times do you want me to say I'm sorry? I can't and won't let Roger down. We arranged the game days ago.'

Poppy gathered up the teapot and cups and strode out of the room.

I wasn't sure what to do. I knew how determined she was. That, apart from her undeniable good looks, was a part of her attraction. But she was coming on far too strong. Sometimes it is acceptable, flattering, when that happens, but I had no intention of giving up my Saturday afternoon four-ball with three good friends.

I have lost count of the number of people I have met who, when the subject turns to sport and especially golf and cricket, say: 'Oh, I gave it up when I got married. I'll start again when the children grow up.' They never do, of course. For a partner in a marriage to give up something he or she enjoys seems a negative way to start. I had always told myself that I would never fall for it.

But was this the reaction of a typically selfish single man? Perhaps I was so used to living in my own self-contained world that I had forgotten how to relate properly to other people. And especially someone like Poppy. We had, after all, become lovers and her expectations of me had undoubtedly changed. We both had to learn a degree of compromise.

I went into the kitchen and found her stacking plates and mugs into the dishwasher. I began to speak, but she quickly disarmed me: 'That was very unfair of me, Chris. I'm sorry. I know how important your golf is to you.'

She looked down at the floor and continued: 'My trouble is that I always try to rush things. I always want them cut and dried. And I frighten people off.'

I put my arm around her: 'I don't frighten easily.'

She smiled up at me and said: 'Enjoy your golf. Why don't we meet tomorrow for a swim? As you know, I'm bidden to dinner by the appalling Grant Sadler tonight. So we'll have a swim and then a drink, shall we?'

I did enjoy my golf, mainly because my good form of the previous Wednesday had not deserted me. Five birdies, including two at short holes, ensured that Roger and I took the money. A tea of crumpets, anchovy toast and tea cakes on the verandah and a couple of pints of Bass to follow disposed of our winnings. Easy come, easy go; just like the City in the eighties.

It was delightful to relax and put aside thoughts of the RRA issue. Business and other preoccupations slid into perspective after the cut and thrust of our golf. Most sports afford the players a release from everyday care and golf more than most.

We continued our chat over a few more pints at a pub near my flat. Roger had discovered the place in an unprepossessing back street in Putney. But the landlord and the regulars were friendly and the Marston's was superb.

At home I ate the remains of the chicken casserole which Mrs Bradshaw had cooked for me a couple of days earlier, fell asleep during the edited highlights of cricket's latest one-day international and then went to bed for the sleep of a truly happy man.

My feeling of contentment lasted through my swim with Poppy, who was as accomplished a swimmer as she was a runner, our midday drinks with Mrs Bradshaw and our late lunch. I was beginning to feel very domesticated.

As we plundered a superb apple tart, another gift from Mrs Bradshaw, Poppy asked me to go with her to the *Cap'n Hand* recording on the following evening.

My plans were to leave for Bristol on that evening, so that I could put in two days of practice with Rollo Hardinge in preparation for the Masters. He had not been invited to play in the pro-am but I felt that this was no disadvantage as it meant he could spend a few hours on the practice ground which would be far more beneficial.

'But, Christopher, this is the final recording of the series. I was counting on you to be there. Surely you can go to Bristol on Tuesday morning? It will only take you an hour and a half in your Porsche.'

I explained that one of the main reasons for going there for the week was to spend some time with Rollo to see if I could improve his game. That is, improve his thinking about the game. 'It isn't his talent that's in doubt, it's his golfing brain.'

'You mean you're going down there for a whole week?'

'That's the idea. It's my job, Poppy.'

She made it sound as if I were going off to the Antarctic for several years. But she wanted me with her and I wanted to be with her. So I agreed to commute to and from Bristol each day. It was not an ideal solution but I felt it was time for the sort of compromise I'd been thinking about earlier.

Or was I becoming a wimp? I certainly wouldn't want Toby Greenslade to know how easily I'd capitulated. Nor brother Max.

Chapter 20

As I drove towards Kew, where Eliot Stonehouse lived, at around midday on Monday, I considered how embroiled I was becoming in show business: I was a witness in the death of a famous actress, I was about to have lunch with a notable actor and would pay another visit to the recording studio with Poppy that evening.

Eliot Stonehouse lived in a delightful Georgian house near Kew Gardens. The little garden at the front was manicured to perfection, a mass of bright flowers. The brass knocker on the front door was shining so brightly that I thought twice about sullying it with my fingerprints, but the door opened before there was a chance.

I expected to see Eliot Stonehouse but standing there was a pale-faced man with thinning hair swept straight back. He was probably in his late forties and I noticed how muscular his bare arms were, each with a nautical tattoo.

'You must be Chris Ludlow. I'm Dennis. Come on in.'

He led me through a small hall and I only had time to glance at a beautiful antique table and a couple of oil paintings. Dennis announced me to Eliot Stonehouse at the door of his library-cum-study, which looked out through French windows to a rear garden as colourful and immaculate as the front.

Two walls of the room were covered from floor to ceiling with books and it was obvious that his old Harrovian friend had not totally decimated his collection of first editions. The other walls had a variety of prints, paintings and old theatre bills. Antique tables and chairs were arranged tastefully around the room, and Stonehouse rose to greet me from a delicate-looking sofa which was covered in a deep red velvet.

He was elegantly clad in a dark green corduroy suit and a pale pink, patterned shirt. He made me feel dowdy in my dark grey suit.

Eliot didn't hold my hand. His welcome was warm and he insisted that I sit next to him on the sofa. I tried to make a detour for a straight-backed chair on the other side of the table but Eliot steered me firmly to his side. I wondered what I should do if he put his arm round me.

Dennis entered with a bottle of Veuve Clicquot on a silver tray and two elegant champagne flutes.

'You've met Dennis, obviously. He's my handyman, gardener, butler and friend. He's also a superb cook, as you will shortly discover.'

'Yes,' said Dennis, 'and I try to keep him out of trouble.' He smiled at me. 'Just you relax, Mr Ludlow. Call me if the old faggot starts getting fresh.' He must have noticed my discomfort and his words eased it.

Eliot gave me a concise account of his current investments so that we could 'get the business out of the way and enjoy our lunch'.

It turned out that his Old Harrovian friend and financial adviser had not totally decimated Eliot's savings either. His investments had sent about £40,000 of Eliot's money down the drain. The company's dubious practice was to invest their client's money in highly speculative shares and, even worse, in high-risk companies in which they already had a financial interest.

But Eliot had not been foolish enough to put all his eggs in that flawed basket and had around £200,000 invested in unit and investment trusts, gilts and a catholic array of shares.

He had an excellent working knowledge of the stock market and talked fluently about bull and bear markets, contrarian investing, the random walk theory and the efficient market hypothesis. I asked him how he had attained such a good grasp of the market.

'Actors have plenty of time to read and I've always been interested in how money works. I've spent far too much of it in my time but then I've been lucky with my career.

'I hardly stopped for breath in the eighties – what with television and plenty of character parts in films. But of course I made the real money in TV commercials. Whenever they wanted a solid middle-class, slightly patrician figure for one of the blue-chip advertisers, then they sent for Eliot Stonehouse. I've done them all – the oil companies, the banks, the insurance companies, whisky, gin. And then there were the voice-overs. Big money in those, my boy.

'Not that I don't earn it. Doing the voice of a ricicyle pop, a dancing biscuit or a balletic coffee bean stone cold on a Monday morning with a hangover is no mean feat.'

Dennis reappeared in the doorway and told us that lunch was ready. I knew it was Dennis by his voice, a lightish tenor overlaid with a South London accent. But his T-shirt had been replaced by a smartly pressed pleated white shirt and a bow tie. He had assumed the role of butler and to complete the ensemble had donned a hair-piece to cover up his bald patch.

It was a bit unnerving and I knew that I was staring at it.

Eliot patted me on the shoulder as we went into the small dining room: 'You are honoured. He doesn't put his rug on for many people, you know.'

'Well, there's not much point in putting it on for you any more, is there?'

They smiled good-humouredly at each other.

Eliot had called Dennis's cooking superb but the description did not do justice to what we were served, which was accompanied by an excellent bottle of white Burgundy.

With my promise that I would look at his whole portfolio of investments and try to make some recommendations, Eliot deemed that business was concluded and he was free to entertain. He did so with panache, his scandalous stories larded with references to famous actors, to Johnny and Larry, to Vanessa and Viv.

The conversation turned to Jimmy McCoy and we speculated briefly about who might have murdered him.

'I know who would have liked to have done him in, my dear. Our sexy leading man, Grant Sadler. But despite his on-screen persona, and what he likes to project off-screen, he wouldn't have had the pluck. No, I would imagine it's some cuckolded husband. He mixed with some very rough types, you know.'

Eliot was very balanced in his view of McCoy: 'A very coarse man, with his taste for empty-headed starlets with well-endowed bosoms. But he had a real talent as an actor, an unrealised talent, because he had a lot to learn. But it was there, he had natural timing. You can't really teach anyone that, I don't think. And there are other members of the cast who shall be nameless, my dear, who wouldn't know about timing if they spent a week in the Rolex factory.'

At one stage I asked him if he had ever worked in Hollywood and this triggered a spate of anecdotes that would have scorched the pages of *Hollywood Babylon*.

'The answer is, my dear, that I could have gone in the very early sixties. I was offered superb roles in a couple of major Hollywood productions. Perhaps I would have become a superstar. After all, I was still young enough, the swinging sixties were upon us and the British were flavour of the month.'

He paused, sipped reflectively at his wine and then fixed me with a sad half-smile. 'But, unfortunately for my career, I fell in love. He was a young and very beautiful Brazilian boy and I fell hopelessly into the abyss. I couldn't leave him and so I stayed in London. Three months later he left me for a Dutch novelist. But it was too late for those parts in Hollywood and I was never offered anything as exciting again.'

Dennis came into the room. 'Come on, Eliot, it's time for your nap. Sorry to fuss, Mr Ludlow, but he's working tonight and he must get his rest.'

'Yes, yes, Dennis. Mr Ludlow knows I'm working tonight. He's Poppy Drake's boyfriend.'

He spoke a little irritably and I thought that the tale of his lost Brazilian love had stirred painful memories to life.

'How are you getting on with dear Poppy?' Eliot asked. 'Be kind to her. She's had some tough times. I sometimes wonder if she's yet got over her husband.'

'She doesn't really talk about him. She's only told me that he died a couple of years ago.'

'You know that it was suicide? Has she told you about it?'

'I know it was suicide, but she's told me nothing.'

'I'm sure she'll tell you the full story when she's ready. He left a suicide note for her. Well, actually a tape not a note and it was heart-rending stuff. It was played at the inquest and it nearly broke poor Poppy.'

On the way out of the house a few minutes later I stopped in the hall to look at the large montage of photographs which encapsulated much of Eliot's career. It was packed with famous faces, but one shot in particular caught my eye. Eliot had his arm around a young man. Judging by their hair styles and the length of their sideboards the time must have been the late sixties or early seventies. They were both in shorts, bare-chested and, laughing, were half-turned towards each other. The younger man looked familiar.

I pointed him out to Dennis and asked who he was.

'Ah, that's the young Grant Sadler. Before he became famous. They were on tour together for a few weeks.'

I looked quizzically at Dennis, but he said no more. He

walked me down the little path and I thanked him warmly for the lunch.

'It's nice to be appreciated, Mr Ludlow. I suppose he told you about the love of his life, did he? The beautiful Brazilian?'

I nodded.

'Quite a performance, isn't it? Tears in the eyes, the whole scene. I'll tell you the real truth. He did have a fling with the boy, gave him lots of money and the boy nicked more, I shouldn't wonder. But he didn't turn down Hollywood in the cause of true love. Oh yes, he was offered the parts, but the sodding Yanks wouldn't give him a visa. They pulled the moral turpitude clause on him. He was a known poof and they wouldn't let him in, Mr Ludlow. He was done for importuning in a public lavatory, a nasty business in those days.

'It makes me laugh when you read about the antics they've got up to in Hollywood over the years, and then they go all po-faced about Eliot. But they were still in shock after what McCarthy did to them in the fifties. Even then, the big studios were still running scared and they weren't going to import trouble in the shape of Eliot.'

As I travelled back into London, an extraordinary question struck me. Just how close had the friendship been between Eliot and Grant Sadler all those years ago? If my guess were right, it certainly wasn't the sort of thing that the macho Mr Sadler would now wish to be common knowledge.

The final recording of the first series of *Cap'n Hand* went through more efficiently than the previous one I had seen. There was, despite the shadow of McCoy's recent death, an end-of-term atmosphere, in which a few fluffs by the cast went unremarked amid the general air of good humour.

Mrs Bradshaw turned up at Poppy's invitation and clearly enjoyed every minute of it. We all went to a local bistro to celebrate the successful conclusion of the show. The camera crews and stage hands monopolised the food, as is their custom according to Poppy, and after a couple of drinks she and I made our farewells in the company of Mrs Bradshaw.

I went to bed that night glad that I was about to re-enter the milieu in which I felt most comfortable. I was looking forward to getting to grips with Rollo Hardinge's golf game and coaxing a good performance from him in the British Masters.

Chapter 21

Rollo was waiting for me on the practice ground of the Churchill Golf Club at ten o'clock. The course, perched on the cliffs above the Severn estuary south of Bristol, is an uncompromising links. The undulating fairways are dotted with the famous 'humps and hollows' which ensure that a golfer never has a level stance from which to play his shots. The rough is fierce. If you stray into it you can be lucky and land in the coarse and clingy calf-length grass and a conservative wedge shot might get you back to the fairway. If you are unlucky your ball will find the heather and more than one despairing hack might be required to dislodge it.

Many golfers never come to terms with the special demands of links golf, but once smitten by its peculiar character other golfers are faithful for ever. It is rarely love at first sight. Bobby Jones loathed St Andrews on his first visit but came to adore the illustrious course as no other.

Rollo told me that he had failed by one stroke to qualify for the final two rounds of the Belgian Open.

'I was unlucky. Missed a couple of short putts during the second round.'

'What did you do with your free weekend? Practice?'

'No, I went to Paris. I fancied some good food and company.'

The weekend in Paris seemed not to have affected Rollo's swing. On the contrary the ball was hurtling down the practice ground through the steady breeze which was blowing off the sea. If it freshened any more it would guarantee a stiff examination of the golfers' abilities.

I know the course well since I have played in several amateur competitions there but, as always, the practice round is my chance to recheck the distances of the holes. As I tramped up and down and compared the results with those written down from previous visits, I was enchanted by the simplicity and effectiveness of the design. The unknown architect had used the natural contours of the ground to produce one of the finest courses in Britain. I noticed how cleverly the bunkers were placed. Many of them were merely pot bunkers but sited in such strategic positions that an ill-directed shot was enfolded by them as if by sublime inevitability.

The design is an object lesson to current golf architects, particularly the American ones, whose eccentricities include a penchant for moving millions of tons of earth, building unsuitable artificial lakes and constructing bunkers as big as football pitches. The size of their egos is only matched by that of the fees which they demand – and get. They should be led by the nose around a course like Churchill before they are allowed anywhere near a drawing board.

Rollo did not enter many of the bunkers however. The practice round confirmed his good form and he recorded a score of well under 70.

He was pleased with his performance. Afterwards, as we had a beer and a sandwich together, he trotted out none of the usual phrases which golfers use to ward off the evil eye. Professional golfers are superstitious beings and take care to persuade the Fates of their humility. A golfer who is on a really hot streak of form will never admit it openly. He might say 'I'm playing nicely at the moment' or 'I'm having a lucky run'. Otherwise he knows that he will get a ghostly tap on the shoulder and perpetrate a series of appalling shots or four-putt several greens.

A golfer who won the Open for the one and only time in the fifties was one of the few to ignore this superstition and get away with it. After two rounds of the Open he was signing autographs with 'Open Champion' written boldly after his name. A famous golf correspondent reported that he moved silently away just in case fate mistook him for an accomplice and gave him the hammer too.

Rollo and I spent another hour on the practice ground while he worked on his short game – a variety of long and short pitches, chip-and-run shots and cut-up shots.

I was back in my flat by late afternoon and found Poppy and Mrs Bradshaw sitting companionably over the remains of their tea together. After a few minutes Mrs Bradshaw withdrew tactfully and we spent a pleasant evening at a local restaurant.

Poppy left at about midnight, having borrowed a spare key to my flat so that she could let herself in if she arrived there before me.

The demands of the pro-am on the following day meant that Rollo did not spend much time on the practice ground, but he managed to fit in a few holes towards the end of the afternoon.

As I entered my flat I was greeted by an enticing smell from the direction of the kitchen and I was soon sitting with a glass of champagne in my hand while Poppy laid the table. We then tucked into some *boeuf bourguignon*.

As I finished the last delicious mouthful, Poppy said 'Chris, I've got a couple of presents for you.'

She brought a package from a nearby chair and handed it to me. I delved into it and found a pair of designer jeans and a colourful sleeveless sweater.

I didn't quite know what to say. I don't wear jeans.

'Thank you, Poppy. Erm, I've never worn jeans. Do you think I'll suit them?'

'Go and try them on.'

I went into my bedroom and to my delight discovered that Poppy had moved in a few of her belongings: some of her clothes were hanging beside mine in the wardrobe and a few items of her make-up were scattered on the top of the dressing table. Seeing her possessions there brought home to me forcibly how important she had suddenly become to me and how welcome she was to move more closely into my life.

I felt a fool in the fashionably baggy jeans. As I re-entered the living room, Poppy clapped her hands and said: 'I knew they'd look good on you. Makes a nice change from those dowdy old cords and golf sweaters.'

'Look here, boss cat,' I said 'you can dress me up occasionally for your show-biz friends, if you like, but tomorrow I'm going back to dowdy.'

She laughed. 'I didn't think I'd get away with it. But you do look beautiful.'

Rollo's excellent spell of form continued in his first round. The wind had freshened considerably and had probably made the Churchill course a couple of shots harder. But I was impressed by the balance and rhythm of Rollo's swing, and he used his one-iron to good effect into the wind. With his score of 69, he was 'the leader in the clubhouse' for about five minutes and we reckoned that he would certainly be in the top twenty by the end of the day. It was a good start and we were both looking forward to Friday's round, when Rollo was teeing off at just after three o'clock.

Poppy stopped work when I arrived home. She had begun the opening episode of the next series of *Cap'n Hand* and her papers were scattered over the dining table.

'It's not easy because I've got to create two new characters to replace Amanda and Jimmy McCoy. And I'm trying to get a feeling for them – what they look like, where they're from, how they talk – all those things that will put some flesh on their imaginary bones.'

We decided to catch the early performance of a film at the Riverside Studios and then had a leisurely meal at a nearby Italian restaurant.

I was in no rush on the Friday morning to leave my bed and lingered over a cup of tea. Poppy had laid out breakfast and then left for a meeting with her agent. She was tirelessly energetic and well-organised. She spoiled me and I loved it.

I had a couple of hours to catch up on some work and was doing quite well when I heard a knock on my door. I knew from its pattern that it was Mrs Bradshaw and welcomed her in.

She said she was sorry to disturb me, I must be busy, but yes she would join me in a cup of tea.

Mrs Bradshaw seemed a little distracted and the conversation, which never flags when she is about, was desultory. In the end, I asked her what was troubling her.

'This is difficult.' She paused. 'Chris, if you didn't want me to clean your flat any more, why didn't you tell me?'

'What gave you that idea? I'd be lost without you.'

'Well, I wasn't able to do my usual bit of cleaning for you yesterday.' I'd never seen her looking so uncomfortable. 'Poppy was working here. She made it very plain that she didn't want me in the flat. Don't misunderstand me, Chris, she was pleasant enough and, anyway, we get on well together. At least, I thought we did. But there was a territorial air about her. She was definitely saying, "Keep out".'

Mrs Bradshaw is a pretty steely character and I could see that her disquiet was genuine.

'It's my flat, not Poppy's. I can only imagine she was feeling a bit fraught yesterday. You know how much I appreciate your kindness and long may it continue. But of course you know you don't need to do it.'

'But I do need to, Chris. You're a friend and you bring something different into my life. I don't want to spend all my time playing bridge with the over-sixties, much as I enjoy their company.

'You represent an extra dimension for me and my little bit of looking after you makes me feel useful. I know that you can look after yourself really but I enjoy mothering you just a bit.'

I was moved by Mrs Bradshaw's words and covered it up like any true Englishman by pouring her another cup of tea.

'Chris, I don't want to seem like a silly and selfish old woman. You and Poppy obviously get on well together, but she disturbed me yesterday. I could see the possessiveness in her and it was not a pretty sight. I've said enough. I'll leave you to your work.'

I know that Mrs Bradshaw is not silly or selfish. On the contrary she is shrewd and good-humoured and a loyal friend. But I also knew that Poppy was taking over a large part of my life. Though we had not touched on the subject we might even be heading for something permanent. But I could not let her upset so staunch a friend as Mrs Bradshaw.

I found it difficult to settle to my work after she left. I was worried about her but was sure Poppy had been tactless rather than unpleasant. She had so many problems to confront. She was playing for high stakes in the competitive and bruising world of television. The trouble was that she was playing the game on her own, without even the support she had every right to expect from her agent. She probably felt besieged and I had become a source of hope and trust for her. She would want to protect that source and perhaps saw Mrs Bradshaw as a threat. She was wrong and I would make her understand that.

I decided to leave early to meet Rollo and sped on my way towards Bristol and the intimidating Churchill golf course.

The uplifting sounds of Smetana accompanied my meandering thoughts and my spirits rose – whether it was the capacity of music to soothe the unquiet soul or the approaching challenge of an important round of golf, I was not sure and I didn't really care. Suffice to tell that my confused musings ceased and I looked ahead with optimism again. 'Seize the Day,' as Saul Bellow put it, and I hoped that Rollo Hardinge would do exactly that.

Compared with the day before the wind had sharpened by a few knots and clouds were flying by overhead as grey as guest-house sheets.

Rollo had been lying fourteenth after the first round and of those who had finished their second rounds hardly anyone had improved his position. A notable exception was Jack Mason who had added a 69 to his opening 71. He was four under par. He is a notably good player in bad conditions and especially when the wind blows. Some say it is because he is a big strong man with a compact swing. But I know that it has much more to do with his strength of character.

Some golfers regard dirty weather as a good excuse for an indifferent score. 'The grips were soaking wet and I couldn't hold the club,' they say. Or 'The wind threw the club head out of line on every shot'. But the good golfers regard such conditions as a challenge to their skills of improvisation and to their determination.

I still did not know enough about Rollo to predict how he would react.

On the first tee he sniffed the wind and said: '"The gale, it plies the saplings double, and thick on Severn snow the leaves."'

Much to the amusement of his two playing partners he then hit a towering hook which put his ball into the wilderness on the left. One of his partners was a friendly and very talented Scottish golfer who had been born, he told me proudly, on the Isle of Arran. The other was a tough and virtually silent South African.

At least Rollo didn't delve into his bag and produce his Bible for guidance.

We were lucky enough to find the ball or, rather, a young boy found it for us and Rollo managed to fluke his par four by dint of a putt of some twenty feet.

Inevitably each of the three golfers was in trouble at various stages in the round, which was not surprising since the wind was variable with sudden gusts upsetting the shot calculations.

There was a sort of grim camaraderie between the players and even the South African was heard to utter some words of encouragement: to himself, of course.

Rollo stuck to his task with courage and concentration and his one-iron was a vital part of his armoury of shots. Time after time he used it to spear the ball low under the opposing wind. Down wind he was in his element and harnessed his three-wood to hit high booming shots. It was an impressive display and he handed in a score of 71.

It was after seven o'clock when we finished and, with only a few players still out on the course, we saw that Rollo was in a tie for fourth place with Jack Mason and an American golfer called Eddie Wayne.

My late arrival home was marked by a long embrace from Poppy, followed by the pop of a champagne cork, which was followed in its turn by a tray with a large piece of onion tart. It had a delicate and creamy flavour and reminded me of dreamy holidays in France.

'Isn't Mrs Bradshaw a fine cook,' I said playfully and put my arm up to ward off the anticipated blows.

'She popped in again today to do some cleaning. I've told her not to bother. I can do anything that's required in that line.'

'Maybe. But go easy. She likes to look after me and we are good friends. Let her if she wants to potter about.'

Poppy shrugged and said: 'OK.' She moved over to a chair and from under it she produced a package. 'I have a little present for you.'

It was a dark blue jacket, beautifully tailored, and a glance at the label showed that it was made of cashmere.

'Poppy, you musn't buy me things like this. It must have cost a fortune.'

'Why shouldn't I? It gives me a lot of pleasure. Talking of pleasure, why don't we have an early night?'

She projected a particularly lascivious leer at me. I didn't resist because I was tired – or thought I was.

We awoke late, not that it mattered as I didn't have to meet Rollo until midday.

As I collected my bits and pieces together for the trip down to Bristol, Poppy asked me for the second time when I would be home. For the second time I told her it would probably be around eight o'clock.

'No earlier?'

'Don't see how. Rollo begins his round at just after one. What's the problem?'

'We've been invited out. Some friends of mine, you'll love them. And they said about eight.'

'Where do they live?'

'Hampstead.'

'Better tell them eight thirty, just in case.'

'Do your best though, Chris, won't you?'

Chapter 22

As I drove west through comparatively light Saturday traffic I reflected on Rollo's chances in the next round. Every round is vital in a professional tournament but the third round of a seventy-two hole championship has a special character. It is when the experienced players know that it is essential not to erode a good position, a time to consolidate at the very worst, before the final push in the fourth round.

I hoped that Rollo would be able to do exactly that; if he went into the last round in the top ten he had the skill and the flair to attain a high finish. It would do wonders for his confidence – and my confidence in him.

Mercifully the wind had dropped to no more than a steady breeze when I reached the Churchill golf club. Rollo had a positively jaunty look and was pounding his shots down the practice area. On the edge of the practice ground I saw Bjorn Carlssen going through his routine and, as well as his caddie, I saw that Toby Greenslade was in attendance.

I left Rollo for a few moments and walked over to chat to him. He saw me coming.

'Greetings, Chris. Your man Hardinge looks in prime form, doesn't he? Lovely swing. The course should suit him today.'

'Maybe. But he's more unpredictable than most. What brings you on to the golf course, Toby? I hope the TVs haven't packed up in the Press tent. There's racing from Newbury and a test match to watch.'

'Very funny. I have assumed my other role as a ghost-writer to young Mr Carlssen here. I am observing his meticulous preparations for the vital third round of a major tournament. Just as I observed the same for the vital first round and the vital second round. I know what he had for breakfast and how he slept, although he has not yet told me about his dreams, if any. No doubt they were suitably wholesome.

'With a bit of luck, he will lift himself today from his position in twelfth place and win the tournament tomorrow. Then I will have a suitably uplifting chapter for his autobiography.'

'How's it going?'

'Like treacle uphill. I've limped and stuttered to another twenty thousand – done about forty thousand in all now. Only thirty thou to go.'

I grinned sympathetically at Toby who was, after all, being rather well paid for his temporary literary purgatory. The ghost-writer has a less than honourable place in publishing circles because so many sporting books, especially by footballers, boxers and jockeys, are churned out merely for the lucrative sale to a tabloid newspaper of the serialization rights: an extract over two or three Sundays of the juicy bits, quickly read and as quickly forgotten. But, as Toby irreverently pointed out, even Jesus had ghost-writers.

I rejoined Rollo who finished his practice with a few three-wood shots and we headed for the putting green, where I caught my first sight of Eddie Wayne, who was to be Rollo's partner. He was a slim-looking man who, dressed as he was in black, looked almost cadaverous. With his droopy black moustache and tanned features he resembled a Western gunfighter. He was a Texan and I knew that he was an extremely determined golfer who had won several tournaments in the USA.

There was nothing wrong with Rollo's putting stroke, and after a few minutes, he wandered towards Eddie Wayne to introduce himself.

'I'm Rollo Hardinge. We're playing together.'

Wayne was crouched low over his putter, his elbows jutting out. He looked like an elongated black stork. He took his putter back slowly and deliberately and knocked his ball into the hole, which was about twelve feet away.

Only then did he look up to drawl: 'Yeah. I know. See you on the tee.'

He bent over his putter again with his eccentric posture and sent another ball straight into the back of the hole.

Rollo shrugged. 'Jack Palance is alive and well and playing golf,' he said quietly to me as we walked away.

On the first tee we watched Jack Mason drive powerfully down the fairway. As she shouldered his bag Zoe Bernini called out: 'Good luck today, Chris. How about a drink afterwards?'

'Bit pushed for time, but I'll try.'

Rollo winked at me. 'I think the lovely Zoe is after your body, Chris. God knows why when she could have mine any time. There's no accounting for taste.'

The sombre figure of Eddie Wayne appeared at Rollo's elbow.

'A bet, Rollo?' he asked.

'Sure.'

'A hundred quids OK?'

'Quid. It's plural. Yes, that's fine by me.'

This was unusual, because not many pro golfers bet during a tournament. They gamble during practice rounds and there have been several golfers whose wagers with well-heeled amateurs have attained the status of legend. However, if the bet were to make Rollo concentrate even harder, all to the good.

Eddie Wayne knew every ploy in the book of gamesmanship and had invented some new ones too. And Rollo fell for them, every one.

The trouble began as early as the third green when Rollo, after unluckily rolling back into a greenside bunker, had a putt of eight feet to save his par. After a couple of practice swings, he addressed his putt just as Wayne edged forward a little from his position ahead and slightly to the right of Rollo.

Rollo stood back from the shot, looked up and said: 'Eddie, you're in my eye-line. Would you move away, please?'

Without a word, Wayne walked several yards further right. Rollo missed the putt.

Anger is the deadly enemy of a golfer and Rollo's face was tight with irritation as we walked on to the next tee. Wayne hit a huge drive down the fairway and, as I handed Rollo his driver, I told him to keep calm. He didn't. His only objective was to hit his ball beyond his opponent's. On the fly, if possible. The result was a destructive hook which went spinning into the rough on the left.

Rollo had been fortunate in that his ball had settled into a spot where the grass was relatively sparse; but he was unlucky because a large and forbiddingly spiky bush was growing about three yards away between his ball and the green.

A golfing savant in the crowd around us told his friend that he'd have to pitch out sideways and I agreed with him.

Rollo surveyed the bush and his ball and peered around the obstruction towards the green. He then repeated the process and muttered to me: '"The hawthorn hedge puts forth its buds, and my heart puts forth its pain."'

'Let's limit the damage,' I said, in my practical caddie role. 'Knock it back to the fairway.'

I handed Rollo a wedge but he told me not to be hasty. I groaned inwardly but did not want to have a disagreement with him at such a vital moment and so early in the round.

Rollo asked me for the distance to the green. It was one hundred and sixty yards to the pin and he asked for his eight-iron.

As he addressed the ball, Rollo looked up at me for a reaction. A caddie should try never to seem negative, because the feeling can so easily be transmitted to his boss. But on this occasion I could not help but shrug my shoulders in resignation.

I then saw a truly remarkable shot. Rollo was aiming about seventy yards to the left of the green. He had to because the bush was in the way. He took his club back slowly and kept his rhythm beautifully under such great pressure. The ball came off the clubhead with a crack and went low towards the far side of the fairway. It then began to climb and the left to right spin which Rollo had imparted began to take effect.

The ball homed in towards the green as if on a radar beam, pitched near the flag, bounced twice and pulled up as if some unseen brakes had been applied. He'd achieved the impossible; you simply cannot control a hook of that dimension and you certainly cannot stop it when it hits the deck.

The crowd was silent for a moment and then the applause and the cheers rang out. Rollo looked hard at me as I shook my head in disbelief.

'"How long halt ye between two opinions?"' he said smugly.

As I shouldered the bag and walked towards the green I said, 'That was one of the most extraordinary shots I have ever seen. And one of the most stupid.'

'It would only have been stupid if it hadn't come off.'

I couldn't really argue with him.

Rollo got his birdie and Eddie Wayne was still muttering about it several holes later.

He really explored his repertoire of needling tactics in the second half of the round. On the tee he stood unnecessarily close to Rollo and, when asked to move, reacted with theatrical astonishment. While Rollo tried a few practice swings in order to regain his concentration, Wayne walked down the tee and asked the crowd to move back because 'you're disturbing the guy – he's the nervous type'.

With a gloomy feeling of inevitability I watched Rollo hit his drive into some cross bunkers, encounter another bunker near the green and end up with a seven. Wayne had a birdie four.

As we moved to the next tee I said: 'Keep calm, Rollo. You'll get the shots back. Just get on an even keel with a couple of pars.'

I might as well have been talking in an obscure Chinese dialect for all the heed Rollo took of me. Eddie Wayne knew that he had won this particular battle but turned the screw by playing beautifully assured golf.

By the end of the round Rollo was way down the field at level par for the tournament. Eddie Wayne was only three shots behind the leaders.

As the players left the scorer's hut, Wayne grinned at Rollo: 'That's the easiest hundred quids I've ever earned.'

Rollo managed a smile, which turned into a grimace. 'I hope, Eddie, that you'll give me the chance to get it back. Double or quits on tomorrow's round?'

'Yeah, I'll take any sucker's money.'

As the American ambled away, Rollo turned to me and shrugged: 'Confident bastard, isn't he?'

'No wonder. So would I be.'

Rollo looked very hard at me and for a moment or two I wondered if our short and so far profitless association was about to end. One part of me was hoping that it would, while another was still determined to unlock his genuine golfing talent.

His golf bag was standing on its base between us and he picked it up and slung it on his shoulder.

'I'm going to practise for an hour or two. Try to sort out one or two things. Will you stay over and have dinner with me? I'm at the George, just up the road. They'll find a room for you, I'm sure.'

I stood and thought for a few moments about my date

with Poppy and her Hampstead friends. I knew that she would be upset if I failed to appear but hoped she would understand that professional responsibilities occasionally had to come first. I was not proud of the way Rollo had played today and I was not proud either of my inability to keep him on the straight and narrow. It was time for some full and frank discussions between caddie and golfer.

I told Rollo that I would meet him in the bar of the George at eight o'clock.

I needed a drink and wandered towards the sponsor's tent. Not that sponsors welcome caddies. On the contrary, they are normally denied admittance as they are to the clubhouse. They have their own tent, with basic facilities; tea and coffee and sandwiches are available. But I hoped that I might spot Toby, whose friends were admitted into hospitality suites without demur.

The uniformed doorman pointed Toby out. He was firmly established at a corner of the bar in his classic drinking position, one arm leaning on the counter and the other with the stem of a glass of champagne pinched between finger and thumb. Well, it was half a glass of champagne. You had to be quick to catch Toby with a full glass. As I moved towards him, it was emptied with gusto.

He was chatting animatedly to several people, among them Zoe Bernini.

'Here's a man who needs a drink,' Toby said cheerfully.

As he waved at one of the barmen, Zoe smiled at me with fellow-feeling: 'A tough time with Rollo, I hear.'

'That's putting it mildly. He's a bright bloke but he played several holes today as if he hadn't a brain in his head.'

'Well, never mind, a good round tomorrow and who knows?'

'He'll have to go some to catch Jack Mason, won't he?'

'Yes, he's playing very well. It'll be a battle royal with Carlssen tomorrow.'

'And don't forget Eddie Wayne. He's only three shots off the pace.'

I finished my glass of champagne and told Zoe that I must go and book a room.

'Why bother, Chris? I've got a nice double room. I don't mind sharing,' she said with a smile.

'My life's a bit complicated at the moment.' Oh, God, that sounded pathetic. 'I'm sorry. Rollo and I are having a strategy session tonight. Got to try to sort him out. Business before pleasure, Zoe.'

As I moved away she said: 'Don't leave it too long, will you?'

The thought of an evening with Zoe was suddenly very attractive and I realised, with dismay, that I was dreading the task of explaining my change of plan to Poppy. I knew that she would take it badly and it irritated me that I felt on the defensive.

After that there remained the problem of Rollo Hardinge. Could I deal with his impetuous personality? Oh well, one hurdle at a time.

I booked myself into a single room at The George and made sure that it was not directly over the kitchens. Hotels seem to have a marked antipathy to guests wanting single rooms, but this time the receptionist put me into a double room at a single rate.

I made myself a cup of tea, gritted my teeth and dialled Poppy's number.

She asked sharply, 'Where are you?'

'Still in the West Country I'm afraid.'

'Well, you'd better get a move on or you'll be late.'

'I'm not going to be able to make it at all. I've got a bit of a problem with Rollo and have to stay down here. We've a lot of talking and planning to get through before tomorrow. I'm sorry, Poppy.'

There was a long silence and I thought for a moment that she had put the phone down. Then she said, 'I fail to understand how some bloody golfer can be more important than a dinner, arranged several days ago, with me and my friends.'

I began to explain that I needed to talk at length to Rollo, that it was part of my job as a caddie to guide his thinking on the course and that he had so far proved unreceptive.

'In a way it's a make or break day for Rollo and me tomorrow. That may sound a bit melodramatic but if he can't get his golfing brain into gear I don't see much of a future as his caddie.'

'You shouldn't even be contemplating a future as a caddie. It's so bloody childish. Grown men knocking a little white ball around a big field.'

'Poppy. You must accept that golf is an important part of my life.'

'God, you're so pompous at times, Christopher. You'll tell me next that golf is a microcosm of life.'

I tried to put my feelings about golf and my commitment to it in the context of hers about her writing. But she wouldn't listen.

'There's no comparison. But if you want to spend your time wet-nursing some third-rate golfer, go ahead. I'll try to make up some vaguely rational explanation for my friends. If I told them the truth they'd think I was mad. But I know one thing, if it were your friends you'd be here. Mine obviously don't matter a damn to you.'

Things were getting very sour over one simple problem, one which I hoped we could sort out sensibly and quietly when she'd calmed down. Now was not the time, though, and I told her so. 'I'll see you tomorrow,' I finished.

'I doubt it,' she said and slammed down the receiver.

Chapter 23

I had half an hour before my rendezvous with Rollo and switched on the radio to find some music. As I rolled the dial past miscellaneous pop and phone-in stations I caught a glimpse of myself in a mirror. I looked flushed and wondered if I really wanted this kind of relationship with a woman? I loved being with her, felt protective and had a strong loyalty towards her. She could spoil everything we had, though, if she thought I was her puppet to be jerked back to London at her behest.

I showered quickly, put on a jacket and tie and headed for the bar.

Rollo was sitting in a corner. The bar was already crowded with a cross-section of the people who frequent golf tournaments: golfers and tournament officials, a couple of agents, several of the pro-am regulars, two or three golf groupies – with *de rigueur* tans, curly blonde hair and curvy bodies – and a solid phalanx of television people, all piling into the booze. Rollo waved me over and reported on his practice.

'It was fine,' he said without much apparent interest. 'I worked on cutting my swing down a shade. Maybe I'll get more consistency that way.'

'That's not a bad idea. You hit the ball as far as anyone. No worries in that department.'

We talked in rather desultory fashion about the course and who might or might not win the tournament and Rollo suggested that we went in to eat.

The George is part of an international chain of hotels but tries to retain its air of tradition as a former coaching inn. The menu was clearly cobbled up to appeal to tourists, with its marked preoccupation with an anachronistic Hollywood-inspired version of Merrie England – Shakespeare, Chaucer and all that.

We settled for some dishes off the set menu, much to the disappointment of the *maitre d'*, who clearly could not wait to singe our eyebrows with one of his special flambé dishes 'cooked at your table'. Wife of Bath Soup (cauliflower) and Will's Home-Made Pie (steak and kidney) were the choices and we decided not to indulge ourselves with a bottle of wine from the absurdly over-priced list. More disappointment for the *maitre d'*.

The best thing about the meal was some surprisingly good English cheese. When we'd had our fill, Rollo said, 'You were obviously as disappointed with my round this afternoon as I was.'

'Yes.'

'Eddie Wayne was a difficult man to play against.'

'Eddie Wayne deliberately made himself a difficult man to play against. You've got to block out the other players. You're not playing them, you're playing the course.'

'But he didn't make it easy.'

'Why should he? He's over here to make money. And he managed to knock out one of his rivals without too much bother. And to add insult to injury he took a hundred quid off you.'

'The hundred quid doesn't matter.'

'It does. It's symbolic of the fact that a rough and determined golfer like him knows he can take you to the cleaners. You fell for all the classic little bits of gamesmanship like a wide-eyed innocent.'

'You're right. I'm not proud of the way I played today, but remember that it's only a game. I can always pack it in and do something else.'

I drank half a glass of mineral water in order to calm

myself and then said: 'If that's really how you feel, Rollo, you ought to pack it in right now, because without real commitment you're wasting your time. You'll never get anywhere near the standard of an Eddie Wayne.'

'Now just a minute,' Rollo interrupted me heatedly. 'I can play shots that Eddie Wayne can't even conceive.'

'You mean that very lucky shot from behind the bush.'

'Exactly.'

'No, he couldn't play that shot, you're quite right. He would've chipped the ball out sideways, knocked it on the green and probably holed the putt for a par. Only an idiot would have tried to play the shot. You were lucky. To be very harsh and a shade paradoxical that shot illustrated how much you have to change your thinking in order to become a good pro.'

'You mean I must shorten my swing and play the percentages and become really boring?'

'It's not boring to be a winner, Rollo. Nobody would want to stifle your imagination but you must remember that you're no longer a gifted amateur with a great future ahead of you. Before you know where you are your future will be behind you. You'll have nothing to show for it. Just a few memories of what might have been. No tournament wins, no Ryder Cup appearances. A few fans might remember you: "Oh yes, Rollo Hardinge. He had everything. A great swing, lovely putting stroke. But he didn't have a brain in his head". They won't remember you for long.'

'I'm not sure I can live up to your high ideals, Chris,' he said sarcastically.

'Perhaps not. But try and remember, starting tomorrow, that you are a professional golfer. Not a bloody amateur playing for fun at Daddy's expense. So, be professional. You've got to be as tough as old boots to win, it's got to hurt. What do you think you are, some latter-day Corinthian, achieving it all by effortless superiority with *Chariots of Fire* raging through your head? Life's not like that and golf certainly isn't.'

The *maitre d'* appeared at Rollo's side and broke the tension between us. No, we didn't want anything else; no, no brandies or cigars, thank you. As he left us, Rollo stood up and thanked me for staying to talk to him.

'You've given me plenty to think about. I'll try my best tomorrow. I want to get my hundred quids back.' He smiled thinly at me: 'I might even listen to my caddie occasionally.'

Rollo was true to his intentions and used his head during the final round of the Masters. He started early since he was positioned in the lower half of the field and when he finished his round at just after two o'clock he had managed to record the lowest round of the day so far: a 65, seven under par, which shot him up the placings. We calculated that he would, with luck, end up in the top twenty, which would ensure a prize of several thousand pounds.

It was also good to think that Eddie Wayne would not find it easy to take another £100 off Rollo, who decided to spend a couple of hours on the practice ground and stay for the finish of the tournament.

I spent half an hour in the caddies' tent over sandwiches and a cup of tea. It is pleasant to hear all the gossip from the band of eccentrics and independent spirits who make up the corps of caddies.

The tales of triumph and disaster, mainly the latter, do not alter much in detail from tournament to tournament, only in degree. 'We had a great eagle at the twelfth and then the bloody fool three-stabbed the next two greens' encapsulates a caddie's view of his master's endeavours. It is said that no man is a hero to his butler and certainly no golfer is a hero to his caddie.

Chapter 24

On the journey home I tuned in to the Sunday sport and, in between the motor racing and the cricket, heard that a relatively unknown Australian called Kenny Crump had won the Masters. Eddie Wayne had a round of 68 and so Rollo had won back his hundred quid.

I was delighted for him, as I had been impressed by the way he had applied himself that morning. He was due to play in the Italian Open the following week at a course near Rome and, although I would not be with him, I hoped that my forcibly expressed views would stay in his head.

I reached my flat shortly before six o'clock, dropped my bag in the hall and gathered up the post which had accrued during my two day absence. Most of it was junkmail but I noticed an envelope which had been delivered by hand, since it merely had my first name written on it.

I found a spare set of keys inside, the ones I had lent to Poppy. There was no accompanying letter.

I then checked my bedroom and the bathroom and saw that all her clothes and make-up had been removed. I felt a real jolt of sadness. I wished she were there.

The light on my answering machine was blinking and I saw that there were three messages for me. The third was from Poppy and she asked me to phone her as soon as I returned to the flat.

With a glass of Beck's beer in my hand as a spurious

confidence builder I dialled her number. As always, Poppy answered almost immediately.

'Have you got some cold beer? I'll bring a curry and we can watch the film.' She had obviously recovered her good humour. I realised how much I wanted to see her again. An hour later she was busy laying out an array of Indian goodies on the kitchen table.

As we piled into the feast Poppy said: 'I was unfair yesterday, Chris. But I was so looking forward to my friends meeting you. They're very important to me and so are you. I was terribly disappointed, but I realise that I did go right over the top. Sorry.'

I did my share of apologising and we agreed that things had moved rather fast and that we both had some adjusting to do.

Poppy did not stay since she had an early start the next morning; a script conference about the second series of *Cap'n Hand*.

'I'll see you next week, Chris. I've booked some seats for that new musical for Tuesday. Will you come with me? And I hope that we can spend the weekend away somewhere. Can we talk about it on Tuesday?'

Poppy was not quite as bossy as usual. She was clearly trying to adjust. Off she went, with a wave from the window of her car; a beautiful and talented woman who could not prevent herself from organising other people but who mostly did it rather well.

I cleared up the debris of the meal and thought about her. Like the coward that I am I had not told her that next Saturday was already spoken for. I was playing in a 36-hole tournament at my own club; the Captain's Prize which I would not dream of missing.

The last few days of wrestling with the differing emotional demands of Rollo's golf game and Poppy's high expectations had left me exhausted. I felt that my reward would be a sound night's sleep but it was not to be. I awoke just after two o'clock with a sour taste in my mouth and thoughts of Poppy spinning and reeling through my head.

Half an hour of that was enough and I sought peace and composure in the pages of P G Wodehouse. It was some consolation to realise that I had only read about thirty of his books and so there were another sixty or seventy to go.

Eventually I fell asleep and awoke at my usual time of seven a.m. feeling rather done down by the Fates, who had denied me the sleep I'd planned. But my mind was clear. I knew that, despite what had been said the previous evening, Poppy would continue to try to reshape my life according to her own pattern. She wouldn't change and only unhappiness would follow. She was beautiful and intelligent and full of fun and interest for much of the time. But she wanted to control me.

I had seen the insidious process affect one or two friends in the past, when the new woman in their life slowly set out to alter them: an emotional remould. At first there were only trivial changes: he was not available quite so often for a game of golf on a Saturday; a quick drink after work was not so easily arranged; the weekend's golf at Le Touquet was out of the question. Within a few months you noticed that 'old Mike' always seemed to be out to dinner or away for the weekend with her friends. A year or two later you were hard pressed to remember what you had in common and certainly you had very little now; especially when the children came along and he gave up golf and rugby for their sakes.

I have never believed in the gospel of total togetherness and my observations of the various happy couples I know suggests that they are happy because they have different rather than common interests.

Poppy was undoubtedly a 'togetherness' person and it had already caused problems, compounded by the fact that she was not only determined but also highly intelligent.

My way out was the cowardly one. I wrote her a letter, or tried to. My fourth attempt seemed even more larded with clichés than the first but I decided that it would have to do: it was my fault because I wasn't ready for a steady relationship; the demands of my two jobs; all the travelling I had to do; I still had a bachelor mentality; I didn't want to give up my freedom; and so on. I didn't mention that I fancied Zoe Bernini.

There was a florist just down the street where I picked out some spring and early summer flowers and arranged for their delivery to Poppy's flat.

As I walked towards the Underground I felt as if I had been relieved of a huge burden; just like Sisyphus if a team of navvies had showed up at the foot of his mountain and taken charge of his boulder.

My newspaper told me that Rollo had finished twelfth in the Masters and had recorded the lowest round of the day, which gave him a bonus of £1000 on top of his prize money of just under £10,000. Jack Mason had finished equal fourth with Eddie Wayne, and Bjorn Carlssen had finished second despite taking an eight at a short hole. Toby could spin that into an interesting paragraph or two in Carlssen's 'autobiography'.

For many reasons I felt buoyant as I entered the office and the Stock Market matched my mood. There was a strong rumour that interest rates were about to be lowered and there were some significant increases in the prices of key stocks in the banking, construction and insurance sectors. The renewed confidence had rubbed off on the rest of the market too and the morning passed in a flurry of business.

Prospects looked even better for the RRA issue which was only three weeks away.

The first call from Poppy came just after midday and, because I was already on another line to one of the pension funds, I truthfully told her that I would have to call her back.

Other calls came in and I was fully occupied for several minutes. She called again about ten minutes later while I was taking an instruction to buy from another client and said she would hold the line for me. When I got to her she said: 'You're trying to avoid me, aren't you? Well, don't think I'll go away, because I won't.'

'Poppy, I'm not avoiding you. We're incredibly busy today. You have my letter and that's says all I want to say. All I *can* say. I'm sorry.'

'It's not good enough, Christopher. You should at least do me the courtesy of talking it over face to face.'

'It wouldn't do any good, Poppy. My way of life doesn't fit yours. A clean break now is better than unhappiness later.'

'You're being immature. Anything can be resolved by rational discussion.'

'We've had our rational discussion, Poppy, and I'm convinced that things can only get worse between us. Better to finish now. Poppy, I'm sorry but I must go. I've got clients queuing on the other line.'

It was almost true; there was actually a queue of one, but he was important to the company.

My lunch hour was only half that. I browsed in a nearby bookshop, bought a sandwich and was soon back at my desk.

Between two o'clock and four o'clock Poppy rang me seven times and I had to ask the head telephonist to intercept all my calls and not put through any female callers unless there were a positive identification that she was a client, my mother or Mrs Bradshaw.

My departure for home was delayed by Andrew Buccleuth, who wanted to discuss the RRA issue: the prospects were looking distinctly rosy.

'Don't quote me, but I'm forecasting a premium of over twenty per cent.'

'That will please the market.'

'Even more important, it will please me.'

In reality Andrew wanted to talk golf and in particular about the Masters tournament of the previous week. He is a real fan, who is fascinated by the minutiae and the gossip of the game.

When I reached my flat there were eight messages on my answering machine and I knew, with a sinking feeling, that they were probably all from Poppy.

Only five of the messages were from her and in each of them she reiterated her wish that I call her.

With no intention of doing so and fearing that she would turn up at my front door – thank goodness she had returned the keys – I went upstairs to Mrs Bradshaw's flat. I took the designer jeans for one of Mrs Bradshaw's good causes.

We occasionally went to see a film together and I thought that would be an excellent way to escape the predatory Poppy. Off we went to the pure escapism of the new James Bond film and then to a cheap and cheerful bistro afterwards.

We toasted each other in the house red and Mrs Bradshaw said: 'Bond has never been the same for me since Sean Connery packed up. He looked just right, didn't he?'

'Yes, but he'd be a bit long in the tooth now.'

'Better that he sticks to golf, eh Chris?'

'Much better. He doesn't need to wear his hairpiece for golf.'

She smiled at me in that familiar and comforting way. 'What's up, Chris? You're not your usual relaxed self. I know you never worry about your golf and rarely about your proper job. I assume that it's Poppy who is furrowing your brow.'

When she'd heard a summary of what had happened over the last few days, Mrs Bradshaw reinforced my determination not to give in to Poppy's persistence.

'It's a kind of moral blackmail and Poppy is obviously used to getting her way. You must not under any circumstances give in to her.'

Then she surprised me by saying: 'Of course I don't have any real experience of the sort of relationship you have with Poppy. I was married young, you know. Straight from home, via secretarial college. And Jocelyn was my only boyfriend, my only lover, too. So you see I haven't got much to go on. But I suppose I have observed the misery that human beings cause each other if they're not honest, or if one tries to dominate or deceive the other.'

Mrs Bradshaw paused and smiled reflectively: 'I must guard against sentimentality, especially in the presence of a young man like you, Chris. I had a lovely time with Jocelyn. We were happy because neither of us tried to force the other to do things which the other didn't want to do. Oh, we argued and occasionally some forceful persuasion might be applied, but we kept our independence. Perhaps that's part of the secret.

'It's something that Poppy cannot, I think, comprehend and you've got to guard against people like that. Sorry, Chris, sermon over.'

Chapter 25

There were four more calls from Poppy on my answering machine when I returned to the flat and, on the following day, I adopted the same defensive tactics, with the help of the telephonist, as I had before.

It was another busy day for the market but Felton Butter hit on a mid-morning lull when he phoned me from the offices of the *Daily News*.

'Hello, Chris,' he said cheerfully and I noticed as I had before how the telephone emphasised his Scottish accent, hardly apparent when you talked to him face to face. 'I see that your man Rollo did well in the Masters. The Ludlow magic is starting to work, is it?'

'He plays the shots, Felton, not me.'

'That's very modest for a caddie. Aren't you supposed to say "we played well"?'

I laughed and Felton continued: 'How's the RRA issue looking? I hear tidings, some good and some, rumour has it, bad.'

'I'm not too worried about rumour so tell me the good news.'

'I thought the market operated ninety per cent on rumour.'

There was a great deal of truth in what he said, but I wasn't going to admit it.

'The good news for RRA is that CBS are about to sign the *Cap'n Hand* format deal for the US network and with a bonus; they're definitely going to use Johnny Storm over there, too.'

'That'll help the shares immensely.'

'Yes, and I should tell your girlfriend, Poppy, to buy some. It'll assuage her disappointment at not getting her slice of the American cake. She's not the sort of girl to laugh it off is she, Chris?'

He could find out for himself that Poppy wasn't my girlfriend any longer.

'However, the good news may be more than tempered by the bad.'

'Go on.'

'Not over the phone. Sex and drugs and rock 'n' roll and so on. Because you're a chum of Toby's I'll give you a little advance information – but in person. Can you meet me in an hour?'

Felton named a wine bar near Liverpool Street station and I decided to tell Andrew Buccleuth the good news about *Cap'n Hand* and forewarn him of the possibility of bad news. The survivor of a thousand crises based on gossip and hearsay, he was unmoved and merely asked me to 'keep him posted'. Some people in the City call Andrew unimaginative but I regard him as having the invaluable knack of remaining calm under pressure.

I got to the bar on time and found Felton at a table with a bottle of Perrier and a copy of *The Times* in front of him. The bar was a conservatory in a new development of offices and shops and was already beginning to fill up even though it was only noon.

I ordered a glass of cider and, as I took my first sip, Felton Butter leaned across the table in true conspiratorial style. His voice was low but precise and I grinned momentarily at the cliché: show-biz journalist gives inside info to broker of new glam-stock.

'It's no joke, Chris. I wonder how your potential investors will react to the news that the Chairman of RRA is implicated in the supply of drugs on a massive scale to the music industry and to show biz generally?'

He paused for dramatic effect, drank some mineral water and continued: 'And that he possibly had a part, indirect though it may be, in the death of Jimmy McCoy.'

I stared at him for several seconds. The repercussions were obvious: the investors would run for cover and the RRA issue would be a major flop. The institutions are traditionally wary of so-called glamour stocks: any company with its core markets in fashion, show business, travel and other such ephemeral activities is regarded with deep suspicion anyway.

There was a slight but apparent look of satisfaction on Felton's face and I said: 'You told me on the phone that the bad news was mostly rumour. Is there any hard evidence to connect Neil Anderson with drug trafficking? Have the police made any arrests in connection with McCoy's murder? How did you get the information?'

I found myself gulping down my cider, such was my agitation, and forced myself to put the glass back on the table.

'How do you think I get my information, Chris? It's a nod here and a wink there. I phone contacts and trade bits and pieces of information. It's like a complicated jigsaw puzzle, except that there's no picture to guide you.'

'So it is conjecture?'

'A lot of it, except that I have a friend in the drug squad who tipped me off that one of the trails leads back via Kevin Lagrange . . .'

'. . . your very good friend who manages Johnny Storm . . .'

Felton grinned. 'Exactly. Who can't take no for an answer and who certainly can't take a punch. Anyway, the trail veers back sharply towards the RRA boardroom and to Neil Anderson in particular.'

'I can't believe that Anderson would get involved in drug

dealing. Why should he? He's filthy rich. He owns a highly successful company. He'll soon be even richer and more successful. What's the point?'

'Chris, you're still naive enough to think that money makes the world go round, aren't you? Well, it may make your world go round but not the world of pop music. Why do you think that RRA have got such a remarkable repertoire of artists on their labels? Do you think it's because Neil Anderson and his boys are better at the business than the other record companies? Or that they pay the most money up front to these yobs? Or that they spot the multi-million sellers earlier than anyone else and nurture their precious talent better?'

Felton laughed: 'Like hell. Of course they're very, very good at marketing. But for the big recording stars in pop and rock, it's not the money. They've got so much money that it doesn't matter any more. No, the unwritten clause in the contract is how much coke or crack can be supplied. Supplied regularly and in quantity. And Anderson has managed to do this better than anyone else.'

'And you're going to tell the world, are you?'

'No, because I can't prove it and I value my skin. I don't want to wake up one day with my kneecaps in pieces in a jar beside the bed – or worse. But I might put some heavy hints in my column this week or next.'

'Can't you save it until after the RRA issue? It's only three weeks away.'

'Not with my editor on my back. He knows something is brewing. He smells the heady mixture of scandal, death, intrigue and mayhem, with famous names thrown in and ambitious, high-profile businessmen. It's nectar to him, an irresistible aphrodisiac. And if I hold out on him, or am beaten to the punch, I'll be out on my ear.'

'Would that worry you?'

'I have to eat, Chris. If you like, I live by my wits. There's no security writing a show-biz gossip column for a tabloid. Which is why I'm trying to break into TV writing, like your friend Poppy. I'm not lucky enough to have two jobs like you.' This was said with some asperity, but he softened the remark with a quick smile and continued.

'Anyway, would it worry you if RRA gets knocked? Should it worry you? Should Andrew Buccleuth be soiling his somewhat patrician hands by making more money for the likes of Neil Anderson?'

'You've got a valid point. But, carried to its conclusion, we wouldn't trade in the shares of certain chemical companies because they fill our rivers with poisons; we wouldn't touch some of the food companies because we disapprove of factory farming of animals. And, anyway, as you've admitted, this is just another juicy story to you. You're not exactly taking an ethical position.'

'You're nearly right, Chris. But it's not just a story. It's a bit more personal than that.'

I asked him why it was 'a bit more personal', but got no more out of him on that subject.

As Felton stood up and prepared to leave, I said: 'One more question. Did you say, at the banquet, that Bill Morris used to represent Grant Sadler?'

'Yes.'

'How long ago?'

'I'm not sure. I think it was in the early days when Sadler was struggling. Walk-on parts and touring in rep, that sort of thing. When he hit the big time he left Bill and went for a big agency in the shape of RRA. Why?'

'Oh, just an idea that's nagging me.'

'Well, don't forget my column if it's a good story. I don't pay money but I can buy you an excellent dinner. Phone Bill, he's always ready to dish the dirt on an ex-client.'

It was a puzzling conversation which had posed more questions than it had resolved. The most immediate threat was to the RRA issue and I was still not clear what Felton Butter had in mind beyond an ill-defined intent to cast the shadow of an insubstantial, if unpleasant, rumour over the reputation of Neil Anderson and his company. But that would be enough in a society as fickle as the City to blight the flotation.

His inference that Anderson was somehow implicated in Jimmy McCoy's death seemed a wild conjecture. The two were good friends who had come a long way from their native Glasgow together. Anderson had even given McCoy a small but ultimately very valuable stake in his company; 'the real McCoy' had been an important client of the RRA agency; and he had a key role in *Cap'n Hand* whose success, in its turn, was of crucial importance to RRA.

I began to wonder about Felton Butter's motives. They would repay some examination. I was even more disturbed by the moral issues surrounding the RRA flotation.

It was all beyond me but I had a clear duty to tell Andrew Buccleuth what I knew.

If Felton Butter's information was true Andrew's firm should not be involved in the flotation of such a company. It was akin to aiding and abetting criminals.

This was almost exactly what Andrew said when I told him of Felton Butter's allegations.

'If it's true we should withdraw the issue immediately. That will cost us an enormous amount of money and Anderson might even consider an action for damages against us. It could get very messy and it just depends how strong Anderson thinks his case is.'

Andrew Buccleuth looked out of the window but probably didn't see the towering buildings that marked, with a vulgar display of philistinism, the vaulting ambition of the City's financial institutions.

He turned back to his desk, picked up a telephone and said: 'Let's ask Anderson whether any of this is true. He's our client and we must be as straightforward with him as possible. Even if he doesn't return the compliment.'

Chapter 26

An hour later we were entering the head office of RRA. Although most of the company operated from some modern offices near Hammersmith, Neil Anderson had retained the building which he had acquired over a decade ago as his London headquarters. It had once been a Presbyterian chapel situated in a quiet street in Earls Court and still housed his personal staff. The focal point was the ground floor whose large expanse was amply filled by an eclectic collection of vast sofas and easy chairs, tables in oak and elm, the occasional desk, a couple of pianos, a bank of stereo sound equipment and numerous television monitors with videos. A large glass dome had been let into the roof, an incongruous piece of design atop the stone walls and stained-glass windows of the old chapel. Modern abstract paintings were hanging here and there on the walls, interleaved with posters of Anderson's clients and many of the pop icons of the past: Jimi Hendrix, Janis Joplin, Bob Dylan, the Beatles and the Rolling Stones. Johnny Storm hung between posters of James Dean and Marlon Brando.

Neil Anderson was sitting at one end of the room, a pile of papers next to him on a low table. He ushered us to a sofa alongside and offered us tea – China, Indian or herbal – coffee, champagne, beer, 'whatever you like'. We both settled for Indian tea, which was delivered to us, while the preliminary small talk was still continuing, by a dark-haired girl with a skirt so short that it could easily have been missed.

'Thank you, Suzi,' Anderson said and, as she left the room, told us: 'Suzi's one of my personal assistants. A very bright girl.' He turned to Andrew. 'Well now, a meeting called in such haste must be important. What's the problem?'

Andrew outlined what we had heard from Felton Butter, without mentioning the source of the rumours and explained how they would affect the RRA flotation. 'We need to know if there is any truth in the rumours. If any of this can be proved the issue will be a disaster. We'd pull out on business grounds but I would take my firm out on ethical grounds anyway.'

Anderson sat up very straight in his chair and looked challengingly at Andrew: 'Do I look like a drug dealer, Andrew? I have been in the music and entertainment business for nearly twenty years and, apart from the occasional puff of marijuana in my youth, I have never touched any drug.'

He gestured at a row of bottles of whisky, vodka, gin and other alcohol on a cabinet a few yards away. 'That stuff gives me enough trouble as it is,' he said with a slight smile. 'I couldn't handle any exotic substances as well.'

I spoke up. 'The rumours don't suggest that you're a user, Neil, they suggest that you're a supplier on a large scale.'

'No, Chris. On the contrary, I hate drugs because I've seen what they do to people. I've seen the misery and the ruin they cause. Anyone in RRA who is found to be a user of hard drugs gets an option: take the cure and keep your job or get out. I only got closely involved with Johnny Storm because I knew that he'd cracked the problem. He's clean now and the more credit to him for it. I know of course that a fair number of our artists are users but I keep them at arm's length. The industry is riddled with drugs but we need their product, we have to sell their records. But that doesn't mean that I approve of their habits.'

'What about Jimmy McCoy and Kevin Lagrange?' I asked. 'They're both hard drug users, aren't they?'

'Lagrange is only an associate and maybe not even that once I've paid him off for Storm's contract. As for dear old Jimmy, well, we went way back together. I couldn't control him, however hard I tried. And, of course, he was like a brother to me. I can't believe he's dead. I keep wanting to pick up the phone for a chat or to arrange a game of golf.'

Anderson looked away and quickly wiped his left eye. Was it a quiet show of emotion or a well-rehearsed move? Andrew took a sip of his tea and said: 'Neil, can you give me your assurances that you are not, and never have been, involved in the distribution of drugs. If so, we'll proceed with the flotation.'

'Surely I've already said enough to convince you of that. I'm a more or less respectable businessman in a pretty disreputable business. That's why I want to go public. It'll be the final seal on my company's achievements, on my achievements too. I wouldn't dream of compromising my position, or yours, Andrew. I haven't sweated blood to build up this firm just to see it all go for nothing because of a rumour, a lie. This is where your company earns its corn, Andrew. You should have sufficient clout with the Press to counteract this nonsense.' He thought for a moment and added, 'I'll use my influence, too. We do an awful lot of advertising in the papers, you know.'

'And the editor of the *News* is a chum of yours, isn't he?' I asked.

Anderson looked at me sharply. 'He is, but he's his own man. He won't pull a story if it's a good one.'

'But it's untrue,' I persisted.

'That won't worry him,' Anderson said dismissively. 'It's really down to you, Andrew. I'm paying you a hell of a sum of money for your expertise. Let's see it working, eh?'

Andrew sat still for a moment and then said: 'We do have expertise and especially in the leisure market, mainly because of Chris. But we also took RRA on as a client on the understanding that your financial affairs were in good order and that there were no skeletons of any kind in the cupboard. In other words that the RRA story would stand very firm. You're really under the microscope in the run up to a flotation. If your company doesn't live up to its assurances, I will pull out of the issue – however much it costs me.'

On that uncompromising note Andrew got up and we prepared to leave.

At the door Anderson said: 'You won't tell me, but I'd love to know who started the rumour. I can cross him or her off my visiting list. I would put strong money on Mr Felton Butter of the *News*. He's a friend of yours, Chris, isn't he?'

'Felton has heard something on the grapevine but he's not the source. You should be warned, though, that he'll refer to it in his column tomorrow.'

'That wee man needs to be careful. Maybe I'll have to talk to him as one Scot to another.'

With that, Anderson shut the huge oak door of the former chapel.

It was the wrong time of day to try to hail a taxi, the time when there's plenty of custom about and when the cabbies subject you to an interrogation of Gestapo-like severity if they think your journey might cause them the slightest inconvenience: 'Oh no, guv, Hyde Park Corner's locked solid, and I'm finishing now', 'I'm on my way home, it's the wrong direction for me, guv', and so on.

Andrew looked at his watch, decided it was too late to bother to travel back to the City, pointed to a rather dingy-looking pub on the corner of a side street and suggested that we had a pint.

We went in through the door whose brass handle and plate had not been cleaned for several years and entered a pub that time had passed by. The L-shaped bar had two beer handles and some assorted lager taps, and only about half a dozen spirit bottles were set up with their optics. Four ragged tables with plastic tops had a collection of folding wooden chairs ranged around them and the only decorations on the walls were a few advertisements for lager and a calendar which was two years out of date.

As we approached the bar a large lady in a T-shirt with a faded Radio Caroline slogan looked at us without a flicker of interest and turned her eyes back to her crossword.

'Good evening,' said Andrew, 'may we have two pints of your best bitter.' He smiled but the barmaid, expressionless, did not respond. She pulled two pints and said: 'Two pounds eighty, please.' Andrew paid, the change was given without a word and we decided to sit at a table in the corner. The jovial barmaid got back to her crossword.

I asked Andrew jokingly whether he fancied a snack and gestured at the food display on the counter. There was a tray with a scratched plastic dome over it, as seen on all self-respecting British Rail stations in the recent past. There was a layer and a half of sausage rolls. I assumed that they were sausage rolls although they looked like plastic representations. Tears of fat had oozed from the ends of the sausages and coagulated over the pale pastry.

The beer, however, was surprisingly good. Andrew drank deep and nodded his appreciation.

'Chris, I'm not sure I'm convinced by our friend Anderson. He's plausible but then he would be. I think he'll repay some investigation. I know someone at Scotland Yard who may be prepared to help. We used to play football together many moons ago. Will you tackle Felton Butter and try to gauge the strength of his information? You get on well with him, don't you? Even though he is a tabloid journalist. Is he making most of it up?'

'I'm not sure. His motives are far from clear. It's not just a case of a muck-raking journalist on the prowl and sniffing an enticing heap of dirt. He made an odd remark about its being some sort of a personal matter but wouldn't expand when I pushed him. I'll ask Toby about him and try and check him out. Beyond the fact that he comes from somewhere near Edinburgh and was at Durham University nobody seems to know much about him.'

We were finishing our beer when an elderly man walked through the door, peered at us in dismay, ordered half a shandy and sat down in the furthest corner from us. We decided he was the pub's only regular customer and that we were occupying his corner.

Chapter 27

My starting point in investigating the history of Felton Butter was to contact Toby Greenslade. It was just before seven o'clock and was therefore prime drinking time for him, but there was a faint chance that he would be at home. He was trying to keep to his schedule to finish the Bjorn Carlssen book within the next couple of weeks.

The telephone rang several times and I was about to give up when the connection was made and I heard Toby's rounded tone.

'Greenslade, scribe, speaking.'

'Your readers wouldn't know that second word.'

'No. I should use the term "hack". It suits me at the moment. I'm particularly hacked off with Bjorn Carlssen. It's not his fault. The dear boy can't help inducing in me vast draughts of ennui. I've written sixty thousand words and without doubt I should be awarded the Pulitzer Prize, the Booker Prize, the Whitbread and probably the Betty Trask.'

'What's the Betty Trask?'

'It's an annual award for a first novel of a romantic nature. Barbara Cartland with knobs on, as someone rudely described it. Well, this Carlssen story is certainly a work of fiction and the author's invention is flagging. Only another fifteen thousand words to go. I'll never do it. I'm reduced to a chapter on "my top ten world golfers". That's just about the kiss of death. Suggested by the editor in question at Scribbler, Pastiche and Yawn or whatever they're called. I had a meeting with him the other day and I just happened to notice that he had odd shoes on. I know that anyone can make a mistake. You're a bit bleary-eyed and you grab what you think is a pair of black lace-ups and one is slightly different from the other. But the amazing thing was that they weren't even the same colour – one shoe was black and the other brown. Mind you, he looks as if he dresses in the dark.

'The annoying thing is that I should be in Italy. I love their Open. Super wines, great food. It gets through to the players, too. They seem to relax and there always seem to be a few really astounding scores, the odd hole-in-one to add to the fun. But I'm stuck here trying to spin gossamer out of old rope. Let's make sure we go to the Italian Open next year, Chris. Put it in your diary now. You can drive; your reactions are better than mine. You can cope with the traditional driving style of the Italian male. You know, off-side wheels three feet the wrong side of the white line, one hand on the car horn, another combing his hair. It's surprising there are any of them left alive.'

He paused for breath. I laughed. But what could I say to such an injunction? Not that I got a chance because Toby continued his train of thought.

'What would you say, young Chris, to sharing a bottle of fizz or maybe two in a nearby hostelry?'

'I would say no because I'm very pushed for time and I can't contemplate even a hint of a hangover, not even for you. But I do need your help.'

'Fire away.'

'Felton Butter. I need to know more about him. Who he is and where he comes from.'

'That is a shade enigmatic, even from you. But I'll do my best.'

Toby's best did not add much to the sum of my knowledge. We ended up quite puzzled since the interleaving of journalism, sport and the City revealed no acquaintances in common. Toby could not name anyone who could be described as a close friend of Felton Butter. Toby knew that both his parents were dead and that he was an only child. There seemed to be no girlfriends or boyfriends and we came to the conclusion that Felton was one of those unusual beings whose work is his play and vice versa. In desperation Toby suggested that I should try the local newspaper in Edinburgh where Felton had begun his career in journalism.

That would have to wait for the next morning. I felt that I ought to turn my attention to the answering machine which had been overworked again. There were half a dozen calls on the tape and I guessed that Poppy would be among the callers. She would have heard by now about the sale of *Cap'n Hand* to an American network. Starting the digging into Felton Butter's past had given me an excuse to put off the moment of having to deal with her anger. Now it must be faced and I poured myself a glass of Ramrod to give me some spiritual strength.

Much to my relief, I got her answering machine and left a rather noncommittal message which almost, but not quite, suggested that I would be out for the evening. I switched my machine back on as a precaution and put a new recording of Bruckner's Fourth on the stereo.

My deep sleep was interrupted at just after seven o'clock the next morning by the insistent buzz of the front door bell. With great reluctance, I swung my legs out of the bed and looked through lids swollen by a prolonged sleep, for my dressing gown. The dim shapes of a succession of dreams flickered through my mind and I knew that my subconscious had been hard at work, sifting through the data bank of dross in my head.

The bell was still buzzing as I trudged along the hall to the door. Surely it wasn't the postman at such an early hour? Or had I forgotten to pay the milkman, an early bird who wore shirt sleeves even in the depths of winter. I opened the door just a crack, as one does when feeling rather defenceless against the early day.

Poppy Drake was standing there, dressed in an elegant dark-green track suit with pink edgings. Her hair was done in a pony tail and she looked a little pink in the face. Surprised as I had been in mid-dream and she so glowing with well-being, I felt at a disadvantage, as if my opponent had been given a two-up start on the first tee.

'I thought you'd never answer. How are you? I jogged over. Aren't you going to invite me in? Where have you been? I've been trying to get you for days.'

Bombarded with questions, half awake, what could I do but let her in? I stood aside and she strode past me, said she'd put the kettle on and I went to have a shower.

Ten minutes later we were sitting opposite each other at the kitchen table, with mugs of tea in front of us. I asked Poppy the reason for her visit.

'Surely I can visit an old friend,' she said coyly. 'The main reason is the news about *Cap'n Hand*.'

'I had heard. It's good news for RRA and of course for the flotation.'

'Sod the flotation. What about me? You realise that I'll get nothing out of this. Those buggers Sadler and Ryan have really tucked me up. Mind you, my agent should never have given in to them.'

'Neither should you, Poppy. You're the client. You have the last say. You didn't have to sign the contract, did you?'

'But that's the whole point. I didn't sign the contract. It's been to-ing and fro-ing between my agent, Sadler's lawyers and RRA's lawyers for several months. I haven't actually signed anything yet.'

'Not even for the first series?'

'No.'

'So haven't you been paid?'

'Yes. That's one thing dear old Victor is quite good at – getting money out of people. They don't like paying any money over until a signed contract is in existence. But in practice Victor makes a fuss about the non-payment of the fee and then refuses to release my script until payment is received. You then find that a cheque is delivered by messenger on the same day.'

'What a way to run a business.'

'Quite. The lawyers are the trouble. All the independent companies think they need them and the result has been more and more complex contracts with reams of superfluous, inappropriate and usually indecipherable clauses, which only another bunch of lawyers can understand. It's one of the best scams of all time. Lawyer shall speak unto lawyer, at vast expense to their clients.'

'It's the same in the City. So what are you going to do?'

'I'm going to screw them in the only way they'll understand. Legally.'

'Tell me more.'

'I'd rather not. It'll be a surprise for you. You'll be highly amused.'

Poppy got up and walked towards me in her graceful way. She leaned over and kissed me and I fought hard to resist a surge of desire. I wanted to pick her up, carry her into the bedroom and spend the rest of the morning in her arms.

She could probably read my none-too-subtle mind because she stood up and looked at me with an inquiring smile. I said nothing and did nothing. There was a longish silence and then she said: 'Let's get together at the weekend. Spend Saturday together. The first episode of *Cap'n Hand* is on the box in the evening. We'll celebrate.'

'I can't make it until the evening. I'm playing in the Captain's Prize at the club. It's a thirty-six-hole event, an all-day job. I can't miss it, it's the event of the club season.'

I saw Poppy's face stiffen, and watched the telltale whitening of the tiny scar by her eye. Then she smiled and said: 'OK, a better idea. I'll come to you on Friday, if that's all right, and you come to me on Saturday.'

I had one very big reason for not wanting to agree to Poppy's plan; I wanted to continue the cooling-off period, as trades-union negotiators always put it. But there were many small reasons which persuaded me to succumb to her charms. I felt sorry for her because I guessed that she needed some support at a difficult time. I could well understand her need for a sympathetic ear and felt the least I could do was to lend one. I also understood how important was the first showing of *Cap'n Hand*, which would be the first outward and visible sign of a prosperous career for Poppy in television. It ought to be a very special evening for her.

So, I fell in with her plans.

Chapter 28

Most mornings at Naylor Buccleuth start with a meeting at which the analysts brief the salesmen on the state of the market. My golfing activities often prevent my attendance but I get to as many as possible. A mass of information and rumour is digested by the analysts whose job it is to identify shares which might move up or down. The aim is to supply good ammunition for the salesmen to use to persuade their clients to buy or sell. Imminent company results, a rumour of some stake-building or a possible take-over, a rise or fall in the pound or the dollar, new unemployment or inflation figures, the likely resignation of a prominent member of the Government, a threat of war in the Middle East, a break-through in the research into cancer – a really creative bunch of analysts can construct half a dozen 'stories' on any average morning to give their salesmen some lures to tempt their clients.

Today was no exception but before I could reach my desk Andrew Buccleuth had intercepted me. He handed me a copy of the *Daily News*, which was folded back to the show-biz page.

The headline read 'Cloud Over RRA Share Issue'. This was of course Felton Butter's lead story:

> Feisty Scottish pop entrepreneur Neil Anderson is having problems with the public flotation of his show-biz glamour conglomerate, RRA. Their big new TV

series, *Cap'n Hand* has been dogged with so much bad luck – the deaths of two of its stars, Amanda Newhart and Jimmy McCoy – that show-biz wags are calling it 'the Scottish series'.

Not a good omen for the sale to the public of Neil's highly profitable company, which would put the seal on his saga of success. A little bird tells me that the McCoy death may turn out messier than most and that many figures in the pop world can expect a visit from their friends with the designer stubble and the torn jeans at the Drug Squad.

'Well, it could be a lot worse,' I said.

'Maybe. But Chris, put everything else aside and get on with your research on Butter. Let's see what his angle really is.'

I was beginning to wonder.

One of my colleagues mentioned that there was an EC butter mountain just outside Tours and was rewarded with only a half-smile from Andrew as he strolled off.

My next move in the Felton Butter research was the newspaper wherc hc had worked before he entered the journalistic big-time with the *News*. I had decided to pose as a freelance journalist who was researching an article on 'how to get started in TV writing' for one of the magazines. Felton would be featured in the article by dint of his writing a pilot episode for a possible new series. I thought that my assumed role would be ephemeral enough to divert any suspicions.

It is remarkable how the mention of television opens doors and loosens tongues. Within a few minutes of explaining what I was trying to do I was speaking to the editor of the *Daily Post*, a man with a strong Lancashire accent.

'Young Felton. Well, I can't tell you much about him except that he had all his qualifications as a journalist when he joined us. He was smart and intelligent, and obviously ambitious. But he worked mostly on the sports pages. You should talk to Alex, the sports editor.'

After a muttered conversation at the other end I was passed on to Alex Murray who had the precise accent of an Edinburgh dweller. He did not waste words but was helpful. Yes, he agreed with the editor's remarks about Felton. He was a good worker who understood sport but always seemed a bit impatient. He always hankered to do other things, he was for instance a mite fastidious for a sports reporter.

'It's all football up here, as you probably know. You're a Rangers fan or a Celtic fan. That's all that matters and every evening paper ensures that its reporter talks to both managers each morning. That was a real chore for Felton. He used to ask the managers about *catenacchio* and the *libero*. They didn't have a bloody clue what he was on about.'

'So how did he get into show-biz journalism?'

'He used his initiative. Did some reviews off his own bat – straight theatre and variety. He was in his element of course at the Edinburgh Festival, and he did a very good interview with Jimmy McCoy. That got him his chance with the *News*.'

'Are there any family I could talk to?'

'Not that I know of but I'll find his file for you. His application form should still be in there. I'll call you back.'

Five minutes later he did.

'Right, Mr Ludlow, this is not a lot of use. His parents are both dead and his next of kin is a Miss Gregson. She lives in Glasgow. No phone number but here's the address.'

'What about his education?'

'Oh, nothing special, one of the secondary schools in the city. But of course he was bright enough to go on to Durham, as you probably know.'

I thanked him and rang directory inquiries for Miss Gregson's number. It was ex-directory.

A few years ago I might have sent a telegram with the

assurance that it would be delivered within a few hours but that civilised and effective form of communication no longer exists. There's something about a telegram. It has gravitas and demands a reply. I could write to Miss Gregson but time was too short and she might not reply for some days.

I went up to Andrew's office to explain the problem, and survived the Gorgon glare of Veronica, his secretary.

He decided to ring 'old Duncan', a stockbroker in Edinburgh with whom we worked occasionally. Old Duncan said he would send 'one of his lads over to see what was what' at once and then the two friends got back to more important matters: a game of golf was arranged for Muirfield in three weeks' time.

Just before midday Andrew phoned me on the internal line and said: 'Miss Gregson has invited you to tea. You'll just about get the two o'clock shuttle. Off you go.'

Three and a half hours later I was walking down a quiet and neat tree-lined street not far from Glasgow Green. Miss Gregson lived in a small Victorian cottage with a bow window alongside the front door which, with its stained glass panels, was probably the original.

Miss Gregson, small and rotund, opened the door. She was dressed for afternoon tea in a dark blue suit with a flower-patterned blouse underneath.

'So you want to talk about Jamie. For a magazine article. Is that right?'

I was slightly puzzled by the name but assumed it was her pet name for him. 'About Felton, yes.'

'Oh, aye, he started to use his middle name when he went artistic. Come on in.'

She led me into the front room, every surface of which was shining bright. Vases of fresh flowers were scattered about. A huge selection of sandwiches, cut into fingers with the crusts off, was laid out under cling-film on the table. In addition there were scones and several varieties of cake.

'Sit yourself down, Mr Ludlow. The kettle's on.'

'You're Felton's, Jamie's, only surviving relative, I believe?'

'Yes. I'm his aunt on his father's side.'

'But your name is Gregson.'

'That's my name and Jamie's. His full name is James Alexander Felton Gregson. He changed his name when he became a journalist and I still don't know why. Some nonsense about a pen-name. Disloyal, I call it and I told him so. But I'm still very fond of him.'

She went out of the room and reappeared a few moments later with a cavernous pot of tea and an equally large jug of hot water.

'Tuck in, young man,' she advised me. I did as I was told – I hadn't had time for any lunch.

'Tell me about Jamie's parents, about your brother. What did he do for a living?'

I noticed that Miss Gregson, despite or because of her rounded figure, had only eaten one sliver of scone.

'Well, John my brother was very energetic. Always full of plans to build up his business. He was determined to be rich and successful. He had ice-cream vans and then some fish-and-chip shops. Then he got into betting shops.'

'When was that? Can you remember?'

'Oh, at the end of the sixties or early seventies. Something like that. He was doing well. I think he had six or seven betting shops. He had a nice house not far from here and everything was doing fine. Then things started going wrong. I wasn't here at the time, I was working up in the Highlands.'

'What were you doing?'

'I was the head housekeeper at a hotel. So I only got everything secondhand. But I remember John phoning me one night. It was late and the hall porter had to get me from my room. I was asleep.

'John was crying. One of his shops had caught fire. All he could say was "they're trying to ruin me, they're trying to ruin me". Now John was a strong man, very determined and I couldn't remember his crying ever. Even when he was a little boy he never cried, he was too proud.'

Miss Gregson poured some more tea and urged me to have a slice of Dundee cake.

'Actually, it's better than Dundee cake because I made it myself. Anyway, six months later poor John was declared bankrupt. He tried various jobs but he was dead within two years. He took to drink and June, his wife, actually left him and took the boy with her.'

'What a dreadful business,' I said inadequately. 'Do you know why his business went down?'

'No, he wouldn't say and June didn't know either. Not that she and I were soul-mates exactly. She was from Edinburgh.' She sniffed her disapproval.

'What happened to her.'

'She died two or three years after John. Cancer.'

'I'm sorry. One last thing, Miss Gregson. Tell me about Jamie's education. He went to the local school, I believe, so he must have done very well to get in to Durham.'

'Yes, he was very bright and a talented sportsman, too. He had a trial for the Rangers, you know, and boxed at Durham, too. If he'd been able to stay on at Fettes, he'd have probably gone to Oxford. That was John's wish. He was absolutely set on that, that Jamie should have all the advantages that he never had.'

I was lifting my umpteenth cup of tea to my lips and nearly spilt it as my head jerked up in surprise.

'Your nephew went to Fettes, you say.'

'Yes, but only for a couple of terms. John had to take him away when he went bankrupt. He never forgave himself for that. He felt that he had failed the boy.'

'How did Jamie take it? He must have been very upset.'

'As I said, I wasn't here very much. I had my own job to attend to, but I heard that he went into his shell for a while. The boys at the local school gave him a hard time, as you can imagine. To them he was a jumped-up little snob from a private school whose father was a failure, a bankrupt.

You know how cruel children are. They're uncivilised at that age. That's when he started boxing. Of course he was also a brilliant footballer and that, above all in Glasgow, brings the ultimate respect.'

'So he won that battle and then set his sights on going to a university.'

'Even more so when his father died. I would imagine that Jamie saw a place at university, even if it wasn't Oxford or Cambridge, as a nod to his father.'

'A sort of posthumous homage?'

'That's a fancy way of putting it, Mr Ludlow, but yes.'

I wanted to catch the six o'clock shuttle and so made my farewells. Miss Gregson told me to call in any time. I thanked her and said I would.

Some pieces of a complicated puzzle had fallen resoundingly into place, or so I thought. I reckoned that I knew who had set out to ruin Felton's father. And he had succeeded. So, maybe Felton was determined to redress the balance in the next generation.

I was glad to get home even though the tiredness induced by air travel was overlaid by my excitement at the thought of revealing my theories to Andrew Buccleuth. Tomorrow would be interesting.

Chapter 29

Because of the time differentials, the salesmen on the overseas desks were accustomed to a very early start. My arrival at the uncivilised hour of seven thirty was greeted with several volleys of good-humoured insults, laced with some vulgar, if ingenious, conjecture as to why I had left my bed so early. My motive in fact was to make Andrew Buccleuth aware as early as possible of my deductions about Felton Butter.

Veronica was touching up her make-up with the help of a tiny compact when I walked into Andrew's outer office. She was too startled to protest as I strode past her and knocked on his door.

He was sitting at his desk and studying a pile of computer print-outs. He smiled warmly and offered me a cup of coffee.

'I assume, Chris, that your early arrival means that your mission to Glasgow was a success.'

'I wouldn't call it that. But I certainly know a little more about Felton Butter and think we can deduce a lot.'

Andrew sat back in his chair and did not interrupt as I ran through what I had learned. I told him that I was certain that Neil Anderson's father had tried to take over Felton's father's business and, when he resisted, had set out to ruin him and had succeeded; that John Gregson's plans for his son's future – Fettes and then Oxbridge – had in turn been ruined by his bankruptcy; and that his death had planted the seeds of revenge in Felton's heart.

'So, I think that Felton has been trying all along to wreck the RRA flotation. I suspect that he may have engineered Amanda Newhart's death and may well have murdered McCoy. I think Sadler is very much an innocent party. But Felton saw his chance, after the fracas at the dinner, to throw all the suspicion on Sadler.'

Andrew studied his fingernails for a few moments and tidied up the computer print-out.

'I think that it's an enormous leap of deduction to get from a lad whose education was interrupted to a ruthless avenger who won't stop at murder, don't you?'

'We don't know what drives someone like Felton – nobody I've spoken to knows what makes him tick. But he knows that one of the keys to Anderson's and RRA's success is *Cap'n Hand*. If it goes well in the States Anderson'll clean up both in the short term and the long. Johnny Storm will be a big star again. The American networks will be ready to take RRA products and Anderson will be in a much stronger position to sell American shows to the UK market. Butter knows that *Cap'n Hand* is the keystone of the arch and he's set out to bring the whole structure tumbling down.'

I was excited by my impeccable reasoning. Andrew looked unconvinced.

'I would have thought Sadler was a much more likely murderer. He and McCoy hated each other. They nearly came to blows at that dinner, as you saw. To call a man a cheat is to invite revenge. Sadler took his revenge.'

'You have a point, Andrew, but I still think Sadler is incapable of murder. You should have seen how he went to pieces when Amanda died. Anyway, he was in bed with his wife when it happened, apparently.'

'Well, she would say that, wouldn't she? And in any case, he could have got someone else to do the dirty deed for him. It has been known. A few thousand pounds into the right pocket and it's done.'

Andrew paused for a moment. 'If Butter wants to wreak revenge on Anderson, why doesn't he simply kill him?'

'Because he's far more subtle than that. Because he wants to see Anderson suffer. First of all by ruining some of his business plans. He knows that the removal of the two big stars of *Cap'n Hand* could mean the end of its appeal. They were going to be in the American series.'

'So is Johnny Storm, but no one's tried to kill him yet.'

'He's not so important as the other two. Anyway, we don't know what else Felton may be planning for Anderson.'

'Well, I can see the thread of reasoning but I think it's tenuous and, of course, thoroughly circumstantial. I'm going to phone Anderson and ask him if he remembers anything about the Gregson bankruptcy. No reason why he should, he's only a couple of years older than Felton Butter.'

He consulted his watch.

'I'll try him at home now.'

I listened in on the conference line as Andrew talked to Neil Anderson, after reassuring him that there were no major problems with the RRA issue. Anderson mentioned that 'the little snide, Butter, is still at it' and then Andrew asked him to cast his mind back to the early seventies.

'Christ, Andrew, I was in my teens. I was only interested in football and trying to get laid. I only had a hazy idea of what my dad did. I can't remember anything about a John Gregson. But it wouldn't surprise me if the old man put the boot in. He was a hard bastard. Nice as pie at home, my mother only had to ask for something and it was done. But, no, I can't help you. He never discussed business with any of us.'

Andrew thanked Anderson and put the phone down.

'That didn't get us very far, did it? Why don't you try a full-frontal attack on your friend Felton. You never know.'

I rang the offices of the *News* at just after ten o'clock and after two mis-routes heard a bored female voice say, 'Show-biz page.' I asked for Felton.

'Not here.'

'May I leave a message?'

'No point.'

'Why's that.'

'Across the pond.'

'Pardon.'

'In Vegas. Sinatra retirement concert.'

She finally deigned to tell me that he would be back in the office on Monday. As I reported my lack of success I wondered how many retirement concerts Mr Sinatra had had. Like the poor, they always seem to be with us.

Andrew suggested that 'old Duncan' might know someone on one of the Scottish newspapers who would be able to recall what happened to John Gregson's betting-shop business. An hour later I was talking to the assistant editor of one of the Scottish dailies.

He told me that he had been a reporter with the *Scotsman* throughout most of the seventies and remembered Anderson well because of his endeavours to get on to the board of directors of Glasgow Rangers.

'Absolutely impossible in those days. It would have been easier for a bricklayer to join Muirfield golf club. There was a lot of take-over activity in the betting-shop sector at the time, particularly by old man Anderson. And I do remember Gregson's little chain. They were well sited with plenty of passing trade and some of them were close to the housing estates.'

'But can you recall any specific reasons why he went bust?'

'Just a couple of things. I remember that one of his shops was burned down and there was a suspicion of arson. Nothing proved, though. And I also remember that Anderson opened up in opposition close to two of Gregson's shops.'

'So he was putting him under pressure. But why would an apparently healthy betting-shop business go down the tubes?'

'If I know Anderson he'd have put him under plenty of

pressure. He'd have offered better odds at his nearby shops, laid on cups of tea and coffee for the pensioners and perhaps given them a free weekly bet. Just a small one – a pound on the nose, that sort of thing. It doesn't take much.'

There was a pause at the other end of the line and I heard the sound of a cup of tea or coffee being drunk.

'But I suspect that the final nail in John Gregson's business coffin was a little coup said to have been orchestrated by Anderson. Rumour was rife in Glasgow at the time. It's relatively easy for a man with Anderson's connections to arrange. You hold a really good, but unknown, horse back for a minor race at one of the smaller courses, Carlisle say, or Ripon. A minute before the start your minions pile in with some hefty bets at all the Gregson shops. Not outlandish bets but enough to sink the listing ship. And of course the poor fellow doesn't have the time to lay some of the action off to Ladbroke's or William Hill.'

I asked him what happened to Gregson's shops and he confirmed that the leases had all been acquired by Anderson after Gregson had filed for bankruptcy.

Not for the first time I reflected on how wicked is the world we live in. I also wondered how I would have reacted if someone had set out to ruin my father and had succeeded. Would I have nurtured a hatred as extreme as Felton Butter's and then waited all those years for my chance to exact revenge?

During the middle of the afternoon I received a call from Poppy who cancelled our date for that evening. She was desperately sorry but something had cropped up. She had a meeting with her agent and her lawyer but we would get together, as planned, on Saturday evening.

'I know that you're playing golf all day, so why don't I come over to you and cook a meal? Can you warn Mrs B? I'll come over during the afternoon and get everything ready.'

I realised that I felt no disappointment that I would not be seeing Poppy that evening.

Chapter 30

The Captain's Day at my golf club is a competition for sixty players over thirty-six holes of medal play. It is the maximum number possible if a convivial lunch is also to be fitted into the day. It is a serious competition, played in a light-hearted way and the volume of claret shifted at lunchtime, followed by the formidable attacks on the club's reserves of port, kummel, brandy and other assorted liqueurs ensures that the afternoon round is lively.

That year's competition was no exception and although I played steadily in the morning to reach third place, the lunchtime alcohol took its toll and I receded down the field to an overall sixth place.

The current captain's generosity was remarkable and it seemed to me that everyone got a prize of some kind, even if it was a booby prize. The latter was a copy of Ben Hogan's 'Modern Fundamentals of Golf' a singularly inappropriate gift for a cheerful and corpulent retired wine-merchant, who described his own swing as being about as reliable as a Moroccan red. He was delighted, of course.

I had to make tracks shortly after the prize-giving. The first episode of *Cap'n Hand* was scheduled for eight thirty on the ITV network and I wanted to be with Poppy in front of the television in good time.

As I dumped my golf bag in a corner of the hall I noticed that there was something different about the room. First of all, my prized print of young Tom Morris had been moved to a position on the wall behind the door and a larger abstract painting had taken its place.

I was irritated. Why on earth couldn't Poppy leave well alone? But the painting was clearly another present and I would rearrange things as soon as I decently could.

I strode into the sitting room and was stopped short by a widely smiling Poppy, standing in a room which I only just recognised. It was the same furniture but it was all in different places.

She looked flushed and excited. She handed me a glass of champagne and said, 'I hope you like it. I spent most of the day tugging your furniture about. Come and see the other rooms.'

Poppy clearly had no idea how intrusive it was to reorganise someone else's flat. My complete lack of enthusiasm for the new arrangements didn't seem to impinge at all on her satisfaction at what she had done. I would have to tell her to stop interfering but tonight – her big night – was not the time. She had done a thorough job and I wondered how she had managed; some of the furniture is hefty and very awkward to handle. She was certainly a big strong girl.

The dining-room table was laid with a very classy cream linen tablecloth and the best silver, or was it silver plate? I wasn't sure.

'We'll eat after the show, Chris, if that's OK. Come and have another glass of fizz. Lift off in a couple of minutes.'

We settled ourselves on the sofa, with the remains of the bottle of Veuve Clicquot on a small table in front of us.

After the commercial break, in which the advertisers tried to persuade us that if we bought the right car, wore the right after-shave or drank the right lager we would have the pick of the most desirable women in the world, the TV network slogan appeared on the screen.

I smiled in anticipation at Poppy as the *Cap'n Hand* title flashed on to millions of TV sets for the first time. Then instead of the catchy theme song, sung by Johnny Storm of course, and the titles of the series, the disembodied voice of a female announcer said: 'Owing to circumstances beyond our control, the first episode of *Cap'n Hand* has been postponed. We apologise to viewers and hope you will enjoy a repeat of the ever-popular *Birds of a Feather*.'

I turned to Poppy with astonishment and dismay. But instead of the anticipated anger and despair, found she was smiling broadly, her eyes shining with pleasure.

'What on earth . . . ?' I began.

She held up both hands and said: 'To use one of your golf expressions, I've stymied the buggers. I took out an *ex parte* injunction against Capital TV and RRA to prevent the transmission of my work. That showed the bastards.'

I realised that I was staring rather foolishly at Poppy, my mouth half-agape, and took a swallow of champagne to cover my embarrassment.

'But how did you do it? Why? When?' I gabbled.

'As I said, with an injunction. Because my contract has never been signed. And I did it this morning,' Poppy said crisply. 'They kept refusing to renegotiate the deal but I was not going to sit idly by and let those greedy bastards spoon up all the cream. So, I've stopped them in their tracks, because the rights to transmit my work have not been properly cleared.'

I could see a glow of triumph in her eyes. I felt that I could almost reach out and touch her aura of determination and aggression. It was unnerving.

'But why on earth didn't RRA oppose the injunction? Have it set aside pending a settlement, or whatever jargon the legal boys use?' I asked.

'Because they didn't take me seriously. Ryan laughed at me yesterday when I warned him what I could do. And then it was too late. We collared a high-court judge this morning at his home. It was rather funny really, he'd just got back with the vegetables from around the corner. He was in a very bad mood because we were going to make him late for his golf. But he had to allow the injunction and that was that.'

I picked up my glass, saw that it was empty and shared out the remains of the bottle with Poppy.

She grinned at me, raised her glass and said: 'Up she goes. Right up Capital TV, you might say.'

She didn't notice that I was not echoing her cheerful, almost ecstatic, mood. I was trying to sort out the various implications for RRA and their imminent flotation.

The story, suggesting as it did gross incompetence at the company, might scare off many of the potential buyers of the shares, particularly the more sophisticated ones. In the bull markets of the mid-eighties it would not have mattered. You could sell canned fresh air to the punters in those days. The junk-bond dealers in America were selling an even less substantial commodity with enormous success. I also reckoned that CBS might have second thoughts about taking *Cap'n Hand* for the US network.

In one horrific flash of imagination I could see the whole of Anderson's carefully calculated expansion plan for RRA and an important slice of business for my company being aborted by the strength and fury of one woman.

I looked up and saw that Poppy was still smiling at me. It was a sardonic smile but also one of anticipation, as if she were waiting for my congratulations. Two conflicting emotions tugged at me: one of grudging admiration for her strength of purpose and the other a wish to strangle her, slowly.

'What concerns me, Poppy, is what you are trying to achieve. Surely this will really put the RRA backs up. They'll try to drum you out of the series altogether. Out of the business, probably.'

'No they won't. They'll renegotiate. They have no choice. For one thing I created most of the *Cap'n Hand* characters. They're my intellectual property, as it is grandly termed, and I could cause them a whole lot of trouble because of that. And I don't want all that nonsense. I just want an equitable contract and that must include a share of the US rights.'

'And you think you'll get it?'

'Yes I do, because too much hangs on the success of the series to muck about. It's better to have seventy per cent of a lot than a hundred per cent of nothing, isn't it?'

I nodded and Poppy stood up.

'Come on, Chris, let's go and eat. No more talk of RRA, unless you must. Let's talk about us.'

Her bubbling mood continued as she spoke eagerly of her plans. She was developing an idea for a new series based around a messenger delivery service; she wanted to do a novelisation of *Cap'n Hand*; and she had dug out from the files a play which she wrote a couple of years ago – would I read it? She was planning some weekends away from London and asked me to join her and began a long discussion on where we could go for a late summer holiday together.

My summer holiday normally encompasses a week at the Open Championship preceded by a week at the Scottish Classic and I told her so. But that didn't seem to dent her enthusiasm and she ploughed happily on.

Her mood was infectious. The evening flew by and we were soon in bed. That was all fun and enthusiasm, too, and we lingered there until mid-morning.

Over Sunday brunch we scanned the newspapers for comments on the postponement of *Cap'n Hand*. To Poppy's disappointment but to my relief there was very little beyond a few lines in one of the heavies that an injunction had prevented the showing of the first episode.

I scanned the sports pages and saw that Rollo was lying in a promising position in the Italian Open: tied for twelfth. Suddenly I had one of those odd lurches, partly in the mind and partly in the stomach. I wanted to be in Italy, carrying Rollo's bag and doing my bit to ensure that he capitalised on his opportunity. I knew the course he was playing; I could picture the holes and I could remember the smell of the flowers, the shapes of the trees and the different hues of the grass. I wanted to make sure that Rollo would be wise enough to use his one-iron at the fifth hole, which was so dangerous if you deviated from the fairway.

I heard Poppy's voice from far away.

'Come on, Chris, we're meeting some chums at Pringles near my flat for a drink.'

'What about Mrs Bradshaw?'

'What about her? Anyone would think you were married to her.'

'But we usually have a glass together on a Sunday.'

'Well, she'll still be here next week, won't she?'

'Yes, I hope so, but I won't be. I'll be caddying for Rollo.'

'Don't be so literal, you know what I mean.'

I was amazed yet again that Poppy, who was so intelligent, was incapable of understanding that she would ruin our relationship by trying to organise my life for me.

I tried to keep the harshness out of my voice as I explained clearly and firmly that my Sunday drink with Mrs Bradshaw is a tradition I enjoy and that Poppy must never again make plans without consulting me.

She agreed with me, a smile on her face. I noticed that she was edging towards the door and wondered if I was getting through to her.

I popped along to Mrs Bradshaw's flat to explain my absence and then headed for Pringles.

It was an agreeable couple of hours with half a dozen of Poppy's friends who were all tickled pink by her victory, temporary though it might be, over RRA.

Poppy suggested a sandwich and a coffee at her flat while she found a copy of the play she wanted me to read.

As I prepared to leave Poppy asked when we would get together next week. I explained that I would be busy carrying Rollo's bag in the PGA Championship.

'Practice day on Tuesday. The pro-am on Wednesday and then the tournament.'

'There are the evenings, Chris. I assume that you don't

have to have dinner with Rollo every evening and then tuck him up into bed.'

'No, I think he makes his own arrangements, especially for the latter.'

Yet again she was putting the pressure on, taking full advantage of the lovely time we had had together during the last few hours. She was a formidable person to resist, in fact it was much easier to succumb but I was determined not to give way. I put my arm around her.

'Look Poppy, we've had a lovely time together but our relationship needs time. You're always pushing things on too fast. I want to come up for some air, so to speak. I'll call you tomorrow. Perhaps we can have a swim together in the middle of the week, what about that?'

'Yes, that's fine. Well, the last bit is fine, anyway. Don't forget to read the play, will you?'

The Monday morning papers had very little to say about the *Cap'n Hand* incident, except for a tailpiece in the financial columns of one of the serious newspapers. Their commentator flagged a clear warning to potential investors in RRA. He concluded his article as follows:

> Mr Neil Anderson has set a dazzling pace of expansion in the volatile world of pop and television entertainment. He has shown a sure, and at times a prescient, ability to anticipate and to lead the market in which his conglomerate is such a force.
>
> But there comes a time in the progress of all companies when it must be demonstrated that all does not depend on one man; that there is a substantial and experienced management team which is also sophisticated enough to deal with increasingly complex problems. The farce which we saw on Saturday night over the postponement of the first and vitally important episode of 'Cap'n Hand' should not have been allowed to happen.
>
> With the flotation of RRA only just over a week

away, this correspondent is not filled with confidence in the ability of the management team to meet future challenges. Investors beware!

I couldn't argue with his conclusions and neither could Andrew Buccleuth, who called me to his office as soon as I arrived that morning.

His usual joviality was a little muted as he told me that he had insisted on a meeting with Anderson yesterday.

'It was a bit of a pain, really. The only time Anderson could make it was at midday in his office in town. I not only had to cancel my golf but drive into London to boot. But it was at my insistence so I had to take my own medicine, so to speak.

'Anderson was extremely downcast, the only time I've really seen his other face. You know how confident he is, irrepressible actually. CBS rang while I was there. He didn't try to hide the truth from me. It was a pretty short exchange. CBS told him to get his act together and get *Cap'n Hand* back on the schedule or they'd pull out of their end of the deal.'

'What was his reaction?'

'Predictable. He'd solve the problem. The series would be back on track. At least nobody can blame Felton Butter for this latest irritation. It's all down to Poppy Drake, I was told. I am also told that she's a very close friend of yours, Chris.'

I felt a little embarrassed but nodded and Andrew quickly said: 'That's none of my business, of course, but can you use your influence with her over this disputed contract? Surely, it can't be too difficult to resolve. In theory there's loads of money for everyone.'

I began to explain to Andrew that it was not entirely about money where Poppy was concerned.

'Of course, the money is important to her. She could quickly become very rich if *Cap'n Hand* goes into several series in the States. But she is convinced that she is fighting for justice as well and for her future prestige as a writer. She's convinced that Sadler, Ryan and RRA have been trying to rob her of those intangible but very important things. She's on a crusade and she's very, very tough.'

Andrew nodded his understanding but asked me again to talk to Poppy. I also agreed to take on the task of reassuring some of the big institutions about RRA's prospects.

As I was on my way out Andrew said: 'By the bye, Chris, that awful creature who manages Johnny Storm – Lagrange isn't it? – showed up at Anderson's office yesterday. I don't know what he's on but it's certainly not aspirin. He was ranting and raving about *Cap'n Hand*. According to him the problem has been caused solely by your girlfriend.'

I explained just how vested an interest Kevin Lagrange had in a successful flotation of RRA: that, according to Felton Butter, he was to be given enough shares to clear his debts, mostly accrued from buying drugs, on the condition that he assigned Storm's management contract to RRA.

As I was nearly through the door and bracing myself to smile through Veronica's laser-like glare, Andrew congratulated me on how well Rollo had done in Italy. I waved an acknowledgement and wondered how well he had done. A glance at the *Daily News* told me that he had finished equal eighth. A good omen for the PGA Championship. Felton Butter's show-business column made no mention of *Cap'n Hand* but contained a long and amusing account of the Sinatra retirement concert and included some remarks about Nancy Reagan which I did not understand at the time.

As I meandered back to my desk I did not relish the task of chatting up those hard-nosed institutional buyers; and I also wondered how I could hope to influence Poppy. She wasn't the sort of lady who would necessarily react well to friendly persuasion.

When Poppy answered her telephone I didn't waste any time on a preamble. I explained how important it was to RRA's future that the *Cap'n Hand* dispute was settled.

'And I think it's important to your career, too, Poppy. Compromise. Make sure you make your point and get a share of the US action, but then accept a reasonable compromise.'

'I'll be as reasonable as they've been,' she said.

Her tone was chilling and didn't bode well for compromise. I transferred my thoughts to the PGA tournament; the practice day on the morrow and then the real challenge on Thursday.

Chapter 31

Rollo was hard at work on the putting green when I arrived at the Brookstone Country Club at ten o'clock on Tuesday morning. As usual he was not difficult to spot, mainly because he was a left-hander, but I would have picked out his smooth, fluid putting stroke in a crowd anywhere. I also noticed that his ponytail had disappeared. Was this symbolic of something? I wondered. He told me that it had been so hot in Italy that he'd had a short haircut. As simple as that.

His week in Italy had added to his tan and he looked particularly relaxed.

'We're off the tee in twenty minutes,' he said, 'with Sam and Scott.' They were two young professionals who, like Rollo, were striving to find their feet in an exacting sporting environment.

It took us well over four hours to play the practice round, as I and the other caddies rechecked our distances from here and there and the three pros played second and third balls from various points near the greens, and especially from the bunkers. They were trying to plan their way around the course and work out how to limit the damage if their shots did go awry.

Not many of Rollo's did and for him it was such an efficient round that it bordered on the mechanical. I didn't want to jog the senses of any mischievous Fates who might be watching and I did not, therefore, count his score accurately. But he was certainly several shots under par and struck every shot with easy authority.

Rollo took me into the clubhouse for a beer and a sandwich. As a caddie I would have been refused entry without his sanction. He was telling me a little about the Italian Open and had just got to the quality of both the pasta and the Barolo that was available in the clubhouse restaurant when one of the barmen walked through the room with a request for Mr Ludlow to go to the telephone.

It was Poppy and she asked if I would attend a meeting at Bill Ryan's house at five o'clock that evening.

'You see, I'm doing what you asked, Chris. Trying to thrash out the contract once and for all. I'd like your moral support and thought you might, in any case, be interested in seeing fair play for the sake of your RRA flotation.' She paused. 'I might also need your physical support, Chris. I've had these phone calls, threatening phone calls.'

'Who from?' Daft question.

'He doesn't give his name, Chris,' Poppy said with asperity. 'But it sounds to me very like Grant Sadler trying to disguise his voice by making it sound a bit yobby.'

'What does he say?'

'Oh, just the garbage they presumably always say. "Behave yourself, darlin', or you'll wake up one morning with a face your own mother wouldn't recognise." That sort of thing.'

There was a pause and then Poppy said: 'I'm trying to laugh it off, Chris, but it's frightening, really frightening.'

I did not believe that the caller could possibly be Grant Sadler and told Poppy so, but I agreed to accompany her. I also protested that I would be like a fish out of water and that the meeting was her agent's territory, not mine. I felt very uneasy about intruding my presence into a situation in which I would have no defined role. The others would have every right to object.

But I could understand Poppy's unease, especially in a city where the ever-present hint of aggression sometimes changes into violence. I was also mindful of Andrew Buccleuth's instructions to try to influence Poppy to settle the dispute. Ludlow, bodyguard and mediator extraordinaire, was ready to go.

At the bar, Rollo was deep in conversation with a dark-haired, slender girl with the tightest trousers I had ever seen. Every contour was clearly outlined and Rollo introduced her as 'Penny, the wife of one of the Brookstone members'.

Strangely enough, he had no plans to practise his golf that afternoon and we made arrangements to meet at midday on the following day, an hour before his starting time in the pro-am.

I had time to drive back to my flat and change my clothes before the meeting. I eased my Porsche out on to the main road and flicked a cassette into the player. As I looked down momentarily, there was a roar of a high-powered car as it went past me. It was a bright red, open-topped Mercedes. Rollo waved regally at me from the passenger seat. Penny was at the wheel. I assumed that she was taking him home to meet her husband over a cup of afternoon tea.

Bill Ryan lived near Ealing Common in one of those tall and chunky Victorian houses which are such a feature of the inner suburbs of London.

It was a few minutes after the stated time for the meeting and I was relieved to see Poppy's car parked nearby. At least my presence would not be a surprise.

I was greeted by the diminutive figure of Sheila Ryan. I remembered her from the charity dinner and especially her self-consciously winsome smile. She led me into a room off the hall and asked me what I would like to drink.

The large, high-ceilinged room was quite full. Apart from Grant Sadler and Bill Ryan, there were also Poppy, Victor her agent, and his friend Tony, and a man who was introduced to me as Nigel, the RRA lawyer.

Bill Ryan, since he was the producer of *Cap'n Hand* and the host, assumed the role of informal chairman. He asked if we all had a drink, smiled a dismissive smile at his wife, who made a dutiful exit, and then said that he hoped we could settle this little problem amicably and quickly.

Ryan smiled at Poppy in a placatory way and said how everyone acknowledged the important part she had played in getting the series off the ground.

'Yes, I created it,' Poppy said.

'Anyone can have an idea. It's getting the money to put it into production that matters,' said Grant Sadler.

As Poppy took breath to snap back an answer, Nigel the lawyer quickly intervened.

'This sort of sniping will get us nowhere. We're all here to hammer out a deal that will satisfy all the parties. So let's stick to the points.'

'A major point is that you,' Sadler said as he pointed at Poppy, 'agreed a contract to assign the rights in *Cap'n Hand* and now you're reneging on it.'

Victor spoke up for the first time: 'Remember, Grant, that my client hasn't signed the contract as yet.'

'But the terms were agreed months ago and, morally speaking, the contract exists,' said Ryan.

'You're a fine one to talk of morals,' Poppy said nastily. 'The contract was foisted on me. It's unfair and I am asking, demanding, that it be changed.'

Nigel spoke up. 'Once again, I must insist that you all stick to the point. Miss Drake, what are you after? Presumably a share of the US income. Well, what percentage?'

Poppy looked at Victor. He studied his fingertips, then glanced for support at Tony. He clearly wanted to be somewhere else, but finally spoke into his beard: 'I am told that RRA and the Sadler/Ryan partnership are sharing the American income fifty/fifty. That being the case, my client is asking for forty per cent of the gross.'

'You must be joking,' said Sadler and Ryan in unison.

Victor held up his hand for silence: 'That is twenty per cent from you – twenty per cent from RRA.'

Ryan said: 'You've still got to be joking, Victor. I'll be honest with you, our contract with RRA is signed and sealed and is nothing to do with Poppy's deal. As a gesture, though, and to get us all off the hook, I'm prepared to offer ten per cent of gross.'

The arguments ebbed and flowed with much bandying of expressions like buy-outs, royalties, gross receipts and producer's net profit. 'Forty per cent of producer's net profit equals sod-all,' muttered Poppy.

Nigel had to intercede on several occasions to keep the exchanges civil, especially those between Poppy and Sadler. Neither made any attempt to contain their mutual hostility.

After nearly an hour Ryan had increased his offer to Poppy to seventeen and a half per cent of the gross, but she was still adamant that this was not enough.

Nigel then assumed a more prominent stance in the negotiations. He asked Poppy and Victor to 'give him five minutes in the conservatory' with Sadler and Ryan.

It took longer than that but he eventually emerged with an offer: thirty per cent of the gross to Miss Drake and an immediate up-front payment of £10,000 on condition that the new contract was signed tomorrow and the injunction withdrawn.

It was Victor and Poppy's turn for the conservatory and, after a few minutes and without any of the puffs of smoke which herald the election of a new Pope, they returned and assented to the new terms.

Nobody wanted to linger in Ryan's home and we were soon on our way back to Kensington in Poppy's car.

'I'll ride shotgun, shall I?' I said facetiously.

'I'll buy you a bottle of champagne, even though you don't look like Steve McQueen.'

We made our second appearance at Pringles within three days and Poppy ordered a bottle of Laurent Perrier.

I asked her if she were pleased with the new deal and she said yes, except that she would have liked to have screwed Sadler even more.

'I imagine that Nigel has kicked in the extra twelve and a half per cent. Of course the ten grand will come in handy. I'm going to buy you a nice present. Something for your flat. To replace those cricket paintings for instance.'

'You will leave my Gerry Wrights alone, Poppy,' I said sharply.

'OK, OK, I was only teasing,' she said cheerfully. 'How are you getting on with your rearranged flat? Much better, isn't it?'

She looked at me expectantly over the rim of her glass and I hated to spoil her mood.

'Oh, I've changed some of it back – Mrs Bradshaw helped me move things around a bit.'

Her face tightened and the minute scar whitened on her cheek in a familiar way.

'You're becoming a stick-in-the-mud, Chris, and Mrs B encourages you.'

'That may be so but she's a good friend.'

'Sometimes I think that, despite her age, she'd like to be more than a friend. I've noticed the way she looks at you. No wonder she doesn't like any other women in your life. She's jealous, she wants you to herself.'

I was startled to put it mildly and looked hard at Poppy to see if she was joking. Her furious expression told me no.

An uncomfortable silence lasted while we finished our glasses of champagne. As we got up Poppy began to apologise but I cut her short and told her that I would walk her home.

At the entrance to her block of flats she asked me to see her safely inside in case the telephoned threats were about to be made more tangible. We did not speak in the lift but at her door she asked me to walk around her flat to make sure that there were no unwanted guests.

We were in the kitchen when the doorbell rang. I told Poppy that I would go. I looked through the spy hole that was stationed just above the central stained-glass panel of the door and saw a motorcycle messenger holding a bunch of flowers.

I opened the door and he said: 'Flowers for Miss Drake, sir.' As I thanked him, he turned quickly away and headed for the stairs.

No problems there. I heaved a sigh of relief. Poppy was standing by the entrance to the kitchen and as I walked towards her she said: 'If those are from that bastard Sadler you can throw them in the bin.'

I handed the bundle to her and she found a note tied to them. As she started to unravel the envelope from the stems of the flowers there was a tremendous crash from the front door, the sound of the stained-glass planel cracking and shattering.

Like an idiot, I rushed back into the hall and caught a glimpse of something fizzing on the floor. A huge and numbing noise, a thudding crunch of sound erupted. A long time later, though it can only have been a second or two, I was picking myself off the floor. My ears were ringing and I was trembling all over, dazed with noise and shock. I looked around for Poppy and saw her crouched in the kitchen doorway sobbing and retching at the same time. I guessed that the explosion was caused by one of those heavy duty thunderflashes that are playfully thrown around at Army exercises. I tried to comfort her and in the end pulled and half-carried her into the kitchen and sat her down. She leaned against me, sobbing, and I stroked her hair and said all the soothing things I could think of.

The doorbell rang again and I found a grey-haired, middle-aged lady in rimless spectacles outside the door. I assured her that all was well, that Poppy was all right (she came inside to make sure) and that we were the victims of a practical joke that had misfired. She was not convinced but went away muttering 'some joke'.

Poppy began to calm down. I put the kettle on to make some tea in the traditional British manner and picked up the flowers which had ended up on the floor. I detached the note, opened it and read the message, carefully written in capitals: THIS IS YOUR LAST WARNING. NEXT TIME IT'S FOR KEEPS.

Poppy had recovered a little and the mug of tea helped the healing process. Her spirited nature quickly reasserted itself. She said: 'It's that bastard Sadler, I bet you.'

'Why should he bother? The deal is settled. There's no point.'

'It's probably his usual bad timing. He fixed it all up earlier and couldn't call it off. Or wouldn't. He's nasty enough.'

I pressed my point, that it must be someone who was vitally interested in the success of *Cap'n Hand* and of the RRA share issue but who was not aware of the recent settlement.

'Anyway, Poppy, Sadler doesn't strike me as the type to go in for threats like that.'

'Oh no? He's still under suspicion for at least one murder, isn't he? Possibly two.'

We did a makeshift repair on the damaged door with some cardboard and tacks and I asked her if she would like me to stay but her natural bounce and determination had returned in full measure. She reckoned that there would be no more excitement and I agreed with her. I was still disturbed by her remarks about Mrs Bradshaw and was irritated by her unsavoury views. I was glad to leave.

It was good that Poppy had been able to renegotiate her contract and I hoped that she would calm her natural aggression and put her energies into her career. It was a tribute to her own determination that the tide had been turned in her favour. I thought, with an inward smile, that she might have given King Canute a pointer or two.

Poppy's friend had left a message on my answering machine. The voice said: 'You should persuade your girlfriend to wise up. She's spoiling things for a lot of people and we don't like it. So both of you ought to be more careful.'

I reran the tape and realised that the voice did sound a little bit like Grant Sadler's but it didn't have his timbre and the consonants were not sounded so emphatically. I made the obvious logical connection that the same person had arranged the truncated fireworks party for Poppy.

Annoyance, rather than any other emotion, affected me, especially since the contractual dispute between Poppy and Sadler and Ryan had apparently been resolved.

Poppy too had called to reiterate her apologies and suggest that we meet for a swim and a drink. Would Thursday be acceptable? There would be no harm in a swim but any thoughts about a continuing relationship with her were receding. Poppy seemed to live her life at a temperature that I could not withstand. It was all too hot and vivid, and I thought I would end up cooked to a cinder. It was time to withdraw quietly to cooler and gentler climes.

The problem of Felton Butter and his possible involvement in the deaths of Amanda Newhart and Jimmy McCoy still perturbed me. Despite Andrew's commonsense view that Felton was an unlikely murderer, I was not so sure. The urge for revenge is a curious emotion and can be harboured for many years. Who could assess how the collapse of his father's business and his subsequent death had affected the young and impressionable Felton? I wondered if the understandable grudge against the Anderson family had grown over the years into an overwhelming hatred, a hatred which had been refuelled by the thought of all the millions that Anderson was about to cull from the flotation of his company.

I was puzzled, too, about Anderson, and began to wonder if he had decided to put the frighteners on Poppy in order to protect the immediate future of RRA.

And what about Sadler? I remembered that there might be a shadow in his past. Had he had a homosexual affair with Eliot Stonehouse? It would be a waste of time to interrogate Sadler, but I might obtain the truth from

Stonehouse. My problem would be to fathom how to ask such a personal question of such a famous and dignified thespian.

Chapter 32

On the following morning I rang Felton's office to try to discover if he would be playing in the pro-am. The same assistant, as dynamic as a week-old blancmange, could not help me but a call to the tournament office elicited the information that he was down to play and had not yet cancelled.

The pro-am at Brookstone Country Club was marked by one of those days that England does so well: the warm and unassuming sunshine, with hardly a tremor of wind, put a smile on everyone's face. The course, in its elegant trim for a major championship, looked gloriously inviting. As we stood on the first tee at midday Rollo rightly said: 'It's beautiful, isn't it? And there for the taking.'

He grinned at his three partners, one of whom was a former England rugby captain. Dean Smith had made a name for himself as an after-dinner speaker since his retirement; the other two were both in the motor trade.

Rollo teed up his ball, stood back and said: 'Gentlemen, I'll just remind you of the format today. We all play our own ball and the two best net scores on each hole count. Sorry to treat you like idiots but it's as well to be sure of what we're about. A score of around twelve under par should win it. But that depends on how many bandits we have out there.'

As all golfers know there are a few players in every club who protect their handicaps; they keep them as high as possible in order to give themselves a better chance in the competitions. They are called 'pot-hunters', 'ringers' or 'bandits', and much ruder epithets are applied to them by their victims. They appear in numbers at pro-ams. You can pick them out easily: players masquerading off handicaps in the early teens who scorch one-irons about 240 yards down the middle of the fairway. And, as all amateurs know, 'even God can't hit a one-iron'.

Rollo checked his line down the fairway, said that he hoped we would have an enjoyable game and hit his drive perilously close to the gardens of the houses lining the course on the right of the fairway.

A marshal found it about five feet from the out of bounds fence. Rollo thanked him and, to his astonishment, gestured at the garden on the other side of the fence and said, '"Japonica glistens like coral in all the neighbouring gardens",' surveyed his shot briefly and hit it through a gap in the trees to the fairway. He next hit a beautifully judged wedge on to the green and holed his putt for a birdie on the par-five hole. The rugby man got a net birdie and we were comfortably on our way.

I knew that all the usual pro-am supporters were playing including Grant Sadler and Kenny Craig, and I had made sure that Felton Butter's name was still on the list too. He was down to play with Luis Dando, the disagreeable Spaniard with whom Rollo had played a couple of weeks ago. I hoped that I would be able to collar Felton after the round since he was playing in a group two ahead of us.

The play, as always in pro-ams, was very slow and we had the added handicap of the marshal who had decided to attach himself, for crowd-control purposes, to our group. The real reason was that he was a rugby fan and had decided to have a chat with Dean Smith. An amiable man, Dean discussed those battles of long ago at Twickenham and the Arms Park and gave his considered opinion as to how England managed narrowly to lose the World Cup final to Australia.

The voluble marshal was able to advise Dean Smith on some of his shots because he'd 'played the course for thirty years'. He had no need to advise Rollo who, after his first wayward shot, was hitting everything straight. The ball was whistling through the air.

After nine holes the team was spot on Rollo's suggested target with a score of 61. The tenth hole is a very tricky par four with a pronounced dogleg to the right. It is essential to hit a conservative shot down the middle of the fairway and Rollo had decided to hit no more than a three-iron. As he set himself up for the shot a small van came around the corner of the service road and skidded to a halt beside the tee. Rollo retreated as the van door opened and an overweight fellow in jeans and an Arsenal shirt stepped out. Oblivious of what was going on around him he walked, whistling, to the rear doors and pulled a large canister of water out of the van.

As he walked across the tee, still whistling Rollo said: '"What dreadful noise of water in mine ears."'

There were a few bangs and thuds as the man replaced the empty drinking container with the new one. He turned round, saw Rollo looking at him and said: 'OK, chief.'

Rollo set himself up again and was about to swing when he heard the glug of the water container. He stopped himself and we all watched as the man drew some water off, tasted it, smacked his lips and threw the paper cup down on the tee. He strode off to his van and drove away, well-satisfied no doubt with his work.

As the marshal deposited the empty cup in the adjacent bin, Rollo, to his great credit, hit a perfect tee shot just past the corner of the dogleg. He scored yet another birdie and the team was still on schedule for his self-imposed target.

There was a long delay on the sixteenth tee as the group in front overtook the group ahead of them, two of whom were in trouble in the trees. One of them was Felton Butter and I was in time to see him drive competently down the last fairway and, as he moved away, he waved a greeting.

We waited on the tee and I saw Felton hit an excellent shot on to the middle of the green. The eighteenth is a stern finishing hole and he had done well to get near the green, let alone to within twenty feet of the pin.

Our group hit their drives into various places on the fairway and Rollo was about forty yards ahead. He needed a four for a score of 63.

We waited together and watched Felton's group. One of them picked up his ball after several hacks in a bunker; another pitched on and holed out for a five; and Luis Dando, hunched over his long putt, tried for his birdie. We saw the ball hit the hole, spin into the air and drop on the edge. Dando swung his putter viciously through the air. His temper had obviously not improved.

'Lovely fellow,' Rollo said facetiously and we watched Dando walk across to Felton, crouch down and study the line.

He said a few words to him and we saw him gesture, a rolling motion with his hand which seemed to suggest that the putt would break towards the hole from the right.

Felton checked the line of the putt once again. Then, to our amazement, he turned away from the hole and faced back down the fairway towards us. His putter described a full arc and there was a meaty crack as he drilled the ball towards us. It is surprising how much distance you can get with a putter and Felton hit a lovely shot. He was beautifully balanced both in his takeaway and in his finish and hit the ball well over a hundred yards towards us.

Rollo smiled and then started to laugh. Dean Smith looked at us, dropped his golf bag and bellowed with amusement.

Felton did not bother to retrieve his ball and I saw him striding decisively towards the clubhouse.

It was surprising that any of the team got their shots anywhere near the green; Dean Smith was still laughing as he addressed his ball. Rollo nearly holed his shot and recorded a superb round of 62 while one of the motor industry men secured a net birdie. The team score was 121, one less than the target set by Rollo. It was by no means good enough to win, as we discovered later, but the team came a very creditable fourth. Rollo came equal first in the individual professional event.

We were all eager to learn the reason for Felton's bizarre behaviour and we found him at an alfresco bar which had been set up alongside the clubhouse. He was being toasted by his two partners. Luis Dando, to nobody's surprise, was nowhere to be seen.

Rollo grinned at him and said: 'Super shot at the last. But, just a tip, if you want a bit more length roll your right hand over as you hit through the ball.'

'What happened?' I asked.

'Oh, I just got fed up with that peasant, Dando. He hardly said a word to any of us all day. What he did say never amounted to more than a loutish grunt.'

'I don't know how his caddie puts up with it,' one of Felton's partners said.

'Is he the nice lad from the North East?'

'No, he's from somewhere in Somerset.'

Felton continued. 'I even tried him in Spanish. I speak enough to make myself understood. But no response. It was definitely a case of "talk among yourselves" as far as we amateurs were concerned. The only time he took any notice of me was on the last. As you know, there is good money for the pro if the team gets amongst the prizes. He helped me, for the first time, with the line of the putt and said, in very passable English by the way, "there's a few bob for me if you hole that putt". And that's when I decided to teach the miserable sod a lesson.'

As Dean Smith ordered another round of drinks I quietly told Felton that I needed to talk to him and that it was urgent. It was about Neil Anderson and the RRA flotation and with some reluctance he agreed to talk to me that evening.

'Would you come to the house? It's a shambles, I'm

afraid. I'm renovating a little mews cottage at the wrong end of Bayswater.'

Felton's house was tucked away well north of the Bayswater Road in a mews that was mostly taken up by dubious-looking car-repair shops. His own house occupied the dead end of the mews and I could see the possibilities that he had also seen.

He came to the door wearing a paint-stained track suit and welcomed me into a surprisingly large living room. The decorations were half finished and there were just a couple of chairs and a small table in evidence.

Felton explained that all the renovations had been done and only the decorating remained.

'I've run out of money, so I'm doing all the daubing myself. Have a drink.'

As Felton twisted the caps off some bottles of Alsace beer we talked about golf and then settled into the two available chairs, the lone table between us. I had just said that I would come straight to the point and wanted to ask him about the Anderson family when there was a knock at the door which, as in most mews houses, opened directly on to the main downstairs room.

'That's probably the plumber,' Felton said as he rose to answer.

I had the bottle of beer to my lips (Felton's glasses were as yet unpacked) as I half turned to see who the visitor was. As Felton unlatched the door it flew open with a fierce momentum. The momentum was supplied by a stocky man with very short hair and the beginnings of a beard. At least he looked stocky because he was so wide and later I realised that he was not far short of six feet tall. He had a baseball bat in his hands. Close behind him, in the same attire of jeans and T-shirt, was his fellow bruiser, a bit wider and a bit taller and with a heavy black beard.

The door's momentum saved Felton because it threw him backwards on to the stairs. The leading assailant (I had decided that he was probably not Felton's plumber) was thrown off balance too and went lurching towards Felton.

I dropped my beer on the floor and leapt towards the door to intervene. At least the number-two bruiser did not have an offensive weapon on him, I thought. He didn't really need it – he was one. For a very brief moment I wondered whose side I ought to be on. After all, I suspected Felton of murder. But my doubts dissolved as, out of the corner of my eye, I saw Felton push himself upright at great speed, drop his right shoulder and then heard the hard 'whump' as he hit his opponent.

I was busy myself by this time and I had an immediate advantage because the assistant bruiser clearly did not expect any resistance. No doubt he had expected his chum to deal easily on his own with the target. Perhaps he was an apprentice bruiser who stood by and absorbed the do's and don'ts of roughing up other people before being rewarded with his own jobs. My determination was also intensified because I was fed up with these intrusions into my life: first Poppy had been attacked, then I had received a threatening phone call and now a couple of thugs were intent on interrupting my meeting with Felton.

I guessed that a haymaker from the bearded one's right hand was going to arrive and right on cue it whistled its way towards me. This was no time for the Queensberry Rules and I ducked underneath and put my knee very hard into his groin. He gave a highly satisfactory scream and I shoved him hard against the far wall. As his head came down I hit his nose as hard as I could with the heel of my right hand. I sent a quick message of thanks to my father, yet again, for paying for all those self-defence classes in my youth. The bone gave way and blood spurted into his beard.

I looked round to see how Felton was faring and his opponent was doubled up, moaning, on the stairs.

The bearded one made for the door, certainly not at speed but in a crab-like way as he tried to bring some comfort to two sore areas of his body.

I let him go but for a moment I thought that Felton had other ideas for his companion. He hefted the baseball bat thoughtfully in his hand and tried a few passes through the air with it.

'Chris, shut the door, will you, I'm going to crack a few of this joker's ribs.'

To give the failed heavy his due, he said nothing and even tried to look defiant. To my relief, Felton winked at me, so I assumed that he was joking. He turned his attention to the heavy.

'Who sent you and why?'

'My guv'nor. Don't know why.'

'Who's your guv'nor?'

'Dave Donovan.'

'Who's he?'

'He runs a team of us. We're security. Look after the door at clubs, that sort of thing.'

'Bouncers.'

'Yeah.'

Felton looked knowingly at me and I realised that he might have made the same deduction as me.

'Right,' Felton said, 'bugger off and thank your lucky stars.'

The man did not delay his departure.

We assured each other that we were both unharmed. As I went over to pick up my fallen bottle of beer I noticed how much my hands were trembling.

Felton slumped into his chair. His face was white and he said that he wasn't built for this kind of mayhem.

'You did pretty well for someone who isn't built for it.'

'Yeah. Not bad. Strictly a short puncher, as Brando said.' He laughed nervously, walked into the kitchen and reappeared with a bottle of malt whisky and two mugs.

'Sorry about the mugs, but I think we deserve something stronger than beer.'

We both drank deeply and Felton said: 'Are you thinking what I'm thinking?'

'Maybe.'

'Anderson?'

'Why?'

'Because I've been giving him and his company so much stick in the *News*? He's let it be known that my comments are not appreciated, that they're affecting public confidence in RRA.'

'No, I don't think Anderson is behind this. He'd have every right to be, mind you, which is why I wanted to talk to you. I think you've tried every which way to ruin *Cap'n Hand*. I think you're obsessed by Anderson. So much so that you haven't even baulked at murder. I reckon that you pushed Amanda Newhart to her death and that you also murdered McCoy. To get back at Anderson. To avenge your father.'

My detective work, with which I was pretty pleased, didn't have quite the effect I'd expected.

Felton stared at me for several seconds and finally spoke.

'What on earth are you on about?'

I told Felton that I knew that Neil Anderson's father had ruined his own father and that I suspected that his grudge had been nurtured through the years until the chance came to get back at the Anderson family and their business empire. His response made me feel rather foolish.

'Chris, Chris, I'm astonished at you. I think of you as a friend. Surely you can't have misjudged me to such an extent. Yes, I detest the Andersons for what they did to my dad. He was an honest man, an upright man, in a dishonest business. And his bankruptcy broke his heart. Not just his own hopes, but above all his hopes for me were destroyed. Fettes and Oxford, that would have been a dream come true for him if I could have done that. I watched his disintegration. Despair, drunkenness, death.'

Felton took a mouthful of whisky and I saw the tears rim his eyes.

'I did dream of revenge. Especially when I had to cope with the taunts at school. But I realised that there was only one way. To get there anyway. To use my brains, to capitalise on my sporting skills. Make sure that I made the best of myself.

'But murder, never. And certainly not after all these years. Oh yes, I admit I've done my best to twist the knife into Anderson Junior. With apologies to you, Chris, I hope the issue goes belly up. But that would only be a slight setback to Neil Anderson. He'll get there in the end, anyway.

'I don't even dislike the man. I'd just like to dig his father up and hang him from the nearest tree.'

My ego was mightily deflated – how wrong I'd been. My precarious construction of conjecture and circumstantial evidence was exactly that, as Andrew Buccleuth had suspected. Felton was no murderer. On the contrary, I felt he was a man you could trust with your life.

I began to apologise and to explain how I'd reached what, I now admitted, was my bizarre conclusion, but Felton cut me short.

'Forget it, Chris. I follow your reasoning. I can understand it. You don't have to apologise.'

He seemed amused rather than angry.

'Stick to golf and finance until you've had a little more practice as a private sleuth. You're not ready to take over Pinkerton's yet. Have another drink. I've a lot to thank you for, anyway. You've just saved me from several broken ribs, maybe worse.'

He poured another generous measure of malt into our mugs.

'Mind you, the ironic aspect of all this is that RRA is the sort of outfit I could well be doing business with in the future.'

'How come?'

'The pilot of my comedy series has been made and it looks as though they're going ahead with six more. So I may be joining your friend Poppy in the ranks of the sit-com writers.'

'That's marvellous news. Congratulations.'

'Thank you. Funnily enough one of the *Cap'n Hand* actors has got a part in it. Eliot Stonehouse. He's very, very funny. But I am biased, of course.'

We talked about the likely source of the attacks on Poppy and himself and Felton agreed with me that it was unlikely to be Neil Anderson. He would not have attacked Poppy because the *Cap'n Hand* contract had been re-negotiated and it seemed unlikely that he would use such an extreme form of persuasion on a journalist.

I told Felton my half-formed theories regarding Grant Sadler and Eliot Stonehouse.

'Follow it up, Chris. Ring Eliot and ask him.'

'I'm probably barking up the wrong tree again.'

'Ring him. Better still, ring his agent. Bill Morris is sure to . . .' He stopped and suddenly said: 'It's Kevin Lagrange. He wouldn't have known about the new deal with Poppy and he's mad enough to do anything. For a start he's as high as a kite most of the time. And he desperately needs the RRA issue to be a success. He wants the money more than anyone.'

I asked Felton if he agreed that logic suggested that the deaths of Amanda Newhart and Jimmy McCoy were connected.

'Not entirely, because I've got a sniff of something happening on the McCoy murder. But there has been no activity on Newhart. It's generally assumed that it was suicide. I have an impeccable alibi, by the way, for the latter occasion,' he said with a smile. He would not be drawn, however, on any likely developments in the McCoy case but promised me the news as soon as it was official. And I promised him I'd ring Eliot Stonehouse's agent straight away.

Chapter 33

As I drove south towards the Brookstone course early the following morning I left my mind in neutral to sift and shuffle the various pieces of information that I had acquired including the hints, tight-lipped as they were, dropped by Felton Butter.

I stopped at a newsagent but the dailies I scanned had no news of the McCoy murder investigation.

The one thing that was certain was that my theory of an elaborate conspiracy to undermine the success of *Cap'n Hand*, and therefore of Neil Anderson and his company, was exactly that: theory, and a foolish and unfounded one at that.

Rollo had drawn two young fellow professionals for the opening two rounds. The lesser-known players are usually concentrated at the beginning and end of the field for important tournaments because of the demands of television. The producer, whose coverage normally extends through the afternoon, wants the big guns to start from mid-morning to about one o'clock, thus ensuring that they will be on the screen for his audience.

The players like to start early in the morning since the greens are likely to be smoother. By the middle of the afternoon, when thousands of spikes have traipsed across them, however good they are they become less reliable, especially near the hole. The corollary to Rollo's early start on the first day would be a late one for the second round, to even things up.

Rollo played, for him, a rather unspectacular round and I was grateful. Apart from a wobble in the middle, when he hit his ball into water and dropped a shot, he scored par or better. The better only amounted to four birdies, because his putting lacked any inspiration. He had one of those days when his stroke looked as smooth and firm as ever but the ball would not drop into the hole. This can have a depressive effect on some golfers, as the ball monotonously pulls up an inch short or veers away on the last roll, but Rollo kept at it in exemplary style. He finished on 69, three under par.

We headed for the putting green and, as Sod's Law would dictate, Rollo began to hole putts from all over the place. After twenty minutes or so he shook his head ruefully, reckoned that he was putting 'quite nicely' and hoped that they would all drop on the morrow. His group was down to play at just after three o'clock in the second round.

Before I joined Rollo for a quick bite of lunch, I commandeered a telephone and called Bill Morris's theatrical agency. I was put straight through to him and heard his cheerful voice.

'Chris Ludlow. The United Charities dinner. A friend of Felton's. How can I help you?'

I was slightly taken aback by his briskness but managed to ask him when Grant Sadler had abandoned his agency.

'Oh, in the late seventies, the toe-rag. As soon as he got a few good parts on the telly. Went to RRA. Why? What's your interest?'

I took a deep breath. 'Do you know whether he had an affair with Eliot Stonehouse? In the very early seventies maybe.'

I heard Bill Morris laugh. 'Christ, I don't know. But what a lovely thought. How much would the *News* pay for that story? It wouldn't surprise me. Eliot couldn't keep it in his trousers in those days. He used to do a very strong line with those young, impressionable actors. Why don't you ask him?'

He gave me a number for a BBC rehearsal room and, still chuckling, he put the telephone down.

I caught Eliot just as he was on his way out to lunch and arranged to see him at around five o'clock.

I rejoined Rollo and watched as he piled his plate high with an assortment of smoked salmon, roast beef, chicken and numerous salads. Before I had finished my more modest helping he had returned to the buffet table and reloaded.

'A bit peckish today, are we?'

He grinned, with a huge slab of well-buttered wholemeal bread halfway to his mouth.

'Got to keep my strength up. I'm having tea with Penny this afternoon.'

'You're as bad as my brother, Max.'

'I hope so,' he said complacently.

My rendezvous with Eliot Stonehouse was hardly ideal for the asking of intimate questions. He took me to the canteen of a tall block of rehearsal rooms in North Acton, where he was working on a play for the BBC. It was packed with actors and actresses amongst whom I recognised many famous faces. After queuing for tea and queuing even longer to pay for the lukewarm liquid, Eliot led me to a corner table.

'Not exactly the Ritz is it, Eliot?'

'North Acton Hilton, my dear. Only the very best when you work for the BBC. I don't want to rush you, dear boy, but I've only got a short break, so how can I help you?'

There clearly wasn't going to be time for tact, even if I had thought up a way of being tactful. I leaned as close to him across the table as I could in order not to share my question with a large section of the acting fraternity and, sensing my difficulty, he too leaned in to the table conspiratorially.

'I noticed the photograph of you with Grant Sadler. My apologies for asking you a very personal question but were you ever more than just good friends?'

Eliot looked at me, eyebrows up quizzically. 'I take it that you are not asking out of prurient curiosity, are you, my boy? That's not your style. So, it's obviously to do with your business role, with RRA and the McCoy murder.'

I nodded and he continued: 'I've got a severely guilty conscience about the whole thing. Grant and I did have a brief liaison. We were touring in *Much Ado* and he was young and ambitious. I suppose he thought I could help him on his way. To me he was just a good-looking boy, if a little rough around the edges. He couldn't act at all. Still can't, not that it's done him any harm. So, I felt sorry for him and, yes, I took advantage of him.'

His smile at the memory didn't suggest too heavy-laden a conscience.

'I'm not a kiss-and-tell person, Chris, and especially not when, years later, Grant got all those beefy TV parts and became a sex symbol. I used to smile to myself a bit, but I wouldn't have dreamed of being indiscreet.

'But I was stupid and did confirm the affair to someone who already seemed to know about it. At rehearsals for *Cap'n Hand* I naturally got to know Jimmy McCoy. In fact he treated me with great deference, coming to me for advice and hanging on my every word. It was rather flattering and I gave way to the flattery and dropped my guard. He took me out to dinner a few times and we naturally talked a lot about our colleagues on the show and their backgrounds. Rumours abound in this business and McCoy seemed to know about Grant and me. But I confirmed it and I suspect now that he was guessing.

'Sadler and McCoy were hardly soul-mates from the start but things went from bad to worse after I let the cat out of the bag. I noticed that McCoy would make crude little jokes about "pooves" and "shirt-lifters" in front of Grant. I believe he was taunting him.'

He paused and smiled sadly at me and I asked him if he thought McCoy would have gone further than that and tried to blackmail Sadler.

'Yes. And that's why my conscience is cloudy, to put it mildly. Sadler has an image to protect. It's the foundation of his career. He's not an actor, because he only plays one part. If McCoy had threatened to reveal all to some rag like the *News*, I do wonder what Sadler might have done to protect himself.'

'Murder?'

'Possibly.'

'But you've said nothing?'

'Good God, no. Well, after McCoy's death I felt I had to speak to Anderson about it, but he swore me to secrecy; he didn't want it to come out.'

Now I was really confused and seemed to have a surfeit of motives. My mind was in turmoil. From my flat I talked at length to Andrew Buccleuth and told him that his own assessment of Felton Butter as incapable of mayhem on the scale so excitedly envisaged by me was correct. He was clearly no killer. On the contrary, his long-term antipathy towards Anderson actually seemed to be softening, probably as the prospects of a career as a television writer brightened and broadened his horizons.

I told Andrew about the attacks on Poppy and Felton and of the latter's theory that they were instigated by Lagrange.

He paused and then said: 'That's a tenable theory, I think. Lagrange is promised a hundred thousand shares and one assumes that is enough to pay off his debts and get him out of the mire. So he wouldn't want any cock-ups over the flotation.'

I saved the best to last and told him of Sadler's past liaison with Eliot Stonehouse. A threat by McCoy to reveal all to the gutter Press could well have driven Sadler to kill him.

As I put the phone down, I also wondered whether

Amanda had somehow learned of the unlikely affair. Had Sadler, after all, decided to keep her quiet in the only effective way?

The phone rang almost immediately. It was Poppy on the line to arrange our swim at 8.30 that evening at a pool in Chelsea. This is always a quiet time when the lanes which are for serious swimmers are nevertheless still in place. 'Serious' would be a misnomer for me but I always prefer to swim, in my laboured way, up and down the lanes rather than in the chaos of the open pool. I am not that keen on swimming. I go strictly out of duty, for the exercise.

Chapter 34

I waited for Poppy at the entrance for a few minutes and, when she did not appear, assumed that she was already inside.

The pool is relatively new, very large and L-shaped. The four lanes, two for slow swimmers and two for fast, were set up in the short arm of the L, and I began my progress up and down the slow lane. There was no sign yet of Poppy.

After ten minutes there were only half a dozen of us and the only other person in my lane was a girl in her early twenties, or so I judged. She had a pretty face and I wondered what her body was like. Most of it was under water so I couldn't tell.

I smiled at her politely as we crossed and I noticed that she swam well. She was stylish and I wondered why she wasn't in one of the fast lanes. As I reached the end of the lane I looked again for Poppy but there was still no sign of her. I checked my memory and the clock above the pool. We had definitely agreed on 8.30.

There were two men in the main pool. They looked a couple of years older than me and were in and out of the pool, doing belly-flop dives and torpedo jumps; all the antics which make public pools uncomfortable for inadequate swimmers like me. Tight and skimpy bathing trunks did nothing to disguise a pair of burgeoning lager bellies, but I could see that they were both powerful swimmers.

I turned and set off on my next series of six lengths. I usually try to do around forty which adds up to about a 1000 yards through the water.

The lanes are a little narrow and I am a clumsy swimmer. As the girl swimmer and I passed each other, I brushed against some part of her body. I turned my head to apologise and was totally unprepared for her reaction.

'You dirty bastard,' she screamed, as she clung to the rope which divided the lanes.

I was about to protest when I heard the crash of two bodies hitting the water and felt the shock waves. A pair of thick muscular arms grabbed me around the neck and pulled me backwards. As I went under the water I made out swirls of tattoos on the arms.

Panic and primeval fears of drowning took over and I struggled and kicked my way back to the surface. I tried to grab the handrail on the side of the bath but a second set of powerful arms detached me and sent me back down below the surface.

I swallowed some water and could feel my strength dissolving. I knew that I was going to die and felt an overwhelming feeling of helplessness. Somehow I managed to fight my way once more to the surface. The two men were shouting and laughing and I knew that, even if anyone were watching, they'd think it was just horseplay. Commonsense should have told me to try and swim away from my attackers, but commonsense had been driven out by the desperation just to get some air. Two pairs of hands reached out to send me down for the third time in a confusion of noise and panic. Later on I asked myself why my life had not flashed at super-speed through my mind's eye. At the time my only thought, as with bursting lungs and head I broke the surface of the water again, was not to go out with a whimper. I lashed out and, with my left hand, found the wrist of one of my attackers, then got a purchase on the base of his thumb with my right. With my last vestige of energy I pushed the thumb upwards and back. I felt the crack and heard the scream and one of my assailants had had enough of the fun. One of his feet kicked me hard in the chest as he thrust away and to my relief the other man, after thumping me hard in the side of the head, followed him out of the pool.

Feeling weak with terror and coughing and retching, I swung myself as rapidly as I could along the rail to the nearest ladder. I had to get out and get out fast. I hauled myself up on the side and lay there, heaving and spitting, half crying with shock and relief.

'What the hell's the matter with you?' It was a laconic Australian voice and I looked to one side to see the trainers and green tracksuit trousers of one of the attendants. He knelt down when I made no reply.

'Shit, I leave the pool for two minutes and you all start drowning yourselves. Can you walk?'

'Give me a minute,' I gasped.

He helped me to my feet and sat me down on the edge of a nearby whirlpool bath. He put several towels around me.

'Did you get cramp, or what?'

'Yes, and then went under and panicked.'

'Where were those other guys? Didn't they help?'

'Not exactly.'

'Now, what's been going on? If there's been any nonsense I want to know about it.'

'Just a bit of fun. Got out of hand. Do you know those two blokes with the tattoos?'

'No, never seen them here before. Look, if you've swallowed a lot of water you should go to hospital. There's a danger of delayed action. Secondary respiratory failure.'

'I'm all right.'

I stood up and sat down again quickly as my legs gave way. The Australian said: 'Wait here. I'm calling an ambulance.'

'No, don't.' I forced myself to stand. 'I'll be OK in a moment. Give me a hand to the changing room.'

Another attendant strolled in and looked at us curiously

as we made our way along the edge of the pool towards the changing room.

'Everything all right, Bruce?'

'Yeah mate, just a touch of cramp.'

Bruce sat me down, told me that he would be back and returned within minutes with a huge mug of tea. Half dressed I sat down on a bench and sipped it. It was very good, mainly because it was generously laced with whisky.

Bruce supervised the rest of my dressing and on the way upstairs said: 'You sure you're OK? No comebacks? You won't drop me in it, will you? I like the job here.'

I reasssured him and, as we went through the swing doors into the entrance hall, I saw Poppy.

'Chris, I'm sorry I didn't make it,' she began, and then realised that something was wrong. 'Chris?'

She took over the escort duty from Bruce who, as he relinquished his supporting hold on me, muttered something like he'd 'go a bit of cramp for a bird like that', grinned and left me for the refreshment area.

I tried to head off Poppy's torrent of questions but did agree to leave my car behind and let her drive me home.

Without frightening her any more than was necessary, I told her about the attack and that she must be on her guard.

My guess was that the source of the attack was Kevin Lagrange. He was obviously reinforcing the threatening phone call. I was heartily sick of these assaults on my person and resolved to have a word with Mr Lagrange, face to face.

Poppy ushered me into my flat and insisted that I went to bed at once as she thought I was in shock. She was probably right. Certainly I felt exhausted and appreciated it when she literally tucked me up in bed. She brought in a bowl of soup and her ministrations helped to dispel some of the horrors. It already seemed impossible that they had really meant to drown me.

Poppy suggested that she should stay the night. I convinced her that it was not necessary and she said she would come by in the morning. I didn't want that either, and told her I must go to the office early before I went off to caddie for Rollo. We agreed that we might meet later tomorrow.

It was not surprising that sleep did not come easily to me. Several times I awoke feeling my life threatened, though I couldn't recall the detail of the threats. At last I dropped into a deep sleep which did not end until well after my usual waking time.

I just caught the end of the *Today* programme and conducted a brief check on my weary body. My back hurt, no doubt because my lungs had been on overtime. My chest felt bruised, as indeed it was, and my neck was so stiff I could hardly turn my aching head. There was only one thing to do; some very gentle exercise. I went into the spare bedroom, did ten minutes of stretching and then went to work on the multi-gym machine. A stirring Elgar symphony kept me company and the blood surging through me helped assuage my aches and bruises. I lolled in the bath and read some of Henry Longhurst's essays. Yesterday's terrors receded further.

I fancied lingering over coffee and brandy and invited Mrs Bradshaw to join me. She was wearing a rather dashing mauve tracksuit, an unusual sartorial departure for her. It suited her.

'You're looking in the pink, Chris,' she said approvingly, 'and I see that young Rollo is doing well. In the top twenty. I hope I'll see you both on TV this weekend.'

Mrs Bradshaw had begun to take a great interest in golf when, a few years ago, she had learned of my involvement. Anyway, she likes the scenery, she says.

We swopped news, though I didn't mention my swimming pool experience, and she gave me an amusing account of her recent battles at the bridge table. I don't play but would guess that she is a formidable opponent.

I complimented her on her tracksuit. 'Yes, it's comfortable. I wear it down to the pool. I'm following your advice to do a little swimming. Actually I've joined a sort of exercise class. Swimnastics, they call it. Not too much of a strain on an ancient body and rather fun.

'I saw Poppy there yesterday. She's a lovely swimmer, isn't she? Very stylish.'

'Did you get together when you'd finished?'

'Oh no. She was with a couple of fellows, so I didn't join her. How are you getting on with Poppy now?'

'So-so. I'm trying to cool things down.'

Mrs Bradshaw insisted on washing up and when she had left I decided to phone Neil Anderson. I wanted to know if Kevin Lagrange was aware that the problems over Poppy's contract had been settled.

He greeted me in friendly fashion and said how glad he was that Poppy had agreed terms and that *Cap'n Hand* was on schedule for Saturday night. I asked him whether Lagrange knew this.

'Oh yes. A strong share price is very important to him and he was going bananas when he thought things were going wrong. So I invited him over so that I could put him in the picture.'

'What time did you see him?'

'Good God, Chris, I don't clock everyone in and out. Some time after seven. Why do you want to know?'

'I'm sorry, can't tell you, but it's important. So he was OK when you told him about the new deal?'

'It's funny you should ask, because he was a bit odd. Dashed out to make a call as soon as I told him. Wouldn't use my phone. Then looked even odder when he came back. Now are you going to tell me why you're interested in Lagrange?'

No, I wasn't. But the information Neil had given me resolved several things. It was now clear that Lagrange had been behind the attack on Felton; he had almost certainly tried and failed to abort the assault via a telephone call from Anderson's office. It was also a safe bet that he had organised the unpleasant and noisy warning for Poppy. But he had plenty of time to call off the aquatic attack on me. So, why hadn't he?

As I was packing my bag, prior to meeting Rollo, a bizarre thought struck me.

I dropped my bag and raced along to Mrs Bradshaw's flat. I rang her bell and then, impatient, rang it again almost immediately.

The door opened to reveal Mrs Bradshaw, looking slightly cross, and then alarmed when she saw it was me. 'Chris, what on earth's the matter?'

'Did you say Poppy was at the pool with two men?'

'Yes. Not very nice-looking men. Not her type at all, I would have thought.'

'What were they like? Did they have tattoos?'

'Yes, they did. They were fat, beery looking. What is it? Do you know them?'

'I rather think I do.'

I thanked her and dashed off with a promise to explain later. I was having difficulty coping with the extraordinary possibility that had formed in my head. I drove towards Brookstone in a daze, which is probably the best way to negotiate Friday lunchtime traffic in the London area.

Chapter 35

If I felt and probably looked quiet and withdrawn, Rollo was the opposite. The warm sun had brought out clothing which was bright with summer hues and he was as dazzling as anyone. He was wearing bright pink cotton trousers and a shirt which was a startling splash of greens, blues and more pinks. It was all topped with a bright green visor.

He didn't make me feel just dowdy; he made me feel middle-aged. As we walked towards the practice ground Toby Greenslade waved to us from the doorway of the Press tent and strolled over.

'Do you issue sunglasses to your friends?' he asked Rollo, and shaded his eyes theatrically. 'You look like the human embodiment of one of those undrinkable cocktails served up in Hawaiian brothels.'

'Yeah, I'm a real swinger,' Rollo replied.

We both groaned and I asked Toby how he was getting on with Bjorn Carlssen's autobiography.

'The sword of Damocles has been removed, dear boy,' he boomed. 'The stone of Sisyphus has been laid to rest on the top of the mountain.'

'I think he might have finished it, Chris,' said Rollo.

'The labours of Hercules have been completed with honour.'

'Yes, OK, Toby. You've finished it.'

He beamed. 'It's utter rubbish of course, but the publisher seems to like it.'

He wished Rollo luck and said we must join him for a glass after the round. As we moved off, Toby called me back and said: 'A message from my fellow scribe, Butter. He has some news. He'll be in the sponsor's bar with me. See you later. Must get back to the racing. They've got Goodwood on the telly.'

He waved cheerfully and strode off.

I already felt a lot better and the rhythm of Rollo's golf cheered me up even more. Once again, several putts did not drop when he had every right to expect them to do so but he returned a score of 67, five under par. He was now lying in a tie for third place with four other golfers.

After Rollo had checked his card thoroughly and handed it in to the scorer we headed towards the sponsor's tent.

'Have you got time for a drink?' I asked innocently.

'Why not?'

'I thought you might be taking tea with the delightful Penny.'

'No. She's strictly a midday, middle-of-the-week girl. Her husband's something in the City.'

'For God's sake, Rollo, don't tell me his name. I probably know him.'

Toby seemed to be in full command of the bar. He was blessed with the great gift of friendliness and would chat happily to anyone within reach. His resonant voice made his reach considerable and a stranger would have taken him for a public relations director, at the very least, of the sponsoring company. He welcomed us into his circle without interrupting the flow of his words or the well-charted progress of his glass to his lips.

Introductions were effected all round and Rollo was presented as 'soon to be the best left-handed golfer in the world'.

'That wouldn't be difficult,' said Rollo drily, 'there are only two of us, and the other guy's on the Seniors' Tour.'

Congratulations on Rollo's golf came thick and fast and he thoroughly deserved them. The portents were good. But the real tournament, as all the old pros will tell you, begins with the final nine holes.

I was anxious to know Felton Butter's news, but couldn't see him in the tent and was glad when he strolled in a few minutes later and, to Toby's mock disgust, ordered a glass of mineral water.

'A disgrace to the profession,' he said. 'If this goes on they'll be employing female sports writers next.'

Felton smiled and said that they already did. He then moved me slightly away from the group, into the anonymity that the surrounding noise afforded.

He thanked me again for my help in fighting off his attackers and I apologised again for so misjudging him.

I told him that his assumption that it was Lagrange's work was certainly correct but the problem had now been removed.

'Thank goodness,' he said, 'my head still aches. I never want to throw another punch in my life.'

He moved a little closer to me and glanced around. A reflex action for journalists, it seems.

'I've got some more news which may or may not affect *Cap'n Hand*. It's not for newspaper consumption, anyway, at least not through the *News*. One of my sources tells me that Grant Sadler's wife has been getting nasty phone calls.'

He paused in a suitably dramatic way and took a gulp of his mineral water.

'You probably don't know Rebecca. She stays well away from the show-biz milieu and she is a devoted mother. One boy, at boarding school, and two girls – about ten and seven, I think. Someone, a woman as it happens, has been phoning her up and asking her if she's aware that her husband is a homosexual.'

I tried to look suitably shocked. 'Well, is he?'

'Well, you never know, but I doubt it. I wouldn't think so, though I suppose he might have dabbled at one time. Wouldn't that knock his image sideways, eh? Poor Rebecca is distraught and so is Sadler, of course.'

He grinned quickly and said enthusiastically: 'Boy oh boy, what a story. If only I could find some hard evidence. And that's not all. Sheila Ryan has had an anonymous phone call telling her that her husband's having an affair with . . . Guess who?'

'I've no idea. Who?'

'Brace yourself. Poppy.'

'Not a chance.'

'No, I know. But all I can say is that it's not too pleasant to be associated with *Cap'n Hand*, so watch out for yourself.'

'Bloody hell, Felton, I am watching out for myself. I've been scared half to death by a thunderflash, been in a punch-up and yesterday evening thought my last moments had come.'

I told him about my near-drowning but kept to myself my suspicions about who had planned it. I also kept the new revelations about Sadler to myself. But Felton was obviously closer to a big and juicy story than he knew.

Chapter 36

I was looking forward to the third round of the tournament. It is often a decisive round as the players jockey for position and it is also a day when the spectators come out in force.

Unfortunately for both the golfers and the spectators the benign weather turned nasty. It could have been February, as cold winds and driving rain swept across the course. These are the days when a caddie really earns his money as he does his best to shield his man from the elements. He must try and keep the grips of the clubs dry, ensure that there are enough gloves available in the bag and have the umbrella at the ready. I was soon cold and wet, but my condition was irrelevant as long as Rollo remained as dry and comfortable as possible.

I was proud of the way he met the challenge of the elements on a course that was at least three shots more difficult than on the previous day. His one-iron was in use a lot more and I noticed how well he played some improvised iron shots into the wind. Instead of trying to hit the ball harder, a mistake that most club golfers make, he simply took a longer club, a five-iron instead of a seven-iron for example, and punched the ball in with a three-quarter swing. It was impressive and he earned his score of 70, two under par, by his intelligent play. It moved him into third place behind the seemingly inevitable Bjorn Carlssen and an imported American golfer called Harry Kronk.

My arrival home coincided with the start of *Cap'n Hand*

and I just had time to pour myself a drink and settle down to watch. I had refused Poppy's invitation to watch it with her, on the grounds that my time of arrival back in London was uncertain. I was relieved to see the episode go out as planned. No doubt Neil Anderson, Andrew and especially the erratic Kevin Lagrange were even more relieved.

The opening episode was fast-paced despite the need to establish the various characters, which Poppy had done with skill. It also made me laugh out loud several times. I rang to congratulate her but declined her invitation to join in the celebrations at Pringles. I had a busy day tomorrow, Rollo was in contention in a major tournament and so on. I realised that I was protesting too much, but I had much I wanted to ask Poppy and wasn't yet ready with all the questions.

The Sunday papers had given *Cap'n Hand* a good critical start. 'A bright opening . . .', 'A promising newcomer . . .', 'Grant Sadler at the helm of a buoyant vessel'.

Just as I was preparing to leave to meet Rollo, Mrs Bradshaw tapped on my door. She said how much she had enjoyed *Cap'n Hand*.

'Such fun. Isn't Poppy a clever girl? But I'm here to wish you and Rollo luck. It's getting so exciting. I'll be watching, so make sure you scratch your right ear for me.'

On the way to Brookstone I wondered how Rollo would react to the extra pressure under which a chance to win a tournament would put him. He had never been there before and I hoped that his swing would not be betrayed by his nerves. It was impossible to predict his reactions. Would he be able to reach that higher level of concentration that really special players can attain? We would soon know.

He certainly looked relaxed when we met on the putting green. In fact golf seemed far from his mind as he chatted away animatedly to his new friend, Penny, who was squeezed into yet another pair of strangling tight trousers, white ones on this occasion.

A man, whom I took to be her husband, stood beside her, clad in corduroy trousers and one of those waxed green jackets worn by town-dwellers who fancy themselves as country-dwellers. He nodded occasionally to demonstrate his part in the conversation. I noted happily that I had not met him in the course of my City life.

To cries of 'Good luck' from the two of them we went off to the practice ground where Rollo's swing looked as sound and relaxed as on previous days.

Rollo and an Australian, Lionel Ferry, made up the penultimate pair ahead of Carlssen and Harry Kronk. There were other skilled golfers just a stroke or two behind, including the extraordinarily consistent Spaniard, Jose Miguel. His speciality was winning tournaments by stealth; without any fuss he would get to fifteen under par and win. Jack Mason was a few shots back too, as were several other proven tournament winners. It was going to be a formidable round.

That would have been a mild description of what was to follow, as Rollo dropped three shots in the first four holes. The tension had tightened his swing and he seemed unable to flow through the ball in his usual uninhibited way. I did what I could to relax him; told him to let the clubhead go, to trust his swing. It worked for a while and he had a birdie and then a superb eagle to put him back after nine holes to where he had started.

In contrast, however, the other players had made progress, especially Carlssen and Kronk. Rollo was now six shots off the lead and in a tie for sixth place with Jack Mason.

He grimaced at me a bit woefully as we surveyed the scoreboard on the tenth tee and said 'I'll have to go for it now, otherwise the rest of them will put me back in the pack.'

To his great credit Rollo lifted his game to a higher plane. By an effort of will he rediscovered the rhythm and power of his swing and began to rip into his shots. Lionel Ferry, who at the halfway point of the round was two shots ahead of Rollo, was surprised to find himself thirty or forty yards behind him off the tee. Three birdies and another eagle pushed Rollo past Ferry and gave him second place alongside Kronk. Bjorn Carlssen won the tournament by two shots.

As we left the final green, Rollo was even accorded the honour of an interview with BBC Television. As I saw the red light on the camera glow, I scratched my right ear for Mrs Bradshaw.

I stood beside Rollo as he answered the familiar questions: Was he pleased with his performance . . . ? Did he think at any time that he could have won . . . ? What were his plans over the next few weeks . . . ?

Finally the interviewer thanked Rollo and told his audience that his recent performances had lifted him to eleventh place in the Order of Merit and that he was an interesting prospect for the Ryder Cup team against the United States.

Rollo's grin got even wider as he took in the interviewer's comments. He turned to me: 'Let's go. I'll see you in the bar after the prize-giving. We'll have some Bolly to celebrate.'

Along with Penny, excited by Rollo's first major success, her friends and Toby, we made some serious inroads into the club's stock of Bollinger. There was no sign of Penny's husband but that was explained when she told Rollo that he had gone to Toronto on business. His grin had by then assumed jaw-breaking dimensions.

Toby, busy refilling everyone's glass, asked me what I was doing on Tuesday, and I replied that I would be in the office anticipating the RRA flotation which was scheduled for Thursday.

'Wrong,' he said, 'you will be playing in the Perrier Pro-Celeb-Am at Le Touquet with Rollo. And myself. It's one of the infrequent outings for one of the civilised world's worst swings. I refer to my own, dear boy. We've been let down and you are the popular choice to fill the breach.'

It was highly unlikely that Andrew Buccleuth would want me away from the office for a day with an important new issue in the offing and I told Toby so.

'Two days, my boy,' said Toby. 'We leave on Tuesday morning and return, no doubt with the trophy, on Wednesday evening. Don't worry about Andrew, I shall speak to him. There won't be a problem.'

Toby's magisterial tone brooked no argument and apparently not with Andrew either, because on Monday morning he told me to go off and have fun. There was nothing more I could do before the flotation and anyway a round at Le Touquet and another at Hardelot were not to be missed.

He talked to me at length about Rollo's performance in the PGA championship. We agreed that he had reacted with a steely brand of determination that might bring him an important victory one day. It was with difficulty that I drew Andrew back to the subject of RRA.

'Everything's fine, Chris. Excellent coverage, on the City and review pages, and Anderson called me to say that the deal with CBS is on. No problems. We should have a success on our hands.'

I had one more pressing task and set about trying to see Grant Sadler. The obvious way to reach him was via Neil Anderson, but I was surprised how easily a meeting was arranged in Anderson's office at RRA. Sadler presumably still felt some obligations towards me as chief witness to his 'innocence' in Amanda Newhart's death.

He looked tired and the puffiness around his eyes was more pronounced, as if he had been drinking more than was good for him.

I felt no need to hold back and said bluntly that all three of us knew about the brief liaison with Eliot Stonehouse, which was unimportant until McCoy heard about it, and that very fact gave Sadler an excellent motive for murder.

Suddenly, I wasn't Sadler's friend any more: 'Caddie turns boy detective,' he sneered.

'Look, I've been roughed up, so has Felton Butter.

Poppy has been frightened half to death. And the whole business has got right up my nose. I couldn't care less about your seedy little life, except as it affects me and my friends. So, I want to know the truth.'

Sadler, shouting angrily, started out of his seat towards me. Come on, I thought, just let me have one good punch at your soft face.

Unfortunately, Anderson did his well-practised mediation act again. At this rate he'd be in line for a top job at the UN.

He got between us and held up his hands for silence.

'Grant has an alibi. He went straight home after the dinner and Rebecca confirms that he arrived at around two a.m.'

I began to interrupt but he overrode me.

'Yes, I know what you're going to say. But one of the girls was ill that night. Grant sat up with her until about seven o'clock that morning and then went back to bed.'

Every time I thought I was getting somewhere, the ideas got knocked on the head. God knows, I wanted the whole thing cleared up, but neither my heart nor my head would accept my renewed thoughts of Sadler having an accomplice.

Anderson saved my face by saying that I was right to follow up the lead and thanked me for 'clearing the air'.

I thanked him in turn, made the merest nod in Sadler's direction and left.

Chapter 37

Toby's grasp of time is flimsy; he has a lordly disregard for it that is infuriating. I had insisted that he spend the night before our rendezvous with Rollo at my flat. We were due at Dover harbour at eight o'clock on the Tuesday morning.

Toby had booked us on to a boat for the short crossing to Boulogne. He couldn't abide 'those ghastly Hovercraft things, too noisy' and by the middle of the morning we were booking into our small hotel on the sea front at Le Touquet.

We were due on the first tee shortly after two o'clock and so had time for an early lunch and a couple of glasses of wine.

'But not for you, Rollo,' ordered Toby, who had assumed the mantle of team captain. 'You're our banker, you'd better stay stone cold sober.'

Rollo took a generous gulp of the house red. 'Just one, Toby, for medicinal purposes.'

I asked Toby who the fourth member of our team was to be. He was vague. All he knew was that someone would turn up. Anyway, he promised us two days of entertainment. Although Perrier was the sponsoring company, other beverages, as well as mineral water, were available. It was all in aid of the Save the Children Fund, and the prizes for both professional and amateurs were generous.

'There are some good pros here, Rollo, and some good amateurs, too,' Toby said. 'And most of your show-biz chums, Chris. Grant Sadler, of course, Bill Ryan, Kenny Craig, all the usual mob in fact.'

'And Felton?'

'Of course.'

We finished our lunch with some coffee, augmented in Toby's case by a glass of Armagnac of 1950 vintage, which Toby pronounced the year of his birth.

Rollo drove us in his smart Italian car up the coast to Hardelot which possesses one of the most attactive golf courses in Europe. It rambles through avenues of stately trees and each hole has its own distinct character. It has a charming clubhouse with an excellent restaurant and a separate bar which is perched above the eighteenth green, as is right and proper. You can sit there, with a glass of Alsace beer, and watch the triumphs and disasters of the other competitors, and either recall or forget your own.

We all warmed up on the practice ground for a few minutes and Rollo was brave enough to give Toby some advice about his eccentric swing.

As we strolled towards the first tee to claim our starting time, there was someone waiting there who, from a distance, looked familiar. He swung a club lazily up and down and I realised who it was. Max, my brother.

Toby grinned as I waved and Max waved back. As we met I said, 'I didn't know you were back.'

'Arrived in Paris on Friday. Fancied a game and got Toby to mastermind this little jaunt.'

I looked closely at my younger brother. He looked even leaner than usual, like a first-class sportsman who had overdone the training a bit. The bones of his face were a shade too prominent.

'How was South America?'

'Fascinating. Frightening. I loved it and loathed it. Nearly died of stomach trouble at one stage. I already miss it, though I'm delighted to be back.'

A slim and elegant woman waved us on to the tee and

mispronounced our names with charm and confidence. Rollo led the way with a colossal hit down the middle and I followed him just fifty yards behind. Max, after three months in the wilds of South America, put his ball between mine and Rollo's. Typical, I thought with an inward smile. Max had an unusual facility to strike a ball, whether it was moving or stationary. Rollo looked at him with interest and checked his handicap.

'Are you sure you're off ten?'

'Yes. But I'm a bit rusty. Not played for months.'

There was no doubt that Rollo was on his game and, despite a couple of misjudged shots which demonstrated his self-assumed rustiness, so was Max. My game was steady but I was hardly needed as Rollo was in such commanding form. He scored a 62 and the team score, for the usual pro-am format of the best two scores on each hole making up an aggregate, was sixteen under par.

From the bar above the eighteenth green we watched the final groups finish. Among them was Grant Sadler. In his team I recognised a young professional, a very talented player who had swept up most of the amateur prizes a couple of years before. I did not know the two other amateurs but the small and energetic figure of Zoe Bernini was unmistakable. She was acting as caddie to a tall, fair-haired man of about my age. The body language told me that any designs I might have on Zoe would now have to be put in the pending file.

When we checked the scores we saw that Sadler's team had beaten ours by a shot. But we won the second team-prize and Rollo won the professional prize. This result made Sadler virtually unassailable in the celebrity Order of Merit.

Toby, enjoying his role as the self-elected team captain, had booked us into an auberge a few miles outside Le Touquet for dinner.

'We've got to get off the beaten track. Too many Brits

spoil the broth and I mean that literally. Many of the restaurants around here have got sloppy because the Brits eat up without complaint.'

When we got there, the auberge was packed. There were a lot of familiar faces from the pro-am, much to Toby's disgust, but a leavening of French families. No wonder it was a popular place; their standards clearly had not wavered and each dish was simply and beautifully cooked.

For a while Max would not be drawn on his trip around South America. He was more interested in catching up on the news 'from civilisation' and especially on the golf and cricket. Anyway, he did not want to get into the 'bore-of-the-month slot with a lot of bush stories'. Eventually he gave us a quirky and understated account of part of his journey. Like the good communicator he is, he left us all wanting to hear more.

As we were drinking coffee and Toby was scanning the list of Armagnacs, we were asked to join another table. Several of them knew Toby and also wanted to toast Rollo's victory.

Max declined the invitation on the grounds that he wanted to talk to his 'big brother' and we settled down with a bottle of Chinon in front of us.

'I hear you're involved with one of my exes,' he said.

'Poppy Drake?'

'Yes. Quite a girl, isn't she? She's had two of the Ludlow males. Do you think she'll be after Dad next?'

We both laughed and Max said: 'I take it that the affair does not run smoothly?'

'No. I'm trying to stop it running altogether.'

'Just as well. She's nuts, you know. Did she buy you expensive clothes? Plan your weekends together? And your holidays? Call you several times a day?'

I nodded and Max continued.

'She's obsessive about her men. It's odd really because she's extraordinarily attractive and she could have whoever she wanted within reason. But she comes on so strong..'

'She's the same with her career.' I told Max about her battles over the *Cap'n Hand* contract.

'That's typical Poppy. She has to have her own way. But she's a walking paradox because she's very bright and great company. Has she attacked you yet?'

Startled, I looked enquiringly at Max.

'I got brassed off with her, fun as she was, very quickly. You're much more tolerant, much kinder than me, Chris. I decided to do the honourable thing and break the news face to face. Over dinner at her flat. I used all the best platitudes. She came at me with a bottle, thought she was going to decapitate me. I almost had to knock her out. She's bloody strong.'

Some more tumblers clicked into place in my head. I told Max about Amanda Newhart's death and McCoy's murder.

'Oh, that's probably Poppy,' he said cheerfully. 'Her husband died, as I expect you know. But I wouldn't be surprised if she helped him on his way too.'

'He threw himself out of a window, or so someone told me.'

'And so did Amanda Newhart?'

'Off her balcony. Yes. How did you know?'

'Just guessing. But did they jump or were they pushed? I wonder where Poppy was at the time.'

'Her husband left a suicide note.'

'They can be forged.'

'Not this one, Max, he actually put it on tape.'

'Oh well. You can't win 'em all.'

Rollo drove us sedately back to the hotel and I thought that my brain, chasing new theories and information, would allow me little sleep. A minute after lying on my bed, it seemed, the alarm was shrieking at me. It was eight o'clock and we were due on the first tee at Le Touquet Maritime in one and a half hours.

Only Rollo really sparkled around the demanding sea course of Le Touquet. He scored a very creditable 66 but our team, 'a little bit jaded' according to Toby, finished in the pack. At a lively buffet lunch we collected our prizes, won on the previous day, and Rollo received a cheque for several thousand francs. Afterwards he endorsed the cheque to the Save the Children Fund and quietly handed it back to the organisers.

As we had a final drink in the clubhouse bar, I saw Felton Butter. He was chatting away to the vivacious Frenchwoman who had announced the teams on the first tee. He introduced me to Claudine, who promised to contact him when she was next in London. She moved off to talk to other players and I asked Felton how I could find out more about the death of Poppy's husband.

'It was a simple suicide, so there won't have been a lot in the national Press. You might do better with the local papers. He wasn't famous. Just an actor, bit parts and fringe theatre, that kind of thing. Let me think.'

As he thought, he ordered another mineral water and a beer for me.

'If you want details you'll have to get at the court records.'

'Which court?'

'Coroner's. He was a suicide, so there would have been an inquest. And there'll be a record of all the relevant evidence at the coroner's court.'

'And I can just bowl up and read it?'

'Doubt it. But I don't know. Let's see, there must be a lawyer in the room somewhere.'

Felton tried to look over and around the surrounding throng and finally hopped on to the iron rail which ran around the lower half of the bar.

'Hah. There's Dennis Doherty. He's a QC. Wait here a minute.'

Off he went, slipping between the crowd and was quickly back.

'No. You can't just turn up and look. You have to have a good reason. You could be a relative but I think your best bet is to be an employee of an insurance company.'

'OK. I could say that we're looking back at some of our settlements in these cases. Some research.'

'Sounds worth a try to me,' Felton said. 'Now, what about RRA? I've had a bash at the shares. Applied for five thousand. Will I get them and, more to the point, will they be worth getting?'

Oh, I could say that we'd [illegible] [illegible]

[illegible]

[illegible]

there but not quite.

[illegible] back to [illegible] and [illegible]. There was a long line of [illegible] [illegible]

We'd have to scale down the [illegible]

Chapter 38

I was eager to get to my office on the following day, the final day on which the general public could apply to buy shares in RRA. The deadline was ten o'clock that morning. In the heady days of the mid-eighties, when the stock market was in a permanent state of boom, the long queues of last-minute investors outside the City banks were a familiar sight.

My various colleagues, after their usual chorus of good-humoured abuse about 'part-timers' and 'professional amateur golfers', told me that the portents for RRA were promising. The applications so far had exceeded expectations and a final burst should ensure success.

Andrew Buccleuth rang down to ask me how I had fared in the pro-am and told me that we would be entertaining Neil Anderson to lunch.

'He'll be here at midday. But I'll collect you in half an hour or so and we'll go and see whether there's a queue outside the Lombard Street bank that's taking the share applications. It's always the best barometer. We're nearly there but not quite.'

A short walk to the bank told us that we were there, and handsomely. There was a long line of potential investors, patient but a little anxious, outside. Andrew smiled happily and predicted a premium of between twenty-five and forty per cent.

'We'll have to scale down the applications of course. A

lot of the bigger private investors may only get a quarter of what they asked for, and we'll have to reduce the numbers going to the institutions.'

It is common practice, when a share issue is heavily over-subscribed, to scale down all the applications. The smaller investor suffers much less than the large one. Someone who puts in for five hundred shares might receive a couple of hundred; whereas someone who wants fifty thousand might only get a thousand or two, or even none at all.

As we strolled towards the office Andrew said: 'A propos of Anderson, I talked to my chum at Scotland Yard. He's as clean as a whistle, it seems, on the drugs front. He's had several very thorough checks. As you know, the boys in blue take a great interest in prominent show-biz people and especially those in the record industry, and he's clean.'

'Or very clever.'

'You're getting cynical, Chris. He actually puts a lot of money into organisations which try to help victims of drug abuse. I had grave doubts about him, as you know. He's a tough businessman in a tough business, but he also has his more likeable side.'

Andrew had arranged a stylish lunch to celebrate the success of the RRA launch. Neil Anderson arrived with several of his directors and he also brought Johnny Storm. 'Good for publicity,' he said.

A dozen of us, with vintage Krug in our glasses, watched the midday television news which showed the long queue of RRA investors. The commentator conservatively predicted a premium of twenty per cent when the shares began trading. The 'grey' or unofficial market, which always precedes the first day of trading, was already showing a gain of thirty per cent.

Andrew proposed a toast to RRA and Neil Anderson thanked him and proposed a toast to all his new investors. It was all very jolly and the food was as lavish as the selection of wines.

While this was going on I was pondering the problem of

how to get at the records of the inquest on Poppy's husband and decided to try a direct approach to the insurance company concerned. But which insurance company was it? Poppy would know of course. I needed, anyway, to see her to try to resolve some of the questions which were troubling me.

I certainly had no wish to alert her to my interest in her husband's death and decided merely to ask her which company insured her life. It was odds on that the same one had insured her husband.

She answered, crisp as ever, on the second ring and, after arranging to meet her at her flat that evening, I asked her about her life insurance.

She laughed and said: 'You're not selling insurance as well, are you, Chris?'

I told her that I was helping our insurance analyst with a research project. She asked me to wait while she checked her file and then gave me the answer. BIC, the British Insurance Company. A well-organised lady.

A few minutes with the firm's insurance analyst procured a friendly contact at BIC and a promise to look into their files for a transcript of the coroner's court proceedings. Ninety minutes later, to my surprise, a courier delivered a package to me. Inside there were copies of the proceedings 'relating to the death of Simon Prideaux'. A compliments slip said: 'You owe me lunch or, even better, a round of golf at Sunningdale. Yours, Roddy.'

I skimmed through the pages, hardly taking in the routine questions and answers. Poppy had appeared on the scene about ten minutes after Simon's fatal fall. She had been shopping. She confirmed that her husband had been depressed, mainly about his career. He had been drinking a lot in the previous weeks. To her distress she had discovered a tape which was Simon's way of leaving a suicide note. This was played in court and the transcription began: 'When you reach the bottom of your despair, about the world, about the people who surround you and, above all, about yourself, it's time to go. I see no more point in inflicting myself on this sad and tortured world . . .' There was more on this theme, a cosmic disenchantment experienced by an over-sensitive man.

His mother testified that Simon had 'never been strong'. The post-mortem revealed that he had a considerable quantity of alcohol and tranquillisers in his body.

I went back to the transcription of the tape. Some faint echoes were sounding in my mind. An itch in the middle of my head. I wondered if Simon, as an actor might do, had consciously or unconsciously reproduced parts of a play or a novel which was known to him – and also to me.

An hour later, as I was walking the last few hundred yards to my home I thought I had the answer. A neighbour, who was taking her dog for a walk, looked at me in startled fashion, her wave and greeting cut short as I suddenly began to run up the road towards my flat.

I found what I was looking for quickly and to calm my feverish mind I decided to give myself an extended session on the multi-gym. It would also help to dissipate the rich lunch which Andrew had served.

There was one more detail to check before I met Poppy. When I reached her block of flats, I walked around two sides and confirmed that there was a door, a fire exit, at the back.

As I rode the lift I wished myself anywhere else in the world; even more so when she greeted me with that wide smile and a kiss. Her opening words were: 'Don't look so solemn, my darling. We'll go out and celebrate. RRA is a great success and so is *Cap'n Hand*. My treat. Where would you like to go?'

I looked down at my feet and said: 'I need to talk to you, Poppy.' She ushered me into the kitchen and told me that we could talk over a glass of champagne.

'No.' My voice was loud and she looked surprised and then hurt.

'What's the matter?'

'You are the matter. This isn't easy so I'll say it all quickly. I think that you killed your husband or at least helped him on his way. You probably killed Amanda and McCoy as well. And I think that you should come to a solicitor with me.'

She was standing with her back to the kitchen window and the late evening sunlight was folding gently around her. I had a lightning flashback to the first time I saw her, when the sun also cast an aura about her.

I walked a couple of paces towards her, my arm out to comfort her. To my surprise she side-stepped and, in a flurry of movement, pulled a broad-bladed carving knife from a rack by the sink. I had used it and knew how sharp it was kept.

Poppy lunged at me and I saw the knife flash. I threw myself back and got behind the kitchen table. Thank God she's missed me, I thought, and then felt a slight stinging in my left arm. I glanced down and saw the wool of my sweater darkening. She hadn't missed me.

I felt the onset of panic and put my arms out placatingly. As I started to say her name, she overrode me with a scream: 'You've ruined everything . . .'

I barely registered her tensed body and her flushed face, a globule of spittle on her lower lip, when she was at me again, slashing the knife in front of her.

If only she'd tried to stab me, knife upraised, I might have had a chance to grab her arm and dispossess her. But there can only be one result if you get close to a slashing knife being wielded by someone in a frenzy: certain bloodshed and probable death. I knew that the blade would cut straight through to the bone if she really made contact.

It was terrifying and in my turn I screamed: 'Stop it, Poppy.'

She stopped momentarily and I saw her mouth stretched wide in a dreadful grimace. Christ Almighty, she was growling at me. A horrible, unnerving sound.

The table didn't offer much protection because she could

reach me across its narrow width. She started to push it to trap me against the wall.

I grasped the underside of the table, lifted and hurled it towards her. As she stumbled back I went like the wind for the door, got through and slammed it. If only I could lock her in, I might survive.

Oh God, no key.

I felt the crash of Poppy hitting the other side of the door and her fierce tug on the handle.

I tried to reason with her again, but she was past hearing me. I could hear her though, a mixture of growls, curses and a fearsome keening sound.

I reckoned that I could make it to the front door of the flat before she caught me, but would I get through it in time? Poppy had the laudable habit of locking the front door with a mortice lock even if she was inside the flat. Good security, but unhelpful to me in my present predicament.

As I clung on to the door, I looked around for a weapon and saw nothing very likely. Poppy's strength showed no signs of lessening and, as I felt her tug hard again, I let go suddenly and followed up through the doorway.

She wasn't in a heap on the floor as I'd hoped, but in a crouch, her eyes fixed on me. She hurled herself at me and I was just able to get back into the living room and leap over a sofa out of her way.

She came at me again and I dived across the edge of the sofa and headed for the dining table. A chair, that was the answer. As she set herself, knife whirling and flashing, for another attack, I took her by surprise. I ran at her with the legs of the chair towards her.

I used it as a battering ram, trapped her between its legs, and hurled her against a bookcase. Some glass splintered behind her head. The long back of the chair acted as a barrier between us. Luckily for me, because her right arm was free and she was still slashing the knife from side to side with untiring strength.

The end of the knife was missing me by half an inch and one vicious lunge buried its edge in the seat of the chair.

I took my chance, dropped the chair, forgot my gentlemanly instincts and hit Poppy as hard as I could with the flat of my hand. It gave me a huge amount of pleasure. I'd really had enough. Only then did I remember Max telling me he'd had to knock her out.

Poppy fell hard on the carpet. She was conscious but retching and heaving as she fought for breath.

I grabbed the knife, went into the kitchen and threw it, along with the other knives, into the top of a cupboard. I stuffed some kitchen towel under my torn sweater to mop up the blood.

I helped Poppy from the floor and sat her on a sofa. She looked dazed and so, probably, did I. When she'd got some breath back, she made the first normal human sound she'd made for some minutes. She began to cry, with great wracking sobs. I waited patiently for her to stop and when she looked up I said: 'Poppy, you must tell me everything.'

She nodded and said in a soft, barely audible voice: 'I didn't kill McCoy. But, yes, I did help Simon on his way. He was always whingeing about being a failure, that he had nothing to live for. He'd threatened to kill himself several times and so I made provision. I made up my mind that if an opportunity presented itself I was going to take it. I hate failure and I hate self-pity.

'One day, he was drunk and feeling sorry for himself. I'd just come back from shopping and he was posing by the window, threatening to end it all. So I pushed him; only a gentle push, but he was drunk. I can still see the look of utter disbelief on his face. I felt little except relief. It was like putting a sick animal out of its misery.'

'And you'd already recorded his suicide note.'

'Yes, how did you know that?'

She was very calm and docile now, almost sleepy.

'Your play. You lent it to me, remember? I read the

transcription of the inquest and eventually realised that I'd already seen the words. In your play.'

'Simon and I recorded some of the speeches together and I isolated the suicide speech from the play on to a separate tape. Then, after Simon's death, the distressed widow found it.'

'What about Amanda?'

'She deserved it, Chris. She was trying to take my series away from me. She wanted to cream off the writing credits as well as being the star. The joke was that she could hardly write her name. All her brains were between her thighs. And I was afraid that she would steal you from me, too.'

'Just tell me how you did it, Poppy.'

'Same as Simon, with variations. I knew she was in her flat that day because she was expecting some rewrites from me. I rang her to arrange the delivery and she told me to get the material over before five o'clock because she was expecting someone. So I assumed that she'd be alone before then.

'I sometimes use a little motor bike around London. I hire one over in Notting Hill. I've got the leathers and a crash helmet. Nobody notices delivery men or women any more and they're unrecognisable with their visors down. I'd been to her flat before and knew that the hall porter is hardly ever at his desk. He's usually in the pub. I slipped in at just before five and announced myself at Amanda's door. If anyone else had been there I had an excuse. I was just delivering some rewrites in person. She was alone. She invited me in, of course. It should have been child's play. But someone came to the door and I had to grab her. She was making a hell of a racket so I put my hands over her mouth. The bitch bit me so I hit her. Not too hard. I didn't want to mark her. Luckily, whoever it was – Sadler, as I now know – went away. I dragged her to the balcony and pitched her over.'

'Then, visor in place, down the stairs, through the door and away?'

'Exactly. No one notices a courier.'

Poppy now looked almost pleased with herself.

'Someone might have seen you push her. From a building opposite, for instance.'

'No. She's quite secluded, as befits a great star. Nobody directly overlooks her flat. And if they had, they'd have assumed it was a man.'

As I had done, I suddenly realised. Poppy was the figure on the motor bike I had seen at the traffic lights. 'But you didn't kill McCoy?'

'No. He was nothing to me.'

'Any idea who did?'

'No.'

'And the anonymous calls to Sadler's wife and to Bill Ryan's?'

'Yes.'

'And the attempt to drown me in the swimming pool?'

'It was never intended that you should drown, just that you should be badly frightened. I knew I was losing you and I couldn't bear it. I didn't want anyone else to have you. Only me. I had this crazy dream of coming to you like Florence Nightingale and winning you back.'

She had started to cry again. I watched a tear fall from the end of her nose and took her hand. 'Poppy, you know that you need a psychiatrist and a very good lawyer? It's all got to come out.'

'Yes, I know. We'll do it tomorrow.'

'I'd better stay with you.'

'No. Better that you give me some time to myself. Put things in order. I'll ask my solicitor to come here at midday. You'll come, won't you?'

'I'll be here by twelve.'

There were no more words to say. I left her, a small quiet figure sitting in the fading light.

[illegible]

[illegible] came for a short stay had got later and ended up costing about twelve nights.

'You look terrible, Chris. What's up?' [illegible]

He listened quietly while I summarised what Remy had done. He understood my wish to give her as much moral support as I could over the next harrowing weeks.

Max sat thoughtfully looking out of the window [illegible]

Chapter 39

My arm started to throb on my way home, and one or two other joints started up in sympathy. My body wasn't used to impromptu gymnastics.

I washed the cut in my arm, which was superficial, and stuck a plaster on it. I'd been lucky. Then I wandered aimlessly into the kitchen, looked in the refrigerator and decided that I was not hungry. I made a mug of coffee but when I went to drink it found that it was cold. I must have been sitting staring into space for some time.

I felt the need for some support and decided to contact Max, who had gone to visit our parents. Fortunately, he picked up the telephone and saved me from betraying any of my depression to my mother who has infallible antennae for any signs of trouble in her children.

He asked me why I needed his help, but I didn't want to discuss Poppy over the phone. Without questioning me further, he agreed to be at my flat by ten o'clock the following morning.

He was only about half an hour late and said that he'd gone for a short run, had 'got interested' and ended up doing about twelve miles.

'You look terrible, Chris. What's up?'

He listened quietly while I summarised what Poppy had done. He understood my wish to give her as much moral support as I could over the next harrowing weeks.

Max sat thoughtfully looking out of the window for

several moments and then surprised me by saying: 'Are you sure you want to bring in the police? Poppy killed two people, but her husband sounds a pathetic individual and as for Amanda, well, I know that you were fond of her, Chris, but her loss is hardly a great blow to civilisation, is it? I mustn't be flippant but do you think anybody's missed them?'

'Their families, for a start, but that's not the point. You can't seriously be suggesting such an immoral action.'

'I'm offering a practical suggestion. That maybe we should forget the police and put her in the care of a good psychiatrist . . .'

'. . . who is surely bound to tell the law that he has a murderess on his hands.'

'No. The psychiatrist's couch is as sacred as the confessional.'

'I don't agree. If she's to survive, I'm sure Poppy must wipe the slate clean by confessing and paying for what she's done.'

'Catharsis and punishment?'

'Yes. A good head-shrinker and a good lawyer might even get the charges reduced. She probably won't serve anything like a life sentence.'

Max changed tack and asked me again about McCoy's murder and the part Kevin Lagrange had played in the mayhem of the last few weeks.

I told him that Lagrange had undoubtedly launched the attacks on Poppy and Felton Butter, and his motives were greed. He needed the RRA issue to go through smoothly and on schedule. So he had tried to frighten off the two people who might cause problems. But the trouble was that he'd picked two people who were capable of fighting back.

'With the considerable assistance of Chris Ludlow,' said my brother. I did my best modest smile.

'I still don't see where McCoy's murder fits in,' he continued.

'It probably doesn't. It may well be unconnected, whereas

logic tells us, wrongly, that all the *Cap'n Hand* deaths must be linked. But I think that Felton knows something about the McCoy business. As soon as we've dealt with Poppy, I'll talk to him.'

On the way out of the flat Max said: 'I don't like the thought of this fellow, Lagrange, getting away scot free. Why don't we give him a taste of his own medicine? I could arrange it. I've still got some contacts from my days in Ireland.'

Max had spent three years in Army Intelligence, much to our father's horror, after leaving university. Some of that time had been passed doing an obscure and no doubt dangerous job in Northern Ireland.

'Actually, I'd be happy to do the job myself,' he said brightly. I knew that this was true.

'Or I could arrange a drugs bust. I'm still owed a few favours by old Benny. He's still with the drugs squad.'

'Let him be, Max. Lagrange will destroy himself soon enough.'

Our taxi delivered us outside the front door of Poppy's block of flats at exactly midday. As we approached the lift, a slender woman in a business-like dark suit and carrying a briefcase was already waiting. Her skirt was fashionably short and it did her legs full justice. Her black hair fell in ripples on to her shoulders.

We stopped beside her and she gave us both a careful smile.

'I'm Poppy's solicitor, Emily Carrington. One of you must be Chris Ludlow. I don't know what this is all about, but she sounded very troubled, so here I am.'

Max was already hanging on her every word and I sighed inwardly. Here he goes again. As we left the lift I saw him quickly check her left hand for wedding or engagement rings. Not that it ever made much difference to him.

Emily Carrington rang the bell. There was no reply and we tried rattling the letter box and banging on the door. I looked through the letter box and saw no signs of movement nor of disorder.

'I'll break the door down,' said Max.

'Or we could ask the porter for the spare key,' Emily said drily.

'I never get to break doors down any more,' Max said wistfully.

She volunteered to fetch the porter and reappeared quickly with a middle-aged man in a smart brown uniform. He was smiling nervously and clearly could not do enough for Miss Carrington. 'Yes, miss, let's try this key, miss, it should work. There we are, miss, thank you, miss, it's my pleasure, miss.'

Emily thanked him with a dazzling smile but also made it clear in her charming way that he was not required to enter the flat. He almost bowed as he left. He was enchanted by her.

As she closed the door, I called out for Poppy. No reply. Suddenly I felt a chill. I knew what we would find. Max took charge.

'Come with me, Chris, it's either the bedroom or the bathroom.'

He went towards the bathroom and I cautiously pushed the bedroom door.

She was lying in bed, half turned away from me and I thought for a moment that she had overslept. Then I saw the tray on her bedside table. A glass lay on its side, next to a small dark brown bottle and a nearly empty bottle of champagne.

I stood at the foot of the bed looking at Poppy. She was still lovely and elegant, even in death, in what looked like a brand new nightdress. And she looked at peace. I thought of her as I'd known her – full of fun and energy, warmth and anger. I thought too of what might have been; that though it had never been put into words, there had been a moment when I had hoped and expected that we'd spend the rest of our lives together.

My thoughts were interrupted by Max, touching my shoulder.

'All right, Chris?'

'Yes. I think this is better than what we had planned.'

We looked at Poppy in silence, until Emily spoke from the doorway: 'I'll call the police.'

Max looked at the bottle on the tray and said: 'She went out in style. Vintage Veuve Clicquot. Good girl.'

He started to look closely at the various pieces of furniture in the room.

'What are you doing?'

'Looking for the suicide note. No need for confessions now. Come on, give me a hand.'

I wandered into the lounge and found Emily Carrington picking up and checking pieces of paper and envelopes.

'Do you know why she's done this?' she asked and, when I didn't reply, said, 'We must see if she left a note.'

I wandered into the kitchen and found Max already there. He pointed at an envelope on the table. It was addressed to me and was leaning against a jeroboam of Veuve Clicquot.

I sat down at the table, carefully opened the envelope and read the very short note:

> Dearest Chris,
>
> Because this final letter of mine will be made public, I will keep it short. You know why I cannot face the future. You will protect me, even though I have left you.
>
> All my love,
> Poppy

I gave it to Max who said: 'She's left it to you, Chris, as to how much you tell. We'll keep the lid on, won't we? Business pressures affected her, she never got over her husband's suicide and so on.'

As Emily walked in he frowned a slight warning at me.

A few minutes later the well-oiled wheels of officialdom rolled into action: policemen, a doctor, an ambulance, statements, questions. Poppy's suicide note was read without much comment. I was told that it would be returned to me in due course.

Emily Carrington said that she would deal with Poppy's family and Max suggested that we should all go for a late lunch. Emily said she had to return to her office and handed us her card. As she got into a taxi, Max said: 'What a very interesting girl.'

As we walked towards the nearest restaurant I told Max that I was more than ever convinced that Felton Butter knew more about the McCoy murder than he had admitted. I also owed it to him to tell him about Poppy's death. It was time to trade.

I used the telephone in the restaurant and reached him without delay. He was clearly shocked by the news and said he was on his way.

As Max and I toyed half-heartedly with our plates of indifferent pasta, Felton joined us. I gave him a bald account of Poppy's suicide and conjectured on its cause as Max and I had agreed.

Felton smiled at us both. 'So that's the Ludlow party line, is it? I'm betting that there's a lot more to it than you say.'

'Just as there's a lot more that you can tell us about McCoy's death,' I said quickly.

'I'll come to that in a moment. For the sake of friendship I'll toe the line. I was wondering why you were so interested in Poppy's husband. I knew you were sleuthing again and that it wasn't vulgar curiosity. God help me if any of the other tabloid hacks unearth the juicy bits about Poppy.'

'They won't,' Max said firmly. 'Now tell us about McCoy.'

Felton leaned across the table and spoke quietly. 'It'll be in the evening paper anyway. McCoy's wife has been arrested. It was all so simple. Just a case of revenge. And who would blame the poor woman.

'I've always had my suspicions of Hilda McCoy. You

don't know her, but she's the little wifey who got forgotten in McCoy's rise to fame and riches. They married when they were both twenty and guess what? She's a committed Catholic. No question of a divorce. She's looked the other way for the last fifteen years while he's paraded his succession of girlfriends through the squalid pages of the tabloids, poor woman.'

'So why should she get upset this time? They're separated anyway, aren't they?'

'Yes. But you remember when I mentioned Sporran Holdings, which has a small stake in RRA? I told you to look up the directors. Well, if you'd done that you'd have found them listed as J. McCoy and H. McCoy. H for Hilda, his wife. Ninety-nine shares owned by Jimmy and a nominal one for the wee wifey.'

He paused for effect. 'My sources tell me that the understanding between the two of them was that one day, when the RRA ship came in, the spoils would be shared. And the spoils amounted to half a million RRA shares. But in the meantime Jimmy, generous to a fault, gave his latest bit of crumpet, Mikki Boone, forty per cent of Sporran Holdings.'

Felton looked at me with the triumphant air of a man who has just fluked a bunker shot straight into the hole for an eagle.

'So Hilda was deprived suddenly of around a million quid, and probably more, in favour of one of her husband's trollops. Now there's a motive for murder, don't you think?'

Max looked at me and filled up my glass with wine.

'That's the final piece in the jigsaw, isn't it, Chris.'

My mind flashed back over the last few months: the machinations of the show-business crowd; the high stakes which had been gambled on the RRA flotation; and the torments through which Poppy Drake must have lived.

I turned to Max: 'You don't fancy another trip through South America, do you?'

'Not likely. We'll have a friendly game of golf tomorrow. You'll be OK.'